NO STONE UNTURNED

The latest Hennessey and Yellich mystery

Hennessey and Yellich find themselves seeking the body of a man missing for ten years. But the mystery turns into murder – and naturally the bossy widow, nicknamed 'the long-haired colonel' by her husband, is a suspect in his murder. And then a second and third body is discovered – along with a particularly nasty brand of political extremism involving just a few too many respected local businessmen...

NO STONE UNTURNED

Peter Turnbull

Severn House Large Print
London & New York

This first large print edition published 2010
in Great Britain and the USA by
SEVERN HOUSE PUBLISHERS LTD of
9-15 High Street, Sutton, Surrey, SM1 1DF.
First world regular print edition published 2008 by
Severn House Publishers Ltd., London and New York.

British Library Cataloguing in Publication Data

Turnbull, Peter, 1950-
   No stone unturned. -- (A Hennessey and Yellich mystery)
   1. Hennessey, George (Fictitious character)--Fiction.
   2. Yellich, Somerled (Fictitious character)--Fiction.
   3. Police--England--Yorkshire--Fiction. 4. Detective and
   mystery stories. 5. Large type books.
   I. Title II. Series
   823.9'14-dc22

   ISBN-13: 978-0-7278-7842-7

Printed and bound in Great Britain by
MPG Books Ltd, Bodmin, Cornwall.

One

Tuesday, 12 November, 10.45 hours –
Wednesday, 13 November, 11.35 hours

in which a pile of rubble gives up its dead.

Thomas Gunn was a small man and just
twenty years old. He had a firm, muscular
body, which was very heavily tattooed; he
had a pinched face, piercing blue eyes, a
pointed nose, a weak chin. He also had the
'straight ahead' stare of the psychopath. So
observed George Hennessey as he quietly
entered the interview room, softly shutting
the door behind him.

'The time is 10.45 hours and Detective
Chief Inspector Hennessey has entered the
room.' Reginald Webster spoke solemnly for
the benefit of the tape as Hennessey sat
down in the vacant chair beside Webster and
across the table from Gunn and his solicitor.

'I'm behaving myself, sir.' Gunn held both
his hands out in front of him and addressed
Hennessey in a desperate and a pleading
tone.

'I asked you to attend the interview, sir, because Mr Gunn here is offering information.'

5

Webster turned to Hennessey.

'I see.' Hennessey nodded at Gunn. 'What sort of information?'

'But only if the charges in question are dropped or at least reduced.' The solicitor attending the interview was a solid, well-built man in his mid-fifties. Hennessey saw his suit to be grey, expensive looking. His watch was a Rolex. He smelled strongly of aftershave.

'This is Mr Ripon?' Webster began.

'Reginald Ripon, solicitor, of Ellis, Burden, Woodland and Lake, solicitors of St Leonard's Place, attending in accordance with the Police and Criminal Evidence Act 1984.' Ripon completed the sentence for Webster, speaking, Hennessey thought, in perfect received pronunciation, as might be expected of one of his profession.

'Fill me in, please. What's the situation?'

'The situation, sir,' Webster began, 'is that Mr Gunn was arrested this morning at York station, having stolen a suitcase from a passenger train. He was detained on suspicion by the Transport Police; they thought Mr Gunn's appearance did not gel with the large and pricey looking suitcase he was seen carrying. There have been many thefts from trains in the last few weeks, sir ... all the thefts seem to have occurred when the train stopped at York and so the Transport Police have been extra vigilant.'

'Yes, I remember the notice,' Hennessey growled, keeping his eyes firmly focused on

Gunn; his long straggly hair, T-shirt which exposed the tattoos on his arms, old, faded jeans. Yes, he could see why the Transport Police would have 'acted on suspicion'. The absence of a jacket too would have pigeon-holed Gunn in the eyes of the officers, the 'hard men' of the underworld being reported to eschew jackets and warm clothing as 'nesh'. Youths like Gunn, he had learned, give and take 'tankings' in brawls and see feeling the cold and damp as a sign of weakness. It was, to date, recognized as being a mild autumn but he felt that Gunn would still have had to steel himself against that morning's weather if all he was wearing was a T-shirt and jeans.

'Well, it transpired that Mr Gunn couldn't tell the officers what was the name and address on the label attached to the suitcase handle and he was arrested.'

'I see.' Again, Hennessey growled.

'He was also found to be in possession of a return ticket to Darlington.'

'Ah...' Hennessey smiled. 'So that's how it's done, is it? Buy a ticket to the next mainline stop ... Darlington to the north, or Doncaster to the south ... then get a return train and sight up the train, looking for a likely bag ... or suitcase, or rucksack ... watch a member of the public put the case in the luggage rack in the vestibule at the end of the coach and then take his or her seat, facing away from said vestibule...' He raised his eyebrows.

'Easy pickings for a thief.'

'No comment.' Gunn had a thin, high-pitched, squeaky voice.

'So the thefts? All down to you, or are you part of a team?'

'No comment.' Gunn pierced Hennessey with a stare. 'I've got something over me, sir...'

'Ah...' Hennessey realized Gunn's stare was one of desperation, not of challenge or defiance.

'A very lenient judge sentenced Mr Gunn here to two years imprisonment, but sentence was suspended for two years,' Webster advised.

'When?' Hennessey turned to Webster. 'How long ago was this?'

'About six months ago.' Webster sat back in his chair.

'Ah ... so the theft of a suitcase from a train would not normally invite a two-year sentence ... but having committed the crime, you will go down for two years for the earlier offence on top of the sentence for theft. I see why you are worried. What was the two years suspended for?'

'Possession of cannabis.' Reginald Webster spoke quietly but with calm authority. 'Mr Gunn has quite a track record ... hence the two years, so probably not so lenient.'

'Oh, I think so.' Hennessey again turned to Webster. 'The suspended part makes it lenient. I mean, I can see Mr Gunn is a regu-

lar customer of ours ... by his attitude...'
Hennessey paused, 'by his manner, his familiarity with an interview room.'

'I can't go down, sir,' Gunn pleaded. 'I can't do two years.'

'Well, perhaps you should have thought of that before you stole that suitcase. So what will we find when we turn over your drum?'

Gunn looked crestfallen. 'You're going to search my flat?'

'Of course we are ... you know the drill very well by now ... you know we are.'

'My client has information which he feels you would be very interested in ... very interested indeed.' Ripon spoke softly, holding eye contact first with Hennessey and then with Webster.

'You seem to know what it is, Mr Ripon?' Hennessey asked.

'Well, we talked briefly, Mr Gunn and I, so I can tell you what he told me. I have his permission.'

George Hennessey leaned back in his chair, he glanced at the tape recorder with the red recording lights glowing softly, the twin cassettes slowly turning. He glanced at the smooth, darkly stained tabletop, then at the hardwearing hessian floor covering, the two-tone orange of the interview room wall, light above dark, the opaque pane of glass which was the only source of natural light, the filament bulb in the ceiling which shimmered behind the perspex cover. 'So, what can you tell us?'

'So, what can you offer me?' Again the squeaky, pleading voice of desperation.

'Depends what we find in your flat.' Hennessey opened his palms. 'All depends...'

Gunn sank his head into his hands which had 'love' and 'hate' tattooed across the knuckles. 'I can't go back...'

'Oh, but you are going back ... no question of that at all ... we can't drop charges but we could put in a good word or two for you if you start working towards your parole, attend all the courses, good citizenship, victim empathy. You'll easily get a parole hearing within twelve months ... out for next Christmas. And if you provide good information, well then, in that case, we'll certainly inform the parole board.'

'That's all you can offer?' Gunn paled. 'I thought I could ... what's that term? "Plea bargain", like on television.'

'Our American cousins plea bargain ... we don't.' Hennessey spoke firmly.

'Significantly more lenient sentencing in the UK though,' Webster offered smiling, 'so you're quite lucky really, even if we don't plea bargain.'

'It's the best you can do?' Gunn seemed close to tears. 'Two years...'

'It's all we can do, Thomas. So spill. Anything you tell us will help you, not in the way you want to be helped, but it will help you.'

Gunn glanced at Reginald Ripon, with

pleading, fearful eyes.

'My advice is to co-operate, Mr Gunn.' Ripon spoke without returning Gunn's look. He didn't want eye contact with Gunn, that was plain, thought Hennessey. Ripon seemed to Hennessey to be a solicitor who thought legal aid work was beneath him. His advice was sound and good but his attitude seemed to Hennessey to be perfunctory. If the man did have the capacity to fight for his clients and do so with fire in his belly he wasn't, observed Hennessey, going to do it for Tom Gunn.

There was a silence for perhaps fifteen or twenty seconds.

'I could do Category D ... you know, minimum security.'

'That's up to the Prison Service, Tom,' Hennessey replied. 'You don't mind me calling you Tom?'

'No –' Gunn slowly shook his head as if in resignation – 'I'll get used to it again. The prison staff use first names, I'm only ever Tom when I'm tucked up inside ... on the outside I get called Gunny ... sometimes just Gunn depending on who I'm talking to.'

'Again ... you help yourself. Start working towards parole and Cat D once you get to Franklyn. That's the job of Franklyn ... it's an assessment prison.'

'Oh ... don't I know.' Gunn looked up and held eye contact with Hennessey. 'All those courses, like the ones you've mentioned, sir,

11

and the Reflection and Rehabilitation course and the Alcohol Awareness and Drug Awareness, I've done them all ... I'll be doing them all again, I expect. All over again...'

'Well, all over again starts here.' Hennessey allowed an edge to creep into his voice, 'and if you aren't going to tell me something I don't know, Tom, something I really need and want to hear, I'll leave you and let Mr Webster here complete the charging for the theft of the suitcase and organize the search of your flat.'

'OK ... OK...' Gunn held up his bony hands. 'It was when I was in Full Sutton ... that's where they sent me after Franklyn. I mean the last time I was tucked up ... they sent me to Full Sutton.'

'Yes?' Hennessey leaned forward showing interest.

'Well, a geezer there, an old geezer, told me he done a murder that the police didn't know about. In this area ... round York.'

Hennessey leaned further forward. 'Go on.'

'Well, he didn't do it –' Gunn forced a smile – 'so he says ... but he helped get rid of the body, that's what he claimed anyway, to anyone who'd listen.'

'Name?'

'Don't know...' Gunn shrugged. 'He just talked about "the body".'

'The con ... his name, I meant.'

'Oh...' Gunn forced another, weaker smile. 'Phil ... Big Phil Buchan.'

'Big Phil,' Hennessey echoed, 'Big Phil Buchan.'

'Yes ... he's a big guy ... I mean big, spends all the time he can in the gym. Hard man ... gets left well alone. Has it easy inside. Easier than most.'

'And he's there now?'

'Yes,' Gunn said with a nod, 'he's not due out for a while ... a good while. He's in for armed robbery. They done a security guard and hurt him bad. I told you he was hard. He got ten years.'

'Don't recall that incident.'

Gunn shook his head. 'It was down London way. Don't know why they transferred him up here, but it suited him, he's got family here. He wasn't complaining.'

'I see.' Hennessey leaned back in his chair. 'This sounds interesting.'

'You won't tell I told you?'

'No.' Hennessey smiled. 'That I can promise. It didn't come from you.'

'OK.'

'But will he know you informed us? Is that a danger for you? Do you need protection?'

'No.' Gunn shook his head confidently. 'Big Phil's muscles and chest size aren't the only thing that's big about him. He's got a big mouth. After a while inside, people start to run their mouths off, and Big Phil ran this off like big time, in the canteen, in the gym, someone will tell you the same story if I don't. Just don't tell him it was me, I don't

13

want to get slashed in the showers.'

'Agreed.' Hennessey interlaced his fingers. 'So, what did Big Phil say he had done?'

'Helped hide a body. Like I said. Got rid of it. No body, no murder.'

'Of?'

Gunn shrugged. 'Never said his name, some one...'

'Male? Female?'

'Male ... a big, tall old geezer, so Big Phil said.'

'Did he say where,' Hennessey pressed, 'where the body was concealed?'

'East of here, village called Pendwick.'

Hennessey glanced at Webster, who shook his head as if to say, I don't know where it is.

'You said hide?'

'Yes ... that's what he said,' Gunn sniffed. 'Big Phil said it was hidden.'

'Not buried it, or burnt it?'

'No, sir. Hide, he always said they hid it.'

'They? So a team ... Big Phil plus others?'

'Yes, sir.' Gunn looked at Hennessey. 'Big Phil and others ... not by himself.'

'And "always" ... he said this more than once?'

'Yes ... he was proud of it, "took us all night" ... talked about shifting stones ... "big pile of loose rubble".'

'So, a pile of loose rubble in a village called Pendwick.' Hennessey spoke more to himself than anyone else. 'Shouldn't be too difficult to locate.'

14

'Reckon so,' Gunn smiled. 'Reckon so...'

'If he was telling the truth,' Webster commented. 'That has to be seen.'

Again Gunn shrugged. 'Well, his story never altered ... always the same details.'

'Which were?' Hennessey pressed the interview forward.

'Driving out of York in a van or some sort of vehicle, went to some big house, did not know where that was, just some big house, picked up the body, heaved it into the back of the van, still dressed in this suit, the boys in the back of the van went through his pockets, as you would...'

'As *you* would,' Hennessey sighed. 'As *you* would, but carry on.'

'His wallet was bulging ... Big Phil said the boys shared out the cash and Big Phil reckoned he got the geezer's gold watch. He pawned it. Got more that way than by taking a share of the cash, he said.'

'OK ... and then?'

'Drove out to Pendwick. So he said.'

'So ... Big Phil didn't know where the body was collected from, just that it was a large house, but he knew where it was buried? Or hidden?'

'Yes, sir.' Gunn nodded. 'That was the deal. They pick up the body and get rid of it. Got paid a thousand pounds each.'

'How many men?'

'Big Phil didn't say, but five or six ... I think it was that sort of number. It was a van they used ... so two in the front then a couple of guys in the back with the body. Oh, and Phil said somebody took the guy's shoes because they fitted him.'

'Dead man's shoes,' Hennessey groaned deeply. He had often wondered at the provenance of shoes offered for sale in charity shops, but to actually slip the shoes off a very fresh corpse to try them on ... Big Phil's friends were clearly desperate men but that, pondered Hennessey, that could be useful, very useful indeed. Desperate men break more easily when questioned. 'So it was up to Big Phil and his mates to get rid of the body?'

'Yes,' Gunn replied sullenly. He clearly resented having to provide information. 'That's why Big Phil knew where they went because they did a recce a day or two beforehand, so he told us. The deal was, he reckoned, that the body shouldn't be found. Not right away. Couldn't leave it at the side of the road, and payment for the job was kept back like, you know what I mean ... five hundred on the night and the rest one month later if the body hasn't been found by then. I reckon they must have thought that if the body wasn't found inside a month, then it had been well hidden ... well enough anyway. So they put it under a pile of rubble that one of them knew wasn't going anywhere anytime soon. So Big Phil said.'

'When was this? Do you know?'

Again, a sullen shrug of the shoulders. 'Years ago ... had to be. Big Phil was sent down for the robbery in the smoke about three or four years ago ... so, sometime before that. So, I have helped myself? I've done myself a favour?'

'Yes ... if the story is true.' Hennessey stood slowly and left the interview room, moving at his own pace, on his own terms.

'Mr Hennessey is leaving the interview room at 11.07.' Webster spoke clearly for the benefit of the tape.

Hennessey and Yellich stood side by side and looked at the pile of rubble as the blustery autumn wind tugged at their hair and made their coat collars flap against the side of their chins. The rubble had been easily found by enquiring of local knowledge in the form of the cheery landlord of the Yorkshire Hussar, who denied knowing of such a pile of rubble anywhere in the village, but added that that was understandable since, as he explained, he rarely left the pub except to drive into York, 'That's the way of the pub trade, the village comes to you'. Then he suggested that Hennessey and Yellich should try Old Roger, and nodded to an elderly man who sat in isolation in front of a pint of beer in the far corner of the saloon bar. 'He's lived in Pendwick all his life and does odd jobs for folk now to top his income up ... pensioner, you see ... Old Roger, he's the man to ask.'

Hennessey and Yellich had crossed the floor of the saloon and introduced themselves to Old Roger and explained their quest. The man had listened patiently and then, without speaking, reached for his cap and walked out of the pub indicating that they should follow him. Hennessey was about to say that there really was no need, simple directions would be sufficient, but Old Roger was clearly determined to lead the outsiders to the pile of rubble they sought. They had left the pub, turned to their right into the main road of Pendwick, lined with shops with sun awnings, a post office, another pub. Old Roger then turned right again, down a narrow side road lined with small cottages. Beyond the cottages was a flat landscape, fields and woodland. Between the last cottage and the beginning of cultivated fields was an area about half the size of a football pitch, so Hennessey guessed, and in the centre of the land was a pile of rubble. Hennessey asked Old Roger how long the rubble had been there.

'Ten, twelve years.' Old Roger spoke with a strong, regional accent. 'Dumped one night by fly tippers ... no value in it ... it's asphalt, you see, like a car park has been ripped up to be re-laid or the land built on or such like. If it was proper stone, it wouldn't have lasted, folk would have helped themselves to it over the years, stone being valuable but, asphalt ... no use to anyone. So it stayed.'

'Who owns the land?'

'A bloke who lives in New Zealand.' Old Roger pointed to the cottage adjacent to the parcel of land. 'He also owns that cottage. Tried to sell before they left, him and his wife, but couldn't get the right price, so they rented it out, it was all they could do. It's managed by a letting agency in Driffield. The council won't shift the rubble because it's on private land.' And with that, Old Roger turned and walked away, back in the direction of the village centre, doubtless, thought Hennessey, back to the Yorkshire Hussar, and another pint of beer.

'Well, we have a mound of rubble,' Hennessey said, 'just where we were told it would be. How many constables, do you think?'

Yellich considered the rubble, about five feet high, ten feet wide, twenty feet deep, he estimated. 'Ten, I'd say, boss, any more than that and they'd get in each other's way.'

Hennessey glanced at him. 'Ten ... you think?'

'I'd say so, sir.'

'The body can't be buried that deeply,' Hennessey argued, 'just deeply enough to conceal it. Four, five constables should be enough, don't you think?'

'The whole thing has to be taken apart, sir, we don't know if a body is in there ... and if it isn't, well, we'll have to take the whole thing apart until we know it isn't and if we find one body, we'll then have to check for

19

others. Every lump has to be lifted. I thought five officers starting this end, and five at the other end, working towards each other ... so ten ... that was my thinking. Ten, plus a sergeant.'

Hennessey winced. His sergeant was, of course, correct. Once again, Yellich was thinking correctly, and he, the senior man, wasn't; once again the younger man was ready to climb out of his detective sergeant's shoes; and once again, Hennessey heard his pension calling his name, as he often did of late, and with noticeably increasing frequency and volume. 'Yes ... ten...' He plunged his hand into his coat pocket and extracted his mobile phone. 'Ten and a sergeant,' he repeated.

The body was found, as Hennessey had predicted, buried within the rubble but only sufficiently enough to conceal it. It was male, so Hennessey determined by the remnants of clothing, and almost totally skeletal. It was photographed by the Scene of Crime Officers and then delicately lifted by four grim-faced officers on to a stretcher and laid reverently at the side of the parcel of land.

The curious crowd of villagers that had slowly gathered as news had spread by word of mouth were kept at bay, but Hennessey could do little about the individuals who stood brazenly at their windows overlooking the scene which was unfolding under a grey and cloudy sky. Piece by piece the mound of rubble was dismantled but, with no little measure of relief for George Hennessey, no other corpse was found.

Dr D'Acre arrived, as requested, and stated that no useful work could be done in situ. 'The best thing to do,' she said quietly and authoritatively as she stood, having examined the corpse, 'is to take it back to York district and conduct the PM.' She glanced at Hennessey and allowed a usual and a brief moment of eye contact. He relished the short hair, the face without any make-up, save for a very light-toned lipstick. 'Will you observe for the police, Inspector?'

'Yes ... yes, I think I will. When will you be doing it, ma'am?'

Dr D'Acre glanced at her watch. 'Not today ... not now ... tomorrow forenoon? Would that suit?'

'That would be most convenient,' Hennessey said with a smile. 'Sergeant Yellich and I have to go to HM Prison Full Sutton, interview an allegedly large man with an allegedly large mouth.'

'Oh?' Again, a brief but exquisite moment of eye contact.

'Yes, reportedly he had a hand in this.' Hennessey nodded to the skeleton, presently being zipped into a heavy-duty plastic body bag by two young and ashen-faced constables. 'See what he has to tell us.'

Phillip 'Big Phil' Buchan revealed himself to

be just as Tom Gunn had described him: barrel-chested, fiery red hair, striking red beard. He sat in the chair in the agents' room of Full Sutton prison looking perplexed, glancing at Hennessey and then Yellich, then back to Hennessey.

The room itself was cold, clinical, thought Hennessey, lifeless, in a word; a room where all was done to focus everything on the interview. Two metal, brown-coloured, upright chairs on one side of a metal table, two similar chairs facing them on the other side of the table, plaster walls painted dark blue, and, as with the interview rooms at Micklegate Bar police station, the only source of natural light was via a slab of opaque glass set high within the wall, the room being illuminated by a filament bulb in the ceiling behind a perspex shield. A metal door set in the wall opposite the opaque glass was the only entrance and exit. Occasionally, from the other side of the door, the distinct rattle and jangle of keys could be heard.

'So, what's this about?' Buchan spoke with a slight trace of a Scottish accent. 'It's better than being in the Anger Management class, that's for sure, but what's it about?' He, like Tom Gunn, was heavily tattooed.

'Your name was mentioned,' Hennessey spoke calmly, 'just this morning, by someone trying to do themselves a favour.'

'Oh? Grassed me up?' Buchan's eyes hardened. 'Is that what you're saying?' Hennessey thought him not a man to be trifled with and felt further, that despite what he had said, the youthful Tom Gunn, the suitcase thief, might, in fact, need protective custody. 'That's what you mean ... isn't it? Grassed up.'

'Well, you grassed yourself up, really,' Hennessey explained.

'Meaning?' Buchan growled menacingly.

'Given to boasting,' Hennessey explained. 'So we hear...'

'You like an audience,' Yellich added. 'You like to entertain.'

'Go on.' Buchan leaned forward. 'Ask me what you want to know ... whether I tell you or not is another matter, but explain to me why you're here.'

'We took apart a very large pile of broken up asphalt today ... in a village called Pendwick.'

'Not too far from here.' Yellich smiled. 'Half an hour's pleasant drive across autumn fields. Ring any bells? A pile of rubble...?'

Buchan shot a cold glare at Yellich as if to say, *I don't need reminding that there are no seasons in the slammer, I don't need reminding that I'm in here and you are not.* Buchan was dressed in a blue striped shirt, blue jeans, jogging shoes and was beginning to stink. Hennessey assumed his weekly shower was due.

'Anyway ... we found him,' Yellich continued, holding eye contact with Buchan.

'Him?' Buchan sneered.

'The guy you had buried ... hid ... concealed in the rubble.'

Buchan remained stony-faced. It was suddenly very hard for Hennessey to imagine this man boasting about his exploits. He seemed to know how to keep his mouth shut despite earlier reports.

'So, what we want to know is, who the man was? We'll find that out anyway ... and we want to know who else was involved,' Hennessey pressed. 'Our source said that you said there were four or five of you.'

'He did?'

'Yes ... he did.' Hennessey instantly regretted what he had said and attempted to salvage something. 'Or she ... or they.'

'Too late,' Buchan said and produced a very menacing smile. 'He it is.'

'Narrows it down to about thirty million people.'

'Narrows it down a lot further than that,' Buchan growled but still held the smile, 'but that's for me to work on. I have a wire in here and there.'

'So, do you have anything to tell us?'

'I don't think so.'

Both officers got the impression that Big Phil Buchan was smugly toying with them.

'When are you due for parole?' Hennessey asked.

'While yet.' Buchan looked momentarily uncomfortable at the mention of parole.

'This could help you.'

'Oh?' A look of alertness flashed across his eyes.

'Provide information. Helps us and you help yourself.'

Buchan sneered. Then he leaned forward confidently. 'Let me get this right...' He rested his elbows on the tabletop. 'You have found a body of some guy ... buried under a pile of rubble in some out of the way village I never even heard of, and some nasty wee cretin gave you my name as being a part of the burial team? Is that it? Is that what you are saying?'

'Well, it's not a burial, but yes,' Hennessey confirmed with a nod, 'that's what we are saying.'

'Well ... was that guy murdered?'

'We don't know yet.'

'He will have been topped ... you don't hide bodies of folk that go naturally.'

'Fair point.'

'So, my understanding of the law,' Buchan growled, 'is that anybody who gets himself involved in disposing of a murder victim is part of the crime ... part of the murder?'

'Accessory after the fact ... yes, that's the case.'

'Which carries a life sentence?'

'Yes. A life sentence,' Hennessey repeated.

'So, you are here wanting me to admit to something which will have me sent down for life ... and that's *helping* me?' He shook his head slowly. 'Are you mad or are you mad?'

'If you were involved, we'll find out ... and we will prove it. A cough now will definitely be reflected in your sentence.' Hennessey continued to speak calmly.

Buchan grinned. 'We're a long way from that – a very long way from that.'

'From what?'

'Being charged. You know that and I know that. I've been bouncing in and out of the pokey since I was fifteen, and I got form even before that. I have just the one rule: cough to nowt. Any blagger here will have the same rule, cough to nowt ... until ... until –' he held up a fleshy finger with the nail bitten to the quick– 'until the filth can prove it ... and they can show you that they can prove it. Then cough to everything that can be proven. That way you begin to shave your sentence, but only when you know that they can prove it. Only, only, only then. And you ... you are a long way from proving anything. I plan to be out of here in three years. You think I'm going to cough to something that could see me in for life?'

'Well, give it some serious thought.' Hennessey sensed the interview was drawing to a close. 'Depending on your involvement in this...'

'If I was involved,' Buchan added with a smile.

'If we can prove you were involved, your stay as a guest of Her Majesty will continue,

26

but think ... think on. Help us now ... any prison sentence you invite upon yourself could be easily swallowed up in the same time you're serving now.'

'You wouldn't even notice it,' Yellich offered. 'Bargain of the century.'

Buchan's jaw dropped. He looked at Yellich. 'Seriously?'

'Think about it,' Yellich added, 'but the meter is ticking ... as you say, the person in the rubble will have been murdered. This is a very hot murder inquiry, doesn't get any hotter. We'll be giving it all we've got and if we get to you before you come to us...'

'Think about it, Phil.' Hennessey stood. 'Life can mean as little as three years with good behaviour. Sergeant Yellich is correct ... you might not notice it, much better than walking out of here only to be bounced back for a ten stretch, that's a real rubber ball number.'

'No one can survive ten years.' Buchan looked up. 'The system gets you. Destroys you. I've never served more than five ... and this one'll be about seven in total and that is tough going.'

'So I believe and so I can imagine.' Hennessey tapped the door. 'You know how to contact us.' He paused. 'A single phone call from you could save your sanity.'

In the foyer of the agents' room, when Buchan had been escorted away amid the sound of jangling keys and slamming doors,

Hennessey asked the hall officer if Big Phil Buchan was given to boasting.

'Big Phil!' The hall officer smiled. 'He's a con of the old school, keeps quiet. Plays his cards well close to his chest.'

Driving back to York across dimming landscape of long shadows, Hennessey, in the passenger seat said, 'I think we reached him, I think he was involved.'

Yellich, both hands on the wheel, eyes focused on the road, nodded in agreement. 'I think we'll hear from him ... and quite soon.'

Hennessey glanced to one side and watched a rabbit hop across a ploughed field. 'Yes. Tom Gunn's going to need watching though. Buchan will know it was Tom Gunn who grassed him up. He'll work it out. He'll put the word out through the prison telegraph system ... the wires he mentioned. Gunn will have his face slashed open. I'll notify the governor of Franklyn.'

It was Tuesday, the twelfth of November, 16.35 hours.

George Hennessey signed out from the red-bricked Micklegate Bar Police Station after a morning departmental meeting and walked across the road junction, when the traffic lights permitted, to Micklegate Bar where the heads of traitors to the Crown were once impaled upon spikes. The last such impalement took place as recently as 1745. At the Bar he climbed the narrow stone stairway and joined the walls, knowing as does every citizen of the famous and faire, that walking the walls is by far the most speedy and convenient way to cross the city centre. Only when the city is being flayed by hail and sleet-bearing easterlies in the depths of winter do the pavements make an attractive alternative. But that day was a calm, warm November day, blue sky with white cloud at, in RAF speak, five tenths. Leaves gathering on the grass and in the gutter were occasionally added to when a stray zephyr bent the trees backwards and forwards for a minute or two causing further leaves to fall, confetti-like.

There were, Hennessey observed, few other foot passengers on the walls that morning, one or two citizens like himself, walking purposefully, an occasional group of tourists strolling and looking from left to right as they did so, frequently stopping to take photographs at places of interest, or of themselves.

Hennessey left the walls, as he had to, at Lendal Bridge, crossed over the Ouse, which on that day, looked both exceedingly cold and exceedingly sullen and was understandably without any traffic. He turned left into the graceful curve of St Leonard's Place, home of firms of solicitors, the opera house and the art gallery, and at the far end, Bootham Bar. From Bootham, he walked down narrow Gillygate with its small shops and houses and which, being just outside the walls, was of little interest to tourists and was thus the home of specialist shops and un-fashionable cafes. Gillygate gave to wider Clarence Street at the junction with Lord Mayor's Walk, and Clarence Street, in turn, gave to Wigginton Road, also known as the B163, which carried the traffic out to Sutton on the Forest, Huby and the Yorkshire Wolds.

To his left stood the medium-rise, slab-sided building that was the York District Hospital. He entered the hospital grounds and walked across the car park, searching for, and finding in a heart-leaping, flushing-with-pride-and-joy moment, a red and white Riley RMA circa 1947, an elegant, graceful, stylish car which Hennessey had ridden in, as a passenger, never being allowed to take the wheel, and had always found the passenger compartment cramped by the standards of modern saloons, and also cramped despite the promise of room strongly suggested by the car's lines.

He entered the hospital and walked to the department of pathology and knocked reverently on the door marked 'Louise D'Acre MD, MRCP, FRCPath'. He waited until Dr D'Acre said, 'Come in,' at which he prompt-ly opened the door.

'Good morning, Chief Inspector.' She glanced at him briefly and then returned to her notes. 'Sorry, I am just looking over notes of a previous PM. Do please take a seat.'

Hennessey sat on the chair beside her desk. Her office, he thought, was cramped and much ingenious use was made of the limited space available and also by clearly keeping everything in its place, as if her motto was 'a place for everything, and everything in its place'. He glanced at the photographs on the wall, two teenage girls and a pre-teenage son, and one photograph of a magnificent gleaming coated black stallion standing proudly in a paddock on a summer's day.

'So,' Dr D'Acre said as she leaned back in her chair, 'anything known yet?'

'No, ma'am.' Hennessey held his hat in his hands. 'We delayed making a press release in case we were able to identify the body. That would be more sensitive to the feelings of any relatives.'

Dr D'Acre smiled. 'So how did he die ... that is the first question?'

'Yes, ma'am.'

'And who is he? That is the second question.'

'Indeed, ma'am.'

'Alright, let's get suited up. I'll see you in there and don't ... don't ... don't ... ask me how long he has been deceased.'

Hennessey smiled.

'Because the answer will as always and before be somewhere between the time when he was last seen alive by a reliable witness and the time when his body was discovered, that being as accurate as anything medical

31

science can tell us.'

'Understood, ma'am.'

'Let us not let life imitate art.' She spoke with a serious tone of voice. 'Only pathologists on detective programmes on television can state time of death with accuracy. We mere mortals are much less skilled. I'll see you in there.'

Ten minutes later, Hennessey stood against the wall in the pathology theatre. He was clothed as normally in green disposable paper coveralls, with matching hat and shoe covers. Also in the room were Dr D'Acre and the youthful, rotund and jovial – though, tastefully so, Hennessey had always found – Eric Filey, the mortuary assistant, also both similarly attired in the manner that Hennessey was dressed. The fourth person in the room was not a person as such, he was a skeleton, and lay on the third of four stainless steel tables that stood in a row in the room. A bench ran along the wall furthest from Hennessey, beneath which were drawers containing he knew not what. A stainless steel trolley, containing neatly arranged surgical instruments stood by the table on which the skeleton lay. The floor of the theatre was covered in thick, industrial grade linoleum. The room smelled strongly of formaldehyde and was brightly illuminated by filament bulbs set in the ceiling.

Dr D'Acre stood beside the table on which the corpse lay and adjusted a microphone that was suspended above the table on an anglepoise arm and which was bolted to the ceiling.

'Alright, Janet,' Dr D'Acre clearly spoke for the benefit of the audio typist who would soon be transposing her words to print. 'The date is the thirteenth of November, the time is ten fifteen a.m. and the case number is ... well whatever it is ... I'll leave that to you.' She paused. 'The deceased is an adult of the male sex and is in a near total skeletal condition. Remnants of internal organs are identifiable. By examination of the head, which has sustained injuries, the skull plates are observed to have knitted and so he achieved at least the age of twenty-five years and possibly more. He has the clear racial characteristics of a white northern European, or Caucasian, being a high forehead and narrow face ... possibly Asian, but I think the bone structure of the face is not fine enough to be Asian. Height ... Eric, could you...?'

Eric Filey handed Dr D'Acre a yellow retractable metal tape measure which Dr D'Acre stretched from head to foot. 'Well, in life he was an exceptionally tall man. The tape measures an impressive one hundred and ninety-five centimetres or six feet six inches.' She turned to Hennessey. 'He will have been missed.'

'Indeed.' Hennessey inclined his head as he replied. 'Indeed.'

'Six foot six inches here ... that would be

six foot seven inches in life in Imperial speak or one hundred and ninety-eight centimetres, approx, in metric. A big man, a tall man. Even tall down and outs enjoy their absences being noticed.'

'Indeed,' Hennessey said again for want of something to say.

'The mouth ... the jaw hinges easily, all muscle being deteriorated and hence all rigor gone. The teeth reinforce the observation of a northern European or Caucasian person ... western dentistry, fittings and crowns ... modern dentistry that would be consistent with this being a fairly recent skeleton and also it reinforces the impression that this person will be missed by his family and friends. Death ... well, I won't stick my neck out as you know ... but death occurred within the last ten years. I mean, we are not looking at a well-preserved Roman soldier who passed away over a thousand years ago ... this gentleman saw the same sunsets as we did. So, he is of interest to you.'

'Yes, ma'am.' Hennessey nodded. 'Same sunsets ... of interest, as you say.'

'I know you lose interest if the time of death can be determined to be in excess of seventy years previously ... but this modern dentistry, the clearly identifiable remains of the lungs ... no ... he's a comparatively recent death. Comfortably within your field of interest, Chief Inspector.'

'Yes, ma'am.' Again said for the uncomfortable want of something to say in response.

'Now, the cause of death. As mentioned, injuries are noted to the skull. Two linear fractures which caused depression ... that would have lead to subdural haematoma and death as blood, in large quantities, came into contact with the brain tissue. Both impacts caused the skull to fracture ... a skull fractures outwards from the point of impact and does so very rapidly, at approximately the speed of sound, or about 770 miles per hour ... about 1238 kilometres per hour, under normal atmospheric conditions, though the speed can vary slightly, with environmental variations.'

'Blimey!'

'Oh yes,' Dr D'Acre said as she turned to Hennessey, 'it used to be thought that skulls fractured towards the point of impact and at a slower rate, but an American pathologist used a high speed film to record the effect of striking a skull with a baseball bat and the fracture is clearly seen on the film snaking its horrible way across the skull, away from the point of impact and at a rate of knots that astounded all who viewed the film. So, here the first blow to the top of his head caused a fracture downwards either side of the point of impact ... towards the ears.'

Dr D'Acre moved her hand from the crown of her head towards her ear. 'The second blow was to the rear of the head and caused a fracture to run round the side of his head, but this fracture, or the progress of the same, was arrested by the initial vertical fracture. So, he was struck heavily with a linear object to the top of his head and again, a second time, also heavily, at the rear of his head. The first blow would have caused him to slump forward and as he went down, I assume, the second blow was struck, but both with sufficient force to cause death. Something long and very solid was the murder weapon.' She paused. 'He was murdered. Definitely.'

'Thank you.' Hennessey smiled. 'Murder is confirmed. Now we know what our job is.'

'A quick PM as they go.' Dr D'Acre peeled off her latex gloves. 'He'll be on your missing person's register ... if not yours, then some other force's.

'Dare say.' D'Acre untied her mask. 'Dental records will confirm his identity. Well, that's the nuts and bolts. I'll have my report faxed to you a.s.a.p.'

'Appreciated.'

It was Wednesday, the thirteenth of November, 11.35 hours.

Two

Wednesday, 13 November,
13.35 hours – 23.40 hours

in which a house call is made.

Hennessey sat in his office at his desk reading the missing persons file on Arthur Aldidge. Yellich and Webster sat in the chairs in front of Hennessey, reverential but alert, in silence.

'I think you're right, Webster.' Hennessey put the file down. 'It has to be him. Six feet seven inches tall, forty-five years of age ... yes ... has to be a match ... reported missing ten years ago.' Hennessey tapped the report. 'You know ... I think I do remember this case. The media got hold of it, he was a big fish ... a banker ... a financier ... something like that ... of that ilk.'

'Yes, sir ... financier. I recall the case too, sir.' Yellich leaned forward.

'A wealthy man, whatever he was.' Hennessey pondered. 'No wonder the media were so very interested.' He glanced out of the window of his office as a movement caught his eye. A tightly packed group of tourists

37

were walking the walls, heavy coats and cameras, eagerly looking to their right and left. 'When a wealthy man goes missing, it can only mean trouble of one form or another. That's just the way of it. Either he embezzled all the funds and went to start a new life somewhere with his just-left-school-mistress, passing themselves off as father and daughter until they settle ... or ... or as appears to be the case here, he is the victim of foul play. And it seems now to be clear that there was no new life in the sun for Arthur Aldidge with or without a mistress, but an early end and an ignominious burial under a pile of asphalt. Reported missing by his wife, Audrey Aldidge ... aged thirty at the time ... a bit of an age gap.' Hennessey moved his hands up and down as if comparing weights of two items. 'Fifteen years ... no ... it's not an unduly large age gap. Lived out by Malton way, as he would if he was as wealthy as financiers are wont to be. So, if you two take a trip out there, see what you see, and find what you find. Obtain something to confirm his ID – a full face photograph showing his teeth especially, a sample of his hair from an old comb. You know the drill so I'll leave that up to you. Do you have much else on?'

'I'm working on the string of burglaries, boss,' Yellich informed.

'Oh, yes ... the efficient team, no sign of forced entry ... yet they get in ... somehow ...

frightening ... must have a massive amount of keys.'

'Or they're sneaking in when the house-holder is at home – even more terrifying, I would have thought. We warn and advise folk always to lock doors and downstairs windows, even when they are at home ... but, so many just don't listen.'

Once again Hennessey glanced out of his office window. 'Yes ... well, that will have to take a back seat ... murder is a priority. Ten years ... we deem this a recent murder.'

'Yes, sir,' Yellich answered.

'Webster?'

'Counterfeit money job, sir. A lot of it in York all year ... less now that the tourists have gone but it's still turning up.'

'Getting anywhere?'

'One or two CCTV photographs from pubs and large stores ... but in the main, the gang unload the money on small shops that don't have CCTV or street traders ... or they change the money with unsuspecting street entertainers.'

'Do they?' Hennessey allowed a note of intrigue to enter his voice.

'Yes, sir.' Webster was in his twenties still, young for a plain-clothes officer. Hennessey had quickly grown to like him, having found him keen and dedicated. 'It's in the street entertainers' interest, they're vulnerable at the end of their day with all that loose cash. In fact, I'm surprised more of them aren't mugged.'

'So am I,' Hennessey agreed with a nod. 'They're alarmingly easy targets for the drug addicts who will do anything to get a bit of money.'

'Indeed, sir.'

'So, the counterfeiters are offering them a five-pound note that the entertainer can put safely in his or her pocket, in exchange for a weight of lead ... helps them both out. The entertainer gets to put his money where it won't be stolen, at least where it is less likely to be stolen, and the counterfeiter gets the loose change he says he's looking for. Except, of course, it's not money,' Hennessey continued. 'The entertainers are being mugged ... a gentle form of mugging but it's mugging just the same. Anyway, I'm sorry for the entertainers and the small businesses, but that inquiry has to take second place along with Yellich's team of super efficient burglars.'

'Understood, sir.'

'So, take an enjoyable drive out to this address ... ten years ... a lot can happen in that time ... may have moved by now, but equally may still be there. As I said, see what you see ... find what you find. Try and obtain a more recent photograph than the one in the mis per file.'

The very modest sounding address of 23 Ash Lane, Thaxted Green, revealed itself to be anything but modest in the eyes of both Yellich and Webster though neither commented. It was, they thought, from the point of view of anyone less than royalty, a very desirable residence indeed. The building was, thought Yellich, who had latterly begun to develop a similar interest in Britain's architectural heritage that George Hennessey had developed, mid-to late Victorian. Brick built, the property was cluttered in style, with a roofline interrupted by dormer windows and tall chimneys. It was covered with ivy, which might look pleasing but Yellich knew the plant was doing dreadful damage to the mortar. Unless the ivy was removed, it would suck all the moisture from the cement and the building would crumble. Time, he thought, time for the homeowner to act and act quickly.

The gardens were generous, at least at the front; possibly too small, Yellich reasoned, to be accurately described as extensive but they were generous nonetheless. Too much work for the owner in the garden, unless he could commit himself full time to it, Yellich observed as he pondered the amount of work his own postage stamp size garden entailed. Here was strongly, almost savagely, cut back privet, closely cut lawns, meticulously weeded flowerbeds; here was the work of a professional gardener. The house was not to his personal taste, all that ivy would have to go, the gardener would have to be retained, too much for one man who could only give his free time to the garden; but on the whole, he felt that 23 Ash Lane, Thaxted Green, Yorkshire, was not a property to be sniffed at.

The front door of the house opened as Yellich and Webster halted their car. The person in the doorway was female, about forty, so Yellich guessed, attractive in a below the knee skirt, and expensive-looking blue pullover, black shoes with a modest heel. Elegant, Yellich thought, in a casual but very self-assured sort of way.

Yellich and Webster got out of the car and walked confidently towards the woman who stood firmly in the threshold of her home and showed no fear at all of the two strange men who had arrived unannounced.

'Mrs Aldidge?' Yellich showed his ID.

'Yes.'

'Police.'

'Yes ... I saw you approaching, two men in a car in broad daylight ... I didn't think I had anything to be afraid of, I thought you might be trying to sell me something, but you are the police?'

'Yes ... Detective Sergeant Yellich. This is Detective Constable Webster.'

Webster inclined his head. 'Ma'am.'

'I do hope there's no trouble?' She spoke calmly with received pronunciation so Yellich noted, akin to a television newsreader. Her blonde hair was close and neatly cut.

'Well...' Yellich faltered and cleared his

throat. 'I understand you reported your husband, Mr Arthur Aldidge, as a missing person? This was about ten years ago?'

'Oh...' Her long-fingered hand went up to her mouth, she paled. 'Arthur ... oh ... you'd better come in.' She stepped aside. 'I knew this day would come.'

Yellich and Webster entered the house. Mrs Aldidge closed the door behind them and led them to a sitting room to the left in which a small log fire burned in an iron grate, it gave off little heat and didn't fully take the edge off the chill in the room, but nonetheless it had a welcoming feel to it. 'Please,' she said, 'do sit down.'

Yellich and Webster sat in deep and very comfortable armchairs, as Mrs Aldidge gracefully lowered herself on to a chaise longue.

'I keep a cold house as you might notice,' she explained. 'I believe it is more stimulating, keeps one alert. I refuse to give in to the cold. We are in no danger of freezing in this house but neither will we be lulled into slothfulness by excessive heat. I have visited ... called on people in some houses where one is met by a blast of hot air when the door is opened ... can't possibly be healthy, that sort of heat, sends you to sleep and allows viruses to multiply. We have wood burning fires in all rooms and an Aga in the kitchen which provides central heating ... modestly so. Lovely and cool in the summer, in the winter we

43

wear extra clothing. But, you are here about dear Arthur?'

'Yes.' Yellich, as the senior officer, spoke. 'We believe he may have been found.'

'Found? Alive?'

'No ... I am sorry, I expressed myself badly.'

Webster, observing Mrs Aldidge, as he had been trained to observe when interviewing, seemed genuinely excited at the prospect of Mr Aldidge being alive and equally genuinely crestfallen by Yellich's reply.

'Oh...'

'A body has been found. I am sorry, but we believe it to be that of your husband.'

'Oh ... where is he?'

'The body is in the mortuary at York District Hospital.'

'Can I see it? I will have to see it ... to tell if it is Arthur...'

'That won't be possible I'm afraid ... it is ... well, there is no easy way of saying this ... but the body is skeletal.'

'A skeleton!' Again her long-fingered hand went up to her mouth.

'Yes.' Yellich held eye contact with Mrs Aldidge. 'I am sorry.'

'Oh...' Mrs Aldidge's complexion paled.

'But formal identification still has to be made.' Yellich insisted.

'I see.' Her voice faltered. 'So why do you think it is Arthur?'

'The height ... it's the skeleton of a very tall

44

man, exceptionally tall. The only person on our missing persons database of the height of the ... the...'

'Deceased.' Webster helped Yellich. 'The deceased.'

'Yes ... thanks ... the deceased was a tall, northern European, or Caucasian, male, in life six feet seven inches or about one hundred and ninety-eight centimetres.'

'Yes, that was Arthur's height. He was a very tall man and I am not a short woman ... five ten ... we made quite an impression when we went out together, cut quite a dash.'

'So, I am afraid you must prepare yourself for the fact that the deceased will prove to be your husband.'

Mrs Aldidge nodded. 'Yes.'

'We have been asked to ask you for your help in making a positive identification, Mrs Aldidge.'

'How can I help you?' Again Webster thought her to be genuinely wanting to help.

'Well, a photograph, full face and as recent as possible ... that is to say...'

'Yes, I know what you mean.' She forced a smile. 'Arthur was more than a little vain and did enjoy his photograph to be taken. I can provide whole albums full of photographs of him – no shortage at all in that department.'

'Well, just one would do, full face, if possible, showing his teeth.'

'His teeth!' Mrs Aldidge gasped and seemed to Webster to be a trifle amused.

'Yes, his teeth will help the identification,' Yellich explained. 'The boffins can super-impose the photograph on to a photograph of the deceased's face. If they match up the position of the eyes and so forth, it can con-firm identity ... but the teeth are very useful because they don't decay and if the teeth match, that's it.'

'I see ... so one of my husband grinning, rather than smiling?'

'That would be ideal, if you could provide one such.'

Mrs Aldidge raised an eyebrow. 'I can guarantee it.' She stood and reached for a sash bell pull that hung beside the fireplace and tugged it downwards, twice. She then returned to her seat. 'Molly is a good girl, she'll take you to the photographs.'

'Ten years is a long time.' Yellich read the room, neat, functional, two paintings hung on the wall, a table and chair stood in the window. It was clearly, he thought, a room given over to the receiving of persons upon business, rather than for retiring to with friends and family. 'But would you have a hair sample ... of your husband's?'

'My late husband ... for the skeleton you speak of will be that of my husband ... but a hair sample? As you say, after ten years, that's a tall order.'

'Well, probably not so tall if you have kept his hairbrush and comb.'

'Ah ... I see ... well, yes, I have kept his

46

things ... as a dutiful wife would ... nothing of his has been jettisoned. All has been retained.'

'Indeed.' Yellich was impressed by her piety.

The door of the room opened and an Afro-Caribbean woman entered wearing a conventional maid's outfit of black dress, white cuffs and a white pinafore, black stockings and black shoes. She was, thought the officers, in her mid-fifties.

'Molly,' Mrs Aldidge smiled, 'would you please show these police officers the photograph albums? The ones in Mr Aldidge's study.'

Yellich glanced at Webster. 'I don't think it needs two of us.'

'Alright.' Webster stood and smiled at Molly. 'Just me,' he said.

'We were asked to take her,' Mrs Aldidge had explained in an apologetic tone when she and Yellich were alone 'They need the work, you see.'

'Asked? They?' Yellich was perplexed.

'When we were looking for help, the employment agency asked if we would take a black woman ... they need to work, you see ... so we were told.'

'I see.' He made no other comment but began to feel uncomfortable.

'So we were delighted to help. Do out bit, all helps to create a multi-racial Britain. She's been with us for fifteen years.'

47

'Ah...'

'We have two.'

'Maids?'

'Yes, both black ... Molly and Prudence ... both utter delights.'

'I see,' Yellich said again but couldn't prevent himself from growling. 'Well, on the assumption?'

'Dangerous,' Mrs Aldidge interrupted as she held up a slender, straight admonishing finger although she did add a smile. 'Arthur would always caution about that. Never, ever, ever ... he would say, never ever, ever proceed upon an assumption and would always enjoy citing the Penistone railway disaster as a near perfect example as could be had.'

'Which was?' Yellich was intrigued. He had never heard of the incident.

'Happened in the nineteenth century. In those days there was just a single railway line between Sheffield and Manchester and they ran to timetable as closely as they could. On a dark and stormy night the express from Manchester was two hours overdue so the officials at Sheffield despatched a locomotive to look for the train from Manchester...'

'Along a single track?' Yellich said in amazement.

'Yes ... but see it from their point of view ... two hours overdue and the storm ... you can understand their thinking, the way their imagination allowed worry to set in. Anyway, the express had just had the journey from hell, delays and setbacks, setbacks and delays and was doing its best to make up lost time, and because of the bad weather visibility was poor and the two drivers didn't see each other until the last minute ... head-on collision at speed, many fatalities ... but it was Arthur's favourite example of the danger of proceeding on an assumption.'

'Interesting story ... but I think it's a fair assumption that the deceased will indeed prove to be your husband, Mrs Aldidge, so while DC Webster is looking through the photographs, I wonder if I could ask a few questions?'

'By all means.' She said this with a dazzling smile, if a little forced, thought Yellich.

'So, you are?'

'Me? I am Mrs Aldidge, Mrs Audrey Aldidge.'

'Audrey.' Yellich took out his notepad and took a ballpoint from his pocket. 'And the indelicate question, if you don't mind?'

'Delicately put. I am forty-two,' she replied with a smile. 'You are very tactful.'

'Thank you.' Yellich also smiled. 'You mentioned "we" a number of times ... who else lives in the house?'

'Just myself and the maids, and cook, but I do also have visitors who stay for varying lengths of time. None here at the moment though.'

'I see. So, your husband's disappearance...?'

'Yes ... nightmarish, the stuff of nightmares. It's the not knowing that is the worst. Now I hope I might be able to bring some closure to it ... have a headstone to visit, a grave to lay a wreath upon – such things are so important.'

'If the corpse proves to be that of your husband, I suppose that is some compensation.'

'I feel it is going to be.' She shook her head. 'No ... it will be him. It will be poor Arthur.'

'So, tell me about him?' Yellich probed as gently as he could.

'Arthur ... well, what can I say? He was a money man, that was his world, a financier, a Mr Ten Percent ... a bit like a private banker or an upmarket moneylender. He didn't lend money to individuals, of course, but only to businesses, corporations who wanted to expand or had a new project to launch and which needed a little extra cash for the advertising costs for example ... that sort of thing. He did very well out of it ... as you see.' She waved an open hand indicating the room, the house, the grounds, the location. 'He had a modest background. He was self-made.'

'Yes.' Yellich looked round the room. 'It is very impressive, the house ... as a police officer, I confess I rarely get the chance to call at houses like this.'

'I can imagine. Not a lot of crime takes place in houses like this unless visited upon by burglars, of course.'

50

'Not a lot,' Yellich conceded, 'but some ... a little. We must remember that the only person who cannot be charged with committing an offence is Her Majesty the Queen.'

'Ah, yes ... because people are prosecuted in Her name. She can't prosecute herself. I read that somewhere, a long time ago. In a magazine in a doctor's waiting room.'

'But crime covers the whole of the social spectrum and in my brief time I have already seen one or two very spectacular falls from grace, but let's press on.'

'Of course,' said quietly, giving Yellich the impression that milady likes speaking more than she is spoken to.

'What were the circumstances of your husband's disappearance?'

'The circumstances? He disappeared. That was the circumstance.'

'Anything happening at the time that would cause someone – some person or persons – to want to harm him, can you recall?'

'Persons, I would think ... he was six feet and seven inches tall ... but I didn't know of anything ... he never mentioned anything or anyone. He disappeared, as people sometimes do. He just didn't return home from work one evening. Simple as that, just as simple as that. He worked in York ... he often said he could have worked at home but he liked to separate home and work and he bought a small house in the city and he used

51

it as an office. I am not sure how lawful that was, turning a domestic dwelling into a place of business. I think something in the by-laws might prohibit that.'

'I think so too, but … carry on.'

'Well, the business concerned was all paperwork and faxes and telephone work, it wasn't as though he turned the house into a shop or anything like that. He also travelled and so he wasn't always there.'

'OK, it isn't an issue for us. Please carry on.'

'So he went to work one spring morning, kissed me … as he usually did, no … as he always did, he always kissed me as he left to go to work, got into his car and drove to York, but didn't drive back. His car was found parked where he usually parks it … in the drive of the "office", as he called it.'

'Was there anyone employed by him or a business partner?'

'His secretary, the good Mrs Gentle. Gentle by name and gentle by nature, or so I always found her. A middle-aged lady with three grown-up children. Mary Gentle. He hadn't got a business partner.'

'We'll have to interview her.' Yellich wrote the name on his notepad.

'I have her address.'

'Thank you. So, when did you report your husband as being missing?'

'As soon as I could, what wife wouldn't? I remember it all so very clearly, as one would.

The curiosity as to why he is late very soon turns to worry, and then the worry turns to fearing the worst. I phoned the police at ten p.m. asking if there had been an accident, the police officer told me to report him as a missing person if he still hadn't come home within twenty-four hours. Quite cold I thought ... emotionally speaking.'

'Yes.' Yellich nodded. 'That's the standard procedure – sorry if it seemed a bit ... unfeeling.'

'It is?'

'Yes, because most "missing" persons turn up within twenty-four hours – adults that is. Children are treated as mis pers, as we call them, as soon as we are notified. We search for children but we can't search for adults except in exceptional circumstances until twenty-four hours has passed.'

'I see.' Audrey Aldidge shifted her position on the chaise longue, curling both legs under her on to the piece of furniture. 'So, of course I reported him as being missing at six p.m. the following day. I took the twenty-four hours as being twenty-four hours from the time he was expected home, not from the time I first contacted the police. A police officer came and took a statement and a recent photograph and then left, and that was the extent of the police investigation.'

'Well, that's really all we can do ... as I said,' Yellich explained, feeling awkward, 'we can't search for missing adults, except on the rare

53

occasions such as when the missing adult in question is vulnerable in some way or the circumstances of their disappearance are very suspicious. We did once search for a young woman of about twenty years who failed to come home after being dropped off by her friends at eleven thirty at night, just a hundred yards from her home. She was vulnerable at that time of night and failed to travel the short distance from the car to her parents' house and witnesses a-plenty to attest to where and when she got out of the car.'

'I see ... that's very interesting.'

'And we were right to search ... her body was found hidden a few days later. In that few hundred yards she crossed the path of a man who killed her on a whim ... wrong place, wrong time. It happens.'

'Oh ... how tragic for her ... and for her family.'

'As you say, but a forty-five-year-old businessman ... a wealthy man ... sane ... tall ... unlike a twenty-year-old girl who vanishes when she's walking home at night, if a man like that disappears it is not anything we can be at all alarmed about.' Yellich sat back in the chair. 'Can I ask you another indelicate question, please?'

'About money?' Audrey Aldidge smiled. 'It has to be about money.'

Yellich also smiled. 'Yes ... well anticipated. Who would ... who did benefit from your

54

husband's disappearance?'

'Nobody, really.' Audrey Aldidge held eye contact with Yellich. 'He was the bread-winner. He left enough money to enable me to survive and survive quite comfortably. We had a joint account and there was, shall we say, sufficient in there ... the house is in joint names and the mortgage was fully paid.'

'Convenient.'

'Very. Or lucky ... probably just lucky. It meant I had a roof over my head and I could keep the domestics and cook. After two years he was presumed deceased according to law and I was then able to assume power of attorney and access the other money he left, though that wasn't very much. I also author-ized the sale of the house in York ... the one he used as his place of work ... his opera-tional base because, as I said, Arthur did travel very widely as part of his job.'

'I see.'

'No life insurance was payable. Arthur did have life insurance of course ... quite a large policy, six figures, but the insurance com-pany will only pay out on production of a death certificate ... no body means no certifi-cate, and no certificate means no cash. That is, apparently, the rule of the game.'

'Well, that might change in this case ... some small measure of compensation for you ... perhaps.'

The door opened and Webster entered the room holding a photograph. He showed it first to Audrey Aldidge. 'I thought this one, if that is alright, Mrs Aldidge?'

Audrey Aldidge nodded. 'Yes, that's alright ... you can have that one.'

Webster then handed it to Yellich.

'Seems ideal.' Yellich looked at the photograph. It showed a bronzed male, short, silver hair, open blue shirt, grinning at the camera. 'Ideal.'

'It was taken in Corfu ... believe it or not that was taken in the January of that year. We went on holiday to the Mediterranean each winter to escape the British winter weather ... it was Arthur's idea ... just a couple of weeks in January, once all the Christmas and New Year parties were over and done with the winter weather really sets in ... we jetted off somewhere. We did it one year and enjoyed it and it became a regular thing. That year, that was the year he disappeared, we went to Corfu and we took one of each other ... you take one of me and I'll take one of you. I had no idea it was going to be so tragically useful.'

'Useful is the word, I'm afraid.' Yellich slipped the photograph into a cellophane envelope. 'The full face ... as I said, it is ideal.'

'Also got this, sarge.' Webster held up a comb and turning to Audrey Aldidge, he asked, 'May we take this as well, please?'

'Of course, please do ... anything that helps.'

'Still has a few strands on it, visible to the naked eye, as you see.' He handed it to Yellich. 'Very helpful I would think.'

'Just what we need.' Yellich dropped the comb into another cellophane bag and sealed the top. 'We'll return these, of course.'

'There really is no hurry ... the photograph ... the comb ... really, no hurry at all. Can I help you with anything else?'

'Not at the moment, thank you.' Yellich stood. 'But we will be calling back. This is early days yet ... early on in the inquiry.'

Audrey Aldidge got up as well. 'I'll see you out. Seems a pity to disturb Molly to do something that I can quite easily do myself.'

'Impressions?' Yellich asked as he halted the car at the foot of the driveway of the Aldidge home before turning into Thaxted Green, and the road to York.

'The maid was helpful ... very.' Webster kept his eyes on the road. 'The photographs were kept in envelopes, not mounted in albums, but the envelopes were dated, made it a bit easier.'

'Yes, the photograph you obtained couldn't have been more recent. Well done.'

'The maid said something interesting. She said that she thought there was something wrong in the house. She was working there when Aldidge disappeared ... long-serving lady ... but she didn't elaborate. Just said something was wrong ... something was not right.'

'Interesting, as you said. Did you ask her what she meant?'

'Yes, but she didn't give anything away. She seemed a little frightened of something or of someone. I think she'll be worth a chat with later ... once we establish the identify of the deceased.'

'We also have a secretary to interview ... one Mrs Gentle, by name and nature, apparently, but let's not rush our fences ... one step at a time.'

The woman stood reverentially as George Hennessey entered Commander Sharkey's office. She was tall, slender, conservatively dressed, short hair. She was black: Afro-Caribbean. She smiled softly at Hennessey. She was late twenties he guessed.

'George,' Sharkey greeted Hennessey warmly. 'Please take a seat.'

Hennessey nodded at the woman and sat in the vacant chair in front of Sharkey's desk. The woman pointedly and politely waited until Hennessey had seated himself before she resumed her seat.

'George –' Sharkey indicated to the woman – 'this is Detective Constable Carmen Pharoah, she's joined us from Leif Vossian's team upon Leif's retirement.'

'Leif's retired!' Hennessey was genuinely surprised. 'Why, he had a few years left ... more than me in fact.'

'Ill health.' Sharkey opened the palms of

58

his hands in a gesture of helplessness.

'Oh?'

'A mild heart attack ... he sensibly heeded the warning signs. You know all too well what I feel and fear about heart attacks and men in their pre-retirement years?' Sharkey was a small man for a police officer. Hennessey had always found him to be perfectly turned out. His desk was of an everything-in-its-place neatness. On the wall behind him were two photographs, one showing Sharkey in the uniform of a junior officer in the British Army, the other showing him in the uniform of an officer in the Royal Hong Kong Police, as was. He was in his forties, about ten years younger than Hennessey.

'Yes, sir.' Hennessey had often heard the tragic story of Johnny Taighe and doubted that it would not be long before he heard it again.

'Well, DC Pharoah has joined us here at Micklegate Bar, and I'm allocating her to your team.'

'Another team member!' Hennessey beamed at Carmen Pharoah. 'Excellent.'

'Yes –' Sharkey turned to Carmen Pharoah – 'for a long time DCI Hennessey worked only with his sergeant DS Yellich – just the two of them ... then DS Ventnor joined, rapidly followed by DC Webster ... answerable directly to Mr Hennessey.'

'I see.' Carmen Pharoah had a soft, southern counties accent.

'And you'll make the third new addition. It's a good time to join, everybody is still getting to know each other, all still in a state of flux.'

'Yes, sir.'

'Pharaoh ... as in ancient Egypt?' Hennessey asked.

'Spelled differently, sir. The "o" and "a" are the other way round in my name.' She spoke with a calm self-assured, self-possessed manner. 'The origins of the name are obscure and it's my married name.'

'I see ... a very interesting name anyway whatever the origins.'

'I grew up as plain Carmen Bennett in Leytonstone.'

'Yes ... I thought I recognized the London accent. I'm from Greenwich originally ... we have that in common, two Londoners in the frozen north.'

'Yes, sir.' She had a pleasant smile, so thought both Hennessey and Sharkey. 'Well, I married and became Carmen Pharoah. I am now single once more but have retained my married name.'

'I see.' Hennessey smiled. 'Well, again ... welcome aboard.'

'This will mean more supervision for you, taking the overview, George, less time in the field ... less leg work.'

'Sir ... I am capable,' Hennessey appealed to Sharkey.

Sharkey held up his hand. 'I know what

you are going to say, George, and it's no reflection on you. I am in fact increasing your workload if anything. Supervising a team of officers will mean more deskwork but that is also more pressure on you – you are invited to take it as a compliment. I understand there's a spare desk in the DC's room?'

'Yes, sir.' Hennessey sighed with resignation.

'Well, that will be DC Pharoah's accommodation.'

'So,' Hennessey leaned back heavily in his chair, having made all introductions. 'Impressions?' He sipped his tea, which was contained in a large mug embossed with the image of a pair of scales.

'Well, boss, we found the body where Big Phil Buchan said it would be. He was cagey as you'll recall. He'll need a revisit but our impressions...' Yellich hesitated. 'Well, I thought Audrey Aldidge a mite slippery.'

'Slippery? Care to explain ... care to elaborate?'

'I didn't get the impression that she was letting me get hold of her personality.' He too sipped from his mug of tea. 'It was the old story of being like trying to nail jelly to the wall ... or of soap on a rope.'

'That's interesting.' Hennessey nodded. 'Could be very interesting.'

'Yes, sir. Said the right things, full of co-operation but ... something was missing.' Yellich paused as if in doubt or hesitation.

'There's something else, I think,' Hennessey said and then smiled. 'Go on, let's have it ... it all goes into the pot, everything is of value ... nothing is irrelevant.'

'Well ... she kept referring to "we"...'

'We?'

'Yes, sir ... said as if she was living with someone, as a permanent thing ... or as if there was family in the house ... but when I pressed her on the point, she said the "we" meant her and her two maids and the cook.' Yellich shrugged. 'I don't know, sir, it just didn't seem a wholly truthful answer. I don't employ servants or maids or anything, of course, but I have never come across monied people including employees in the concept of their family or partners. It seemed odd somehow.'

'I can understand that. It does seem a little strange.' Hennessey put his mug of tea down on his desktop surface. 'Tell me about the house? The building itself.'

'Well, definitely talking money, I mean big money,' Yellich said. 'The modest address of ... what was it? Twenty-three Ash Lane, turns out that it is the address of the type of house that would normally invite a name, by which I mean Something or other Hall ... or Manor. It is an ivy-covered nineteenth-century pile ... very large gardens that are most probably cared for by contract gardeners. Big money alright.'

'Her source of income?'

'Didn't ask ... sorry, but she indicated her husband left her comfortably off ... didn't enquire if she was employed or self-employed herself.'

'No matter, we only called to determine the identity of the deceased, but it sounds like we'll be returning.'

'Yes, sir. In respect of the identification, the comb and the photograph were sent to Wetherby by courier, we ought to get a result tomorrow.'

'Good.' Hennessey smiled and nodded. 'Webster, anything you'd like to add?'

'Well, sir, much the same impressions as DS Yellich. One of the maids took me to Mr Aldidge's study where the photographs were kept.'

'In a study?' Hennessey raised his eyebrows.

'Yes, sir.'

'Odd, don't you think? A strange place to keep photographs.'

'Possibly, sir, but a recent photograph of Mr Aldidge was rapidly found and at the time that was all that was sought.'

'Fair enough.'

'But I did get the distinct impression when we were driving away, I mean the impression came in hindsight, that the photograph had been placed there ... as if for the convenience of the police.' He leaned forward and picked up the missing person's file from Hennessey's desk, adding, 'Excuse me, sir.'

'You have thought of something, Yellich?'

'Yes, sir ... just comparing the photograph in the file with the photograph Mrs Aldidge gave us ... they are identical ... if not identical, then similar – same background, same blue shirt, taken on Corfu, she said, the January of the year Mr Aldidge was reported as a missing person. No, it's different, a different background, but that smile ... it is as if ... I don't know ... seems strange.'

'Go on ... all in the pot.' He grinned. 'Nothing is irrelevant.'

'Well, it is as if the photographs were taken in readiness for a police inquiry into his disappearance and subsequent finding of the body ... the full face being shown in both photographs ... it's very neat ... and placed so easily to hand as DC Webster has reported ... ready to provide the police with it.'

'The pot's getting bigger, which is what brainstorming sessions are about. What do we know of the deceased ... little or much?'

'Financier, sir. Chose to work in a house in York, rather than from home,' Yellich said whilst still reading the missing person's file. 'He disappeared in the February, says here.'

'Yes?'

'They went on holiday in January, getting some winter sun after the Christmas and New Year parties ... escaping the sleet and the snow.'

'That's what she said?'

'Yes, sir.'

'So, they were not recluses ... they were socially integrated, in fact party animals.'

'It would appear so, sir.'

'Next of kin other than wife? Any issue of the marriage?' Hennessey pressed.

'Nothing known, sir, not yet ... we didn't explore those areas.'

'Alright, if the comb and photograph prove to be a positive match, that will be the next stage of this investigation. Somebody murdered this man ... but according to Tom Gunn the body had to be concealed for at least a month ... all very peculiar.'

'The maid said something quite interesting, sir.' Webster spoke. 'She said she thought something strange is going on, as I recounted to DS Yellich in the car ... or was going on. She has worked there for fifteen years and remembered Arthur Aldidge going missing. She'll be worth chatting to – and she seemed timid.'

'Sounds like it. Sounds like one to chat to.'

'As will the secretary, Mrs Gentle.' Yellich replaced the file, lying it carefully on Hennessey's desk.

'He had a secretary? That sounds useful, secretaries know a great deal, often a lot more than they should.'

'Apparently, sir. Mrs Aldidge said she would provide us with her address.'

'You didn't obtain it?'

'No, sir, as Webster said, we were only there to ascertain identity.'

'Alright. Identity will be established; we all know that ... so some work to do starting tomorrow. Thompson Ventnor will be with us by tomorrow, he's giving evidence today at Bradford Crown Court. This takes priority over anything else any of you are working on. You're plunging in at the deep end DC Pharoah.'

'Yes, sir.'

Carmen Pharoah walked home receiving a few not unexpected but rather unpleasant and hostile glances, because tall, elegant black women are an unusual sight in York. York, she had come to learn, is not at all a cosmopolitan city, it isn't London, or Liverpool, or Birmingham. She was, however, settling in York and saw herself as a pioneer; being a good neighbour, and an efficient police officer would make it easier for the next black woman to follow her, and the next black woman to follow her, and slowly the black community in York would be established. That was her thinking, her attitude, her determination. She coped easily with the odd hostile look by keeping in mind her sisters, and her brothers, coming behind her. She saw herself as a pioneer.

Home for her was a modest two-bedroom, neatly decorated flat just beyond the walls on Bootham, close to the house in which Guy

Fawkes was reported to have been born. She entered the flat and changed from her uncomfortable work outfit and into a tracksuit. She prepared an elaborate dish of spaghetti, savouring the preparation of the meal as much as the eating of it. Long gone were the days when, as a young woman in a hurry, she felt that a meal should take less time to prepare than the eating, and had lived quite contentedly on ready-made meals which just required heating. Now, more leisured, she bought the ingredients and relished the cooking.

Curled up on her couch after the meal, sipping a glass of chilled Frascati, and listening to Mozart, she wondered if she would ever return south. The move north had been a grief-stricken, emotionally driven reaction to her sudden widowhood. Every woman prepares for widowhood upon marriage because men die young and women live on and on and on, there being so many more women in nursing homes than there are men, and thus widowhood for her was not unexpected in itself. What was unexpected was its unfairly, even cruelly, early arrival and its dreadful suddenness. She had been a detective constable in the Metropolitan Police, her husband a chartered accountant, both young, both black, both successful, both ambitious and deeply in love with each other. Both eagerly anticipating a golden future ... then, in an instant, she was alone.

Later still that night she lay in bed listening to the sounds of the night, the solitary click of a woman in heels making her way slowly and apparently unconcerned for her safety, along Bootham, the group of merry-making university students, she guessed from their accents, the whirring of the late night buses, the distant 'ee-or' sound of a railway locomotive arriving or leaving the station.

It had been a long, interesting day, she felt, and allowed herself to drift into the welcoming embrace of sleep.

It was Wednesday, the thirteenth of November, 23.40 hours.

Three

*in which two home visits are made and a
sea change occurs.*

Hennessey leaned back heavily in his chair
and dropped the fax on his desk with a
gesture of finality. 'Well, that clinches it,'
he said. 'The deceased is indeed Arthur
Aldidge. We never had any doubts that it
would be he, but this confirms it. So, Arthur
Aldidge was murdered.' He drummed his
fingers on his desktop. 'Ten years ago he was
struck twice on the head and his body buried
in a large heap of asphalt, to be kept hidden
for "at least a month" as Tom Gunn alleged,
and was in fact hidden for ten years. I must
say, Wetherby came back quickly ... overnight
... that is quick. Very quick. Good for them.'

'Rapid match, I'd say, sir.' Yellich sipped his
tea.

'Has to be the reason,' Ventnor offered. 'A
simple and an easy job to round off their day
yesterday, but nevertheless, still good for
them.'

69

'So, we have an ID for the victim,' Hennessey pondered aloud. 'We have very suspicious circumstances. Who what's for action?' He glanced at his expanded team, Yellich, Ventnor, Webster and Pharoah. 'Right, we need to start ferreting, we know so little. So, I think the sensible thing to do is that we'll split into two teams of two. Let's see ... Yellich and Pharoah, and Ventnor and Webster ... so you two, and you two.'

'Yes, sir.'

'Yes, sir.'

'Webster and Ventnor, go and see Buchan in Full Sutton, lean on him ... it won't be easy, but see where you get to, feel your way forward, go as far as you are able to go.'

'Yes, sir.' Webster replied for both he and Ventnor.

'Yellich and Pharoah, back to the reportedly modestly addressed Twenty-three Ash Lane. What was the name of the village?'

'Thaxted Green, boss,' Yellich responded. 'Quite a picture postcard village, in fact.'

'That's it ... picture postcard Thaxted Green. Go back there ... you also see where you get, you also probe your way forward, you also go as far as you are able. Notify Mrs Aldidge that she is now Widow Aldidge and then probe from there ... gently does it, firmly, keep it focused, but gently does it.'

'Yes, boss,' Yellich said, again.

'I also want the two maids interviewed, and also the cook. We will also need to speak to

70

the secretary. I'll do that, so as soon as you have the secretary's address and phone number, please let me have it ... I repeat, as soon as you are able.'

'Understood.'

'Rendezvous back here at ... shall we say ... two p.m.?'

Hennessey reached forward and picked up the phone on his desk, having deliberately and with some sensitivity let it warble for a second or two. 'Hennessey.'

'Yellich, sir.'

'Ah...' Instinctively he reached for his ballpoint pen.

'We have just arrived at Mrs Aldidge's house.'

'Yes?' Hennessey pulled his notepad towards him.

'I am sitting with Mrs Aldidge and DC Pharoah now.'

'Understood.'

'The secretary...'

'Yes...' Hennessey held his pen poised over his notepad.

'It is one Mrs Mary Gentle, Ingram Drive, number thirty-seven that is ... thirty-seven Ingram Drive, Clifton.'

'Got it, thanks.' Hennessey scribbled on his notepad whilst holding the phone trapped between his ear and his left shoulder. 'See you back here.'

'Yes, sir.' Yellich switched off his mobile and

slid it into his jacket pocket. 'That was our boss,' he explained, 'he's going to visit Mrs Gentle.'

'I see.' Mrs Aldidge remained stone-faced as if absorbing the certainty that she was now a widow. 'So it all starts now, I assume?'

'*It*?' Yellich inclined his head and raised his eyebrows.

'The police investigation ... isn't that what you call it? Now you have a body ... now you have a crime. I am sorry if I sound a little angry but I feel ten years has been lost somehow.'

'Well, as we explained to you yesterday...'

'Oh ... was it only yesterday?' Audrey Aldidge glanced up at the ceiling. 'Somehow ... so much has happened.'

'As I explained, we can't search for missing adults, unless their disappearance is suspicious, and clearly so. I am sorry but it is just the way of it.'

'I can appreciate that and I dare say you could not have prevented anything ... Arthur would still have been murdered.' Audrey Aldidge was dressed more casually than she had been the previous day; now she wore white slacks, blue training shoes, a lemon coloured jersey and a man's sports jacket, which indeed, Yellich had to concede, looked quite fetching. He reflected again how women have more latitude than men when it comes to clothing; there is not a single item of women's clothing that a man can wear and still enjoy social acceptance, but women can wear flat caps, sports jackets, jeans and, as with Mrs Aldidge at that moment, also what are, to all intents and purposes, trousers. 'So, how can I help you?' She spoke as if mustering emotional strength from somewhere.

'By telling us about your husband.'

Audrey Aldidge sat forward. 'It would be easier if you asked questions, I think. You know, what is relevant ... I could wander off into all sorts of areas that wouldn't be of any help at all.'

'Well, I am sorry to be personal, but how was the quality of your marriage?'

'It was good –' she nodded and smiled as if recalling fond memories – 'very good. Yes, functional in all areas ... we still holidayed together. We hadn't been married long, you see, so it was a good marriage. Not long lasting but very good during its brief life.'

'Oh...' Yellich queried, 'not long married?'

'No ... not long, three years. He was forty-two when we married, I was fifteen years his junior ... so we were still starry-eyed.'

'Yes,' Yellich said with a smile, 'as you still would be after just three years. Mr Aldidge owned this house when you married?'

'He very definitely had the Midas touch, money just seemed to gravitate to him, lucky man. Some people are just like that, I have come to learn and accept, other people just never seem to have two coins to rub together.'

'So I have noticed.' Yellich again smiled. 'To have and to have not.'

'Arthur owned this house outright when he was still in his early thirties. I don't exactly know how he made his money, Mrs Gentle would be the one to advise you there ... but he was in the financial services sector, as I told you yesterday.'

'Yes, as I said, our boss is visiting her as we speak.'

'I wasn't a trophy wife, I want you to know that ... we had a real marriage. We shared on an emotional level, we were partners, it was a real relationship.'

'Yes, we understand, I wasn't implying anything at all, we are still exploring, still trying to get a measure of Mr Aldidge, after all, this only became a murder inquiry about an hour ago.'

'Yes ... I'm sorry,' she said with a smile. 'This is very strange territory for me, new and alarming territory.'

'And you know of no one who would want to harm your husband?'

'No one –' Audrey Aldidge extended an open palm – 'no one at all.'

'What do you know of his colleagues?'

'Colleagues.' Audrey Aldidge raised her eyebrows. 'Arthur didn't really have any. He worked alone, with just Mrs Gentle to keep the office for him and answer the phone and doubtless make the tea. He had contacts in the business community in York and the Vale but no colleagues as such. He was a one-man band. Dare say he would have made a few enemies along the way but what successful businessman doesn't?'

'Friends? Family?'

'Yes and yes. We threw lavish parties and he had one brother. Both parents are deceased now. Alive when he went missing, subsequently died ... that couldn't have been at all easy for them and I shared their grief, he was the eldest and the most successful, they missed him deeply. Agony for them. I visited often, but nothing could ease the pain of their loss, the not knowing ... it was that that made it so bad.'

'I can imagine. Where does his brother live?' Yellich asked. 'We would like to chat to Mr Aldidge's brother.'

Audrey Aldidge smiled. 'He is a publican. Lives out by the coast. I can easily provide his address, but his pub is called the Vine.'

Again Yellich saw a too compliant Audrey Aldidge, too compliant by far, the smile, the summoning of emotional strength suddenly seemed to be an act, the willingness to answer questions all said to him: 'I do not want you to suspect me because I have something to hide'. He then asked, 'No children from the union?'

'No ... we had planned, of course, but...'

'You haven't worked since your husband disappeared, yet you have managed to retain possession of the house?'

75

'Yes, I told you, my husband ... my late husband, was a wealthy man; he left money that I could access and I sold his office in York, that raised a very useful amount that went into a high interest account.'

'Ah, yes, that would help you nicely.' Yellich paused. 'I wonder if we might talk to your housemaids?'

'Of course.' Audrey Aldidge stood and tugged the sash on the wall and then resumed her seat, moving, it seemed to Yellich, with practised grace and ease.

Moments passed and then the door of the room quietly opened and the maid who, the previous day, had given her name as Molly, stood squarely on the threshold.

'These two police officers would like to ask you some questions, Molly. Do take a seat.'

'Yes, ma'am.' Molly moved towards a vacant upright chair.

'In private.' Yellich spoke softly but firmly. 'We want to talk to Molly in private.'

Audrey Aldidge shot a cold glance at him. 'This is my house, this is my husband's murder we are talking about.'

'Yes, but we still would like to speak to this lady in private,' Yellich insisted.

'I protest.' Audrey Aldidge flushed with anger.

'We can talk to her in her own home.' Yellich remained calm.

'She lives here, this is her home, she has accommodation in the attic.'

'Or at the police station. One way or the other, we will speak to her in private.'

Audrey Aldidge stood and walked out of the room with an air of indignation. As she did so, she fixed Molly with a cold stare as if in warning. Both officers saw the stare, both noted it.

'Please, Molly...' Yellich indicated the room with an open palm.

Molly, middle-aged and probably considering herself a little overweight continued to steer a course to the upright chair.

'No ... no...' Yellich said warmly and cheerfully, 'make yourself comfortable.' He pointed to the chaise longue upon which Mrs Aldidge had been seated. 'Sit there ... please.'

'Oh, I shouldn't, sir,' Molly pleaded, 'the mistress is very particular about the servants sitting in easy chairs, she doesn't allow it at all. Not under any circumstances.'

'Well, the mistress isn't here.' Yellich spoke firmly as he experienced the sensation that he was visiting an earlier era, he felt he was having a history lesson. 'Come on, sit down.'

Molly obediently sat on the chaise longue, looking sheepishly at Yellich as if she was tasting forbidden fruit, as if enjoying a treat which wasn't meant to be hers.

'So, Molly...' Yellich began.

'Yes, sir.'

'Molly for Margaret?'

'Yes sir. Margaret. Margaret Coley.' She spoke with a West Indian accent.

77

'We understand you have worked for the household for a long time?'

'Fifteen years, sir.' She crossed her ankles and wrists and sat upright.

'You needn't keep calling me, sir.' Yellich spoke warmly, trying to put the woman at ease.

'No, sir.'

'Yesterday, when I called with another officer, you and the other officer went and looked for a recent photograph of the deceased, Mr Aldidge.'

'He is no longer with us?'

'Ah ... yes, you may as well know, Mr Aldidge is confirmed deceased.'

'Oh...' Margaret Coley put her hand up to her chest. 'Well, after this length of time, it's not a surprise ... like I said ... no ... I should not be surprised. Sorry, I am sorry, yes, I am sorry, but I am not surprised.'

'No. Well, yesterday you told the other officer, DC Webster, that there was something strange going on at the house. What did you mean by that?'

The woman glanced nervously and fearfully at the door.

'Nobody can hear us.'

Margaret Coley opened her eyes wider and shook her head. 'I would not be surprised if this room had a microphone ... you know, is bugged like on the TV .... .She seems to know everything, does that one.' She spoke in a whisper. 'Everything ... everything.'

'If you'd be happier at the police station?' Yellich offered.

'No,' Margaret Coley said as she shook her head, 'it's alright. I'm sure it isn't bugged like you see on the television, just me being nervous, but sometimes you'd think it. The way she knows things ... it's weird ... not natural.'

'Alright ... if you're sure?'

'Yes, I'm sure.' She smiled. 'I am sure.'

'So what did you mean about the strange things going on at the house?'

'The parties that go on here...'

'Parties?' Yellich raised an eyebrow. 'Drug taking, you mean?'

'No, she is clean living in that sense ... alcohol is tolerated but not drugs ... not illegal drugs.'

'What then?'

'They're racists. They have parties with Nazi flags on the walls.'

Carmen Pharoah stiffened.

'For decoration,' Margaret Coley explained. 'Me and Prudence have to put them up before the parties and take them down afterwards.'

'And you are prepared to work here!' Carmen Pharoah leaned forward. 'That makes you ... you are complying with it.' She put her hand to her head.

'I didn't know what to think at first and then me and Prudence ... she's the other maid, she's also black, like me ... now we just giggle about it. I mean, if they want to think they're better than we are because they're white, it isn't harming us.'

'That's not the point,' Carmen Pharoah retorted, angrily.

'Excuse me, miss, but you have a good position, a good income, security of work as a police officer, you can afford to take that attitude. I can't. Prudence can't. I was past forty when I came to work here, so was Prudence. We didn't know each other until we met here but both of us were in the same situation, nowhere to live, no skills to offer, no family, just distant relatives in Jamaica. So Mrs Aldidge offers accommodation, all found, and a wage. That's not bad ... it's a good deal for us. We both get paid quite well considering it's all spending money. Five days a week, two weeks' holiday a year. A roof over our heads. So they like having black servants so they can pretend to be higher than us? Pretend they're back on the plantation like in the old days? It doesn't harm me and Prudence and if we walked out we'd only walk into the Salvation Army hostel and the dole ... nowhere else for us to go.'

Carmen Pharoah remained silent but anger welled up inside her.

'I'm even saving money,' Margaret Coley added. 'So, she likes having black servants at the parties, taking coats, and then keeping out of the way, out of sight. But the group she belongs to, that is another thing entirely,

80

very nasty people. Young, fit, white boys with short hair, being drilled like soldiers on the back lawn, out of sight of the road. They're thugs. I don't like that ... Prudence doesn't either ... some very heavy boys ... very nasty men ... very nasty.'

'What is the name of the group?'

'The British Alliance. I am not supposed to know that but she leaves letters around ... you know, opened and read. She probably thinks I can't read but I can.'

'Alliance ... who with?' Yellich asked. 'What with?'

Margaret Coley shook her head. 'I couldn't tell you, sir, but they've got money ... big motors outside when she has one of her parties here ... black chauffeurs.'

'Black chauffeurs!' Carmen Pharoah gasped. 'What is this?'

'Yes, miss, they have the same attitude as me and Prudence. We have a good giggle together in the kitchen ... me, Prudence and the drivers ... her and her guests and their silly games. The drivers, they are in the same position, accommodated, fed, not bad working hours, good pay, and they have the Salvation Army hostel as the alternative like me and Prudence. So you can be shocked, miss, and if I were in your shoes, I'd be shocked, but I am not in your shoes, neither is Prudence or the drivers either. I'm fifty-six years old and I'm in my shoes. You got to take a step into my shoes, then you see it from my angle ... you got to do that to under-stand it ... step into my shoes.'

Carmen Pharoah sank back in the chair she occupied. Her anger was giving way to dismay.

'This is interesting.' Yellich spoke as much to himself as to the room. 'The young men being drilled ... thugs you say?'

'Like a police force for the Alliance, seems to be. Me and Prudence, we don't know any-thing about that ... the politics ... that is scary, but the parties in the house and letting mistress think we are her slaves in her fine home in the Caribbean in the middle of a sugar plantation ... we get paid for that ... and it don't harm us, like I said.'

'How often are the parties? How often do the thugs drill on the back lawn?' Yellich pressed.

'The parties, once every three or four months ... so not so often. Next one is this coming weekend, we are already preparing for it. The skinheads, they drill every Satur-day ... drill and fighting ... a gang of them ... about twenty.'

'Fighting?' Yellich echoed.

'Practice fighting, in pairs ... don't know what to say it's called.'

Yellich and Carmen Pharoah glanced at each other, as if to say, Wow!

'Alright ... to change the subject a little, what do you remember about Mr Aldidge?' Yellich asked of the now clearly much more

82

relaxed Margaret Coley.

'Mr Aldidge ... well, he was definitely one of them ... the British Alliance. He used to host the parties. You know, sir, and miss, I never got the impression that parties were held in other folk's houses. They never went out as though they were going out to a party. The golf club, yes ... or to a restaurant, yes ... but never to parties as such.' She shifted in her seat. 'They always came back too early. Much too early. Those parties, they went on until well after midnight, all those Union Jacks and Nazi flags hanging from the wall ... in the summer they would spill out on to the lawn at the back of the house.'

'What sort of man was he?'

'Nice enough to me and Prudence and Cook. He and she argued a bit but isn't that marriage? I was married once ... it was like that a lot ... like that too much ... that was in Jamaica.'

'What about the time he disappeared? Anything happen around then ... anything significant that you can remember?'

'A long time ago, ten years ... difficult to remember if some things happened before or after he went missing. I do remember him being visited by a couple of regulars at the parties, and some words being swapped ... happened just the once.'

'You mean an argument ... words being swapped ... arguing ... a fight?'

'Yes, sir ... with raised voices but not a fight

83

... just shouting.'

'Do you know the identity of these two men?' Yellich asked. 'I assume they were men?'

'Yes, sir, they were men alright, but I don't know their names, just recognized them from the parties ... high up though. Mr Aldidge, he always seemed to have a good regard for them he did. They'll be here on Saturday night most likely.'

'So, the parties continued after he disappeared?'

'Oh, yes, sir ... four a year ... just as normal.'

'How did Mrs Aldidge react to her husband's disappearance that you were aware of or able to observe?'

'Mrs Audrey looked worried, as any woman would, but the worry lines faded as she got on with life. She's a go-getter and she was still young.'

'Does she have a partner?'

'I think she does ... in fact she does, a man friend calls and stays overnight. Mr Charles ... only ever called Mr Charles.'

'You don't know his full name?'

'No, sir, just Charles ... as I said, only ever called, Mr Charles.'

'I see.' Yellich paused. 'Is Mr Charles a partygoer ... one of the parties held here, I mean? Is he of the British Alliance?'

'Yes, sir,' Margaret Coley smiled. 'He is definitely ... a regular attender.'

84

'How long would you say it was before he started staying overnight with Mrs Aldidge?'

'Oh, a decent time, sir ... about a year after Mr Arthur went missing but they may have been seeing each other before then, of course.'

'Fair enough.'

There occurred a lull in the interview.

'You don't feel frightened here?' Carmen Pharoah asked, breaking the silence.

'No, miss, been here a long time now. If something was going to happen to me because of my race, it would have happened by now and so long as I do my job, I don't think anything will happen. I have a room of my own ... I am saving money. I don't mind their games ... it doesn't affect me.'

Yellich and Pharoah then asked to speak to the second maid. Molly went to get her.

'Prudence?' Yellich smiled at the woman who sat nervously upon the chaise longue, after initially, like Margaret, making to sit on an upright chair.

'Yes, sir.' She seemed to both officers to be very fearful of something. Or someone.

'Can I have your full name, please?'

'Prudence McVey.' She sat stiffly upright, dressed in a similar maid's uniform to that worn by Margaret Coley and with similar close-cropped hair.

'You were employed here when Mr Aldidge was around?' Yellich asked as gently as he could.

'Yes, sir.'

'Is there anything you can tell us about him ... anything that you think is relevant to his disappearance?'

'No, sir, nothing.' She held a steady eye contact with Yellich, as she shook her head vigorously.

'Nothing unusual happened about the time he disappeared?'

'No, sir.' Again, a quick, rapid shaking of the head.

Prudence McVey had been primed, clearly so, thought Yellich. Listening, and observing but not taking part, Carmen Pharoah also sensed a feeling of disappointment. It was not difficult to imagine, the sort of conversation that Audrey Aldidge had had with Prudence McVey whilst she and Yellich were interviewing Margaret Coley. With Margaret Coley, all Audrey Aldidge could do was give a warning glare, but with Prudence McVey, she had clearly been able to instil into her the fear of the Almighty.

'Well,' Yellich said as he folded his notebook. 'If you should think of anything that you believe might be important, you could perhaps contact us, if you'd be so good.'

'Yes, sir. Can I go now, sir?' She half stood as she asked for permission.

'Yes, thank you.'

Prudence McVey stood and left the room with notable haste.

Yellich and Carmen Pharoah glanced at

each other. Yellich shrugged.

'Got at,' Pharoah said with an incline of her head . 'Very definitely got at. Intimidated.'

'I'll say.' Yellich put his notepad down beside him. 'What is going on in this house? What has gone on?'

'Is there any point in talking to the cook, do you think?' Carmen Pharoah spoke wearily.

'Probably not,' Yellich agreed with a sigh. 'Probably not, but we'll have to for form's sake if nothing else.'

'Cook', as she preferred to be called, though she gave her name as Belinda Sweet, aged fifty years, spinster, proved herself to be equally unforthcoming as had been Prudence McVey. She, too, sat stiffly upright on the chaise longue after also first making for an upright chair and gave 'yes' and 'no' answers, speaking so softly that her voice was barely audible. Yellich had the feeling that he was prising words from her mouth. Unlike the two maids, Miss Sweet was northern European in respect of her race but, like the two previous interviewees, she was definitely 'below stairs' in terms of her status. She too wore her hair in a closely cropped manner as if such was the preferred fashion for female employees to adopt at 23 Ash Lane, and she too seemed to exhibit the same fear of Audrey Aldidge that Prudence McVey had. Although she too remembered Arthur Aldidge very well, she could not offer any information in respect of his disappearance.

The most she offered was, 'I'm Cook, sir, I only know what goes on in the kitchen', and that, both officers felt, had been a response which had been fed to her, with clear instructions that she rehearse it.

Driving away from 23 Ash Lane, after having taken their leave of a cold and disapproving Mrs Aldidge, Yellich said, 'They're not Union Jacks.'

'What?' Carmen Pharoah turned to him. 'What do you mean?'

'They're not Union Jacks,' Yellich repeated. 'Ashore it is the Union Flag, only at sea is it the Union Jack.'

'Oh...' Carmen Pharoah glanced to her left at the houses of the village of Thaxted Green thinking that was the sort of trivia that she didn't want to hear, not at that moment. She found herself profoundly upset by the revelations offered by Margaret Coley, and feared for the woman's safety, no matter what she had said about not being in danger. 'That glare,' she said, turning back to Yellich.

'What glare?'

'The look that Audrey Aldidge gave Margaret as she left the room, as Aldidge left the room I mean, we both saw it. We ought to bring her out of there for her own safety. That look clearly said, "say nothing" and what did she do but give information? She's in danger. She might not have been in danger for the last fifteen years, but the police

88

haven't visited and asked awkward questions in the last fifteen years, just one visit to take a mis per report which was expected and planned for. We have just changed things for her. A Neo-Nazi party ... here in York ... and not just disaffected youth who blame Moslems for the unemployment and Afro-Caribbeans for all the street crime. Here we are talking big money, politics ... this is a serious issue. We've got to take this to the top ... and pull her and the other maid out of there.'

'No!' Yellich slapped the steering wheel. 'We take it to George Hennessey ... nowhere else. It's up to him to pass it up the chain of command.'

The remainder of the journey to York was passed in a strained silence.

George Hennessey graciously accepted the offer of a cup of tea from the sparkly-eyed Mary Gentle who seemed delighted to have a visitor to entertain. Her home was a modest semi-detached house with, Hennessey felt, a cluttered feel about it, and which had a slightly musty smell. Much of the floor space in her living room seemed to be occupied by furniture, many of the surfaces were covered with assorted items though each was placed neatly, as if in its appointed place. Mary Gentle seemed to Hennessey to be a frail-looking, silver-haired lady, now in her seventies, bespectacled, but with a sharp mind and a beautifully warm and generous disposition.

'Your family?' Hennessey glanced to his right at shelves in an alcove, which contained many framed colour photographs of adults and children.

'Yes...' She spoke proudly. 'That's the rogues' gallery, my husband is deceased...'

'I am sorry.'

'Some time ago now. It was shortly after he passed on that I went to work for Mr Aldidge. But we had three gorgeous children and between them they produced eight gorgeous grandchildren and so far, one gorgeous great-grandchild. I am such a fulfilled woman. I am just sorry Stanley isn't here to enjoy what I enjoy. He went very quickly and from natural causes. It was an easy death, that was a mercy, but young ... fifty-three ... still quite young ... too young ... all the plans we had for his retirement...'

Hennessey felt as if stabbed in the side of his chest. 'Yes,' he replied, 'too young.'

'Well, I'll go and put the kettle on.' Mrs Gentle scurried out of the room, clearly eager to entertain her unexpected company.

'So, how can I help you?' she asked when she and Hennessey were seated, each nursing a cup of tea.

'It's really about your ex-employer, as I said on the phone ... Mr Aldidge.'

'Yes ... he has turned up.' She sat forward in her chair in an apparently, eager-to-please

90

attitude. 'That was such a mystery.'

'Why do you say that?' Hennessey stirred his tea.

'Well, otherwise you wouldn't be here ... I mean would you?'

Hennessey smiled. 'Yes, you are correct ... except that he has turned up deceased ... I am sorry to say.'

'Oh?'

This was said with a smile, a tell-me-the-gossip sort of smile, so thought Hennessey, but her warmth was genuine, as was her willingness to co-operate which was all, as a police officer, he could ask for.

'Yes, sadly ... you may hear or read it in the local news.'

'I always catch the national six o'clock news. I'll tune in...'

'We'll be issuing a press release once the next of kin have been notified, my officers are doing that now.'

'I'll watch the local news at six thirty.'

'Yes...' He glanced at his watch: ten forty-five. 'Yes, it ought to make this evening's bulletin. So, Mr Arthur Aldidge?'

'Yes, Mr Arthur, as I called him. I looked after his office.'

'A house in York, I believe?'

'Yes ... sold now, a family live there.'

'Anything at all that you might recall about Arthur Aldidge's disappearance?'

'I remember him leaving the office for an appointment. He never returned ... it was the

91

last time I saw him. It's like that, you often never know the last time you'll see someone ... or the last words you'll say to them. I've learned to be careful what I say to folk, particularly family in case it's the last time I talk to them.'

'Yes, a good attitude to have ... so he arrived from his home that day?'

'Yes ... quite usual ... but he did look worried. I remember he looked worried that morning.'

'That's interesting ... go on.'

'Well, he did seem to be wrapped up in his own thoughts for the few days before he went missing, as though something was preying on his mind.'

'He didn't say what?'

'No ... not to little me ... the little woman in the office ... the word-processor operator, the maker of tea, the opener of mail, the postmistress of outgoing mail ... I never got let into any secrets. I just kept in my place.'

'Alright.' Hennessey sipped his tea. 'Do please carry on.'

'Well, he drove off to keep his appointment ... never seen again. Not alive anyway.'

'Do you remember who with? It would be very useful.'

'Yes ... a client called Redmond. I remember the name because that's my daughter's married name ... my middle child ... she's now Mrs Redmond.'

'Redmond,' Hennessey repeated the name

and wrote it on his notepad. 'Anything else you can tell me about Mr Redmond?'

'He was the manager of the Beaconsfield Hotel in York. The huge new hotel by the racecourse ... you must know it ... huge thing, can't miss it.'

'Ah, yes.' Hennessey nodded. 'I know it. Do you know if he kept the appointment?'

'No, sorry –' Mary Gentle shook her head – 'but I assume he did. Mr Redmond didn't phone asking where Mr Arthur was or if he was late or anything.'

'No matter, I can check.'

'He had a strange phone call I remember now ... it worried him.'

'Oh?' Hennessey again sipped his tea.

'Yes, from a man ... a man called ... unusual name ... not so unusual but fairly unusual. What was it? I will remember it because I do sometimes ... the name just comes to mind for no reason, so I'll remember, if not today, I'll remember...'

'It would be a great help if you could remember it.'

'Dewsnap,' Mary Gentle smiled. 'That's it, 'Dewsnap'. A nice name, I thought. I picture the snapping of twigs underfoot on a dewy morning ... Dewsnap. Unusual, but a pleasant name. I knew I'd remember it. Lovely name.'

'Indeed.' Hennessey wrote the name on his pad and thought it a conveniently unusual name ... very easy to trace the owner of such a name. 'Why do you say that the call from Mr Dewsnap worried him?'

'Because after the call he looked worried, simple as that really. That's when he began to look a bit pre-occupied, after that phone call. Also, after that call, he told me that if Mr Dewsnap called again I was to tell him that Mr Arthur was out. He did call two or three times, then when I said that Mr Arthur was out, he said, "He can run but he can't hide". Not a pleasant voice ... the voice didn't go with the name. He never called again and Mr Arthur disappeared a week or so later.'

'Now that is interesting.'

'Do you think so?' Mrs Gentle said eagerly.

'Oh, yes...' Hennessey tapped his notepad. 'Very interesting.'

'Ten years ago but I recall it like it was yesterday.'

'Anything else strike you as odd?'

'Mrs Audrey clearing the house. That was odd ... I thought that was odd...'

'Odd?' Hennessey glanced to his left, out of the window of Mrs Gentle's sitting room at her small but neatly kept rear garden. He took in the lawn, the carefully weeded border, the closely cut privet and a beech tree beyond, in another property, which glowed a shimmering gold as it was caught by a ray of sunlight. 'In what way ... can you elaborate?'

'Well, I thought it was too soon after he disappeared to assume he wouldn't be returning.'

'How soon?'

'About six weeks, probably less. I thought it a little early to be giving up hope.'

'That is a bit soon, I grant you ... but carry on, please.'

'Upon Mr Arthur's disappearance she obtained power of attorney, took control of all his affairs. She gave me the sack, no redundancy package, "just don't come back", very cutting but she was like that, acid-tongued when she wanted to be. But I did go back, left something of mine behind, so I went back early that same evening. I still had a set of keys you see ... and, well ... knock me down with a feather, as my dear husband used to say, knock me down with a feather, but the house was completely cleared. All Mr Arthur's papers had been burned – they'd had a bonfire in the back garden. It's a bigger garden than my little garden ... the old iron brazier that had been left by the previous owners had been used, it was still full of ash and a few bits of burned paper. The computer too ... I don't and never did understand those things ... but the discs had been burned as well. A pile of burnt discs on the concrete pathway and the machine itself in pieces like it had been smashed with a sledgehammer. Talk about making sure. No one was going to get any information from it by then, nor from the disks, all warped with the heat like they were. I understand there to be neater ways of wiping information from a computer and disks but I dare say she was making sure, like I said, really making sure.'

'It was Mrs Aldidge who cleared the house?'

'I can't say...' She paused. 'I wasn't there ... can't see her doing all that by herself, she must have had help. She'd be the boss but she had to have had help. Gave me my cards at midday that day ... I went back at about eight p.m ... Left a house full of filing cabinets and office furniture, came back to bare floorboards just eight hours later.'

'Bare floorboards? She would have needed help to do all that in just eight hours.' Hennessey pondered. 'What were you doing in the time between Mr Aldidge's disappearance and being made redundant?'

'Minding the shop.' Mary Gentle smiled. 'Mrs Audrey continued to pay me just to be there, answering the phone ... a lot of phone calls to be answered in the early days, folks wanting to talk to Mr Arthur and all I could say was that he was a missing person as Mrs Audrey told me to say to callers ... to tell them he was missing. After a while the phone calls stopped ... perhaps one or two a day ... not from clients by then, just from folk making enquiries and telesales people wanting to sell double-glazing and insurance. After a while I got to take a radio with me and sat listening to Radio Four or reading a book ... quite a good job, I thought, getting paid to read books and listen to the radio. I've never been one for TV especially during the day time.'

'Could be worse,' Hennessey said with a smile. 'I have certainly heard of harder ways to make a living.'

'Well, after a few weeks, Mrs Audrey called and told me to collect my possessions and go. Well, that was me, sixty-two years old. I wasn't bothered, worked longer than most women, had a state pension from sixty. After I was made redundant I gave my life and interest over to my children and grandchildren. Fulfilled woman, as I said.'

Hennessey paused and tapped his notepad with his ballpoint. 'Were there any callers to the house?'

'Clients, you mean?'

'Anybody, anybody at all.'

'Contract gardeners kept the garden neat. My good neighbour does mine ... but Mr Arthur employed contract gardeners ... but apart from that, no one, except Mrs Audrey, she would pop in from time to time if she was in York, as I recall.'

'How were they together? As a married couple, did you get any impression either way? Happy? Unhappy?'

'Happy, I'd say, she always looked cheerful to be calling ... he always seemed pleased to see her. They hadn't been married very long and it showed. Seemed so to me anyway. They never really talked to each other in my presence. He would usher her into his office

97

as soon as she arrived, so it could have been a show of warmth put on for my benefit but I really don't think so ... I have intuition, like any woman.' She sat back in her chair. 'You know, come to think of it, the person to ask about the house clearing ... well, any of the neighbours, but the old lady who lived directly opposite ... used to watch the entire street like a hawk. Never knew her name but she was often at her front window, either upstairs or downstairs ... or in her front garden, pretending to prune her trees.'

'Trees!'

'Shrubs, yes, I should say shrubs, not trees ... but all the while noticing what is going on, those piercing, hawk eyes. She was getting on in years a little then, not much older than me ... but if she is still with us ... and if she's still got her marbles, she'll be the one to talk to.'

'Certainly sounds like it.' Hennessey closed his notebook. 'It certainly sounds like it. Thank you, indeed.'

Philip 'Big Phil' Buchan eyed Ventnor and Webster with transparent distaste. 'You're back soon, sooner than I thought.'

'Updating you, Philip,' Ventnor said and smiled, 'keeping you informed.'

'Where are the other two? You look too young to be law men.'

'Following other leads, they're well occupied, don't worry. We've been asked to visit you.' Webster sat forward and glanced round

98

the agents' room – hard, functional, a table and four chairs. 'So, we've called on you ... as asked to do so by Mr Hennessey.'

'The body has been identified,' Ventnor continued. 'Arthur Aldidge. Very tall man ... you would remember him as being very tall. And he was murdered ... so it doesn't get more serious. You do remember him as being a very tall man?'

'Maybe.' Buchan wasn't giving anything away easily.

Nonetheless the officers ears pricked up; 'maybe' was a step closer to 'Big Phil' Buchan opening up and providing information ... time to apply pressure.

'What does "maybe" mean?' Webster took a packet of cigarettes from his jacket pocket and offered one to Buchan who snatched at it greedily.

'Maybe means maybe.' Buchan put the cigarette hungrily to his lips and leaned anxiously forward while Webster flicked the canary yellow disposable lighter he carried.

'We understand our boss ... Mr Hennessey...'

'He was one of the guys who visited me, right? The older guy?'

'Right.' Webster returned the lighter to his pocket. 'He made you an offer?'

'Did he?' Buchan exhaled through his nostrils.

'Well, he pointed out to you, did he not, that any co-operation you provide to us will be to your advantage. I mean, you've still got three years to serve, and that's allowing for good behaviour.'

'Yeah.' Buchan drew strongly on the cigarette and again exhaled through his nostrils. 'Swallowed up, he said. I remember now. If I was part of the murder of Aldidge I could be charged but the sentence would be swallowed up with what I am serving already.' Buchan leaned back in his chair. 'Dunno ... have to think about it ... could help me out ... it could also harm me. It's a bit like playing poker ... you don't know what cards the other guy is holding. It could be a bluff.'

'So you know something?' Ventnor pressed.

Buchan nodded. 'Yeah, I know something ... but these are seriously heavy boys, a really heavy-duty crew. I mean, I have been a blagger all my life and I know the rules. I get respect in here ... I get left alone ... but I have to watch my step round those geezers.'

'So what did you do?'

Buchan paused. 'These are really, really heavy guys ... it's just not that easy.'

'We can offer you protection.'

'Like you offered "Mule" Mulligan protection?'

Ventnor and Webster glanced at each other. 'You know about that?'

Buchan smiled. 'I hear things ... the blaggers have a community ... word gets round, you know, the telegraph. I met Mule once or twice ... got moved up to Durham ... new name ... he still got the Chelsea smile, though, then they topped him. The milkman found him one morning, door of his house wide open, blood all over the walls, so they say ... that's police protection. I'm going to need more protection than that.'

'Most of the time ... most of the time it works and by most I don't mean fifty-one per cent of the time, I mean ninety-five per cent of the time,' Webster advised. 'We have a good record for effective protection.'

'So ... there's always that chance ... that five per cent. And that's all it takes, all it needs.'

'Yes,' Ventnor said with a nod, 'we don't claim to be perfect. Who is perfect? But a ninety-five per cent chance of disappearing for ever with a new identity is ... well, I'd take those odds if I wanted a clean break ... it's an attractive proposition.'

'I don't want to give evidence ... perhaps I can give information, but I am not giving evidence.'

'You'll have to,' Ventnor said firmly, 'that's what you give in return for protection.'

'It's why it's called Witness Protection,' Webster added.

'So, what do you know?' Buchan drew heavily on the cigarette as he bided his time, still working out if he was going to help them or not. 'I want to know how close you are.'

'Well, we don't know what Mr Hennessey and Sergeant Yellich are finding out at the moment but we do know that Arthur Aldidge was murdered.'

'You said that ... you already said that.'

'His skull was cracked open ... two blows ... with a long, thin instrument. Quite neat but very premeditated. He was a very tall man so he must have been sitting down and taken by surprise. We've seen his house and spoken to his wife ... now his widow.'

'She saying anything?' Buchan forced an unpleasant looking grin.

'Not a lot ... but she's being re-visited ... if she knows something, we'll find out what it is.'

Buchan smirked. 'You won't get any change out of her.'

'Why do you say that?' Webster asked. 'That's an interesting comment.'

'Just won't ... I know her ... believe me, I know her.'

'You're itching to deal.' Ventnor smiled. 'I can sense it.'

'You think?' Buchan dragged on the cigarette once more. 'You can sense it, can you?'

'Yes, I think so.' Ventnor sat back in his chair. 'You said it yourself, Phil, you're a career blagger ... in it for life, in the game if not prison. You know the score, you know the criminal code about grassing ... yet...' Ventnor held up his finger. 'Yet you're beginning to talk to us, you know something very significant about the murder of Arthur Aldidge, you know Mrs Aldidge ... you've mentioned

102

"heavy boys", as you describe them.'

'Possibly I do.' Buchan glanced downwards at the table top. 'I'm fifty-four, I'm getting tired of prison life ... I have spent half my days inside. I was lying on the bunk last night listening to my cellmate mumbling to himself and I thought, What am I doing here? I've never been banged up wrongly, that's fair to say ... never wrongly ... never stitched up by the law. There's some in here that shouldn't be here ... but I'm not one of them. So I have spent half my life in prison – half, and it's all down to me. I got done for about one in ten of all the jobs I pulled but those one in ten were enough to get me to lose half my life ... inside.'

'It's called a sea change,' Webster offered.

'What is?' Buchan looked at Webster in an appealing way. Gone suddenly was the smirk, the unpleasant, defiant grinning. 'What's a sea change?'

'A rapid re-adjustment of attitude. A complete transformation.'

'Sea change ... I'll remember that ... a sea change ... I like that.' He stubbed out the cigarette. 'Well, I don't want to spend the rest of my days inside. I don't want to become one of the sad old ones. When I was younger it was the thing to do, get some prison time under my belt if I wanted to get on ... but I'm heading for the Grey House I hear about and hear about more and more often these days.'

103

'It's a holiday camp compared to Full Sutton,' Ventnor told him. 'A rest home for the burned out cases.'

'Down in the beautiful south, all the lags are north of fifty ... easy regime, very easy they say. I don't want to go there ... fifty-four ... I could live for another twenty years ... longer. Time I screwed the bobbin, I reckon.'

Ventnor smiled and nodded. 'Yes, I think it is ... for your sake. Twenty years of freedom, in a new life, a new identity ... that's a good deal. Don't sniff at it.'

'I could get married ... there's widows ... youngish widows and divorcees out there ... I heard that.'

'Yes, especially in York.'

'Really?' Buchan's eyes brightened. 'Is that true?'

'It has that reputation, Phil, more divorced women in York per head of population than any other town in the UK. So I heard ... many looking for a new partner.'

'That would be nice ... to settle down with a good woman. Do you have another fag? You know, I could quite take to that notion ... put my feet up.'

'So,' Webster asked once the second cigarette had been offered, accepted and lit, 'what don't we know?'

'Plenty, I'd say.' Buchan exhaled lovingly. 'Oh smoke ... fag smoke ... beautiful. I can only tell you what I know.'

'That'll do, for a start ... we'd be happy with that.'

'Dare say I am guilty to accessory to murder after the fact.' Buchan shrugged. 'That's fair ... if you want the truth. I am an accessory.'

Webster held up his hands. 'Careful, Phil ... you are entitled to a lawyer, you don't want to incriminate yourself unknowingly ... that could weaken any defence you might want to use. Let's keep it by the book.'

Ventnor leaned forward and fixed Buchan with a stare. 'You are not obliged to say anything but it may harm your defence if you do not mention, when questioned, anything you later rely on in court.'

'Understood.' Buchan nodded. 'But the sea change ... it has an appeal, I mean it really sounds good. I want to put all this behind me ... I don't want anything hanging over me once I walk out of the gates of this or any other nick. I've done enough bird.'

'Fair enough,' Webster said. 'So ... in your own time, Phil, in your own words.'

'I had a pickup truck.'

'We were told it was a van,' Ventnor queried, 'there is a difference.'

Buchan shook his head. 'A pickup truck ... one of the big ones, about as big as you can drive with an ordinary licence. It had crew accommodation ... driver's seat, front passenger seat and a bench seat behind, enough for three passengers in a sort of cab ... so it could have been taken for a van, then a flat bed behind the crew accommodation to carry the load ... had small sides round it so not a proper flat bed.'

'I know the type of vehicle,' Webster said with a nod.

'Yeah ... see a lot of them on the road ... mine was second-hand, it used to belong to a builder. Could never get the cement dust out of the cab. Anyway, I was asked if I could provide the use of my pickup.'

'Alright now, who asked you?' Webster opened his notepad. 'This is looking useful. For both of us.'

Buchan paused, dragged on the cigarette, then shook his head. 'No ... I won't tell you that, sorry. He was just a go-between anyway ... like a messenger. He's a good lad, got a family, he never was a part of it. He just said some people wanted a motor to do something dodgy. It paid five hundred quid.' He shrugged. 'I was down on me luck then ... no work ... either crookin' or proper work, one of those times. If you have a steady job you won't have experienced that sort of time. It's not clever, not funny. You begin to panic ... down to my last ten quid, things weren't looking up ... didn't seem set to look up either and then the offer of five hundred quid for an evening's work ... it was like a life-line.'

'Alright, we won't push that, not yet anyway.' Ventnor glanced at Webster who nod-

106

ded. 'But tell us how much notice you were given.'

'A week ... I think it was about a week ... a few days anyway.'

Again Webster and Ventnor glanced at each other and Ventnor said, 'Premeditated, like we suspected.'

'Half the money was upfront, half on completion,' Buchan continued, 'and that money was needed. It was really needed. So I drove to the big house, I mean her big house, not the prison, out in the Vale, to an address I was given.'

'What was the address?'

'I couldn't tell you ... I scribbled it on a bit of paper ... this was ten years ago ... my memory is not that good. That's going ... like my waistline.'

'Might the address be a house in Thaxted Green?' Webster prompted.

'Thaxted Green is a village I know, and no, it wasn't Thaxted Green.'

'Alright ... in your own time ... at your own pace.'

'Well, I drove out there one night and I was met by a team of heavy boys ... I mean seriously heavy ... all clean shaven, all as fit as a butcher's dog, all wearing baseball caps ... and none of them with a sense of humour. Not one. All very serious. They asked me my name ... I gave it, then they said get back in the cab and so I did. Then they carried the body out of the house, put it in the back, covered it with a tarp. Got in the cab with me ... serious guys ... four of them, gave me directions. Went to Pendwick, down a side street there ... told me to reverse up to a pile of rubble ... they took the body out of the back, put it in front of the rubble, then started to shift the rubble until the body was covered. Worked like a team ... like watching soldiers, very efficient, formed a human chain ... passing rubble from the back of the pile to the front until it was covered ... I mean, until the body was covered. Heard one of them say, "That'll hide it for a month", and he was told to "shut up". It was obvious that they had a rule about keeping quiet. Then one of them, he comes to the cab and drops a brown envelope on the passenger seat, puts his finger up to his lips and then draws it across his throat ... then nods to his left like telling me to drive off ... I mean, I'm not about to hang around those guys ... so I do. I reckoned they must have had their own transport waiting for them in the village.' He stubbed out the cigarette. 'That's all I know ... nothing else.'

'Did you know you'd be transporting a body?' Ventnor asked.

Buchan shook his head vigorously. 'No ... no way ... I done things but never murder ... and not even a part of murder.'

'You could have driven off when you saw it was a body you were hired to carry,' Webster suggested. 'Why didn't you?'

108

'Yeah ... I asked myself many times why I didn't. I mean, many times ... many times. I think it was that I felt trapped ... these guys were not just blaggers ... they had a sense of pure evil about them, like they didn't have the same code of honour that an old-time blagger has. They were different. They knew who I was, but I didn't know who they were ... I was trapped, like I said, I felt I had to see it through ... I was scared of them.'

'Tell us about the guys,' Webster asked. 'Four you say?'

'Young ... in their twenties.'

'Twenties!' Webster echoed, aghast at the reported youth of the felons.

'Yes, that was something else that frightened me, very young to be topping someone ... and they were calm too ... very matter-of-fact, like soldiers ... again like soldiers.' Buchan shook his head. 'Why me? Why my old pickup? They had organization, easy to get a vehicle of their own. I reckon they thought that they couldn't run the risk of their vehicles being seen, so they hired a stranger and his vehicle ... only explanation ... it was worth more than the five hundred they paid me, the job was.'

'Sounds logical.' Ventnor rested his elbows on the table and clasped his hands together. 'Back to the phone call...'

'Oh ... you said you wouldn't press that question.'

'I said we wouldn't press it for now ... you

have to work.'

'You are doing very well,' Webster said with a smile. 'You didn't know you were going to shift a body, you were intimidated ... under duress, you're giving information ... you might escape charges altogether.'

'You think?' Buchan's jaw dropped. 'Is that possible?'

'Possibly ... no promises, no promises at all, but we have to trace these people, these heavy youths. The guy who phoned you clearly knows them, so you could be charged with obstruction if you don't provide us with his name.'

Buchan groaned and put his fleshy hands up to his forehead.

'He also might escape prosecution,' Ventnor spoke softly. 'It depends on his involvement.'

'And to the extent to which he co-operates with us,' Webster added.

Buchan sighed. 'I can't grass up a mate.'

'Well, it's that or get done for obstruction, Phil,' Ventnor said softly. 'You've done so well for yourself this morning, you're only going to spoil it, by refusing to name this gentleman.'

'Sea change, Phil, remember.' Webster smiled. 'Sea change.'

'His name is Hales –' Buchan shook his head – 'Lester Hales, Lives in York. You know him, he's done time. I have just done what I swore I would never do ... not ever.'

'Lester Hales,' Ventnor repeated and wrote the name in his notepad.

It was Thursday, the fourteenth of November, 12.20 hours.

Four

Thursday, 14 November,
14.00 hours – 23.40 hours

*in which further information is obtained,
and Yellich, Webster and Ventnor are at home to
the gracious reader.*

George Hennessey vigorously scratched an
itch behind his right ear and said, 'Well,
thank you, Ventnor.' He glanced out of his
office window; a lone, middle-aged man was
walking the wall, local, thought Hennessey,
definitely not a tourist. He thought the man
looked pre-occupied, as if with some personal worry, and was not looking excitedly
around him as a tourist would be doing –
definitely local. He returned his attention to
those present in his office, his team, Somerled Yellich, Carmen Pharoah, Reginald
Webster and Thompson Ventnor.

'A productive morning it seems, well done
all of you. I feel a sense of real progress. I
visited Mrs Gentle who told me a few
interesting things.' Hennessey fed back the
details of his interview with Mary Gentle. He
then said, 'So, what's for action? Anyone?'

'Follow up the Lester Hales lead, sir.' Webster was the first to speak.

'Yes, that'll have to be done, you and Ventnor follow that up this afternoon ... that has some priority.'

'We need to know more about that house,' Carmen Pharoah said as she adjusted her position in her chair. 'There's more going on there than meets the eye. I didn't like what we heard. I came away with a horrible feeling about that building.'

'We both did,' Yellich added. 'It has a sinister feel about it.'

'The cook and the second maid were too scared to talk, that woman had obviously put the fear of God in them, and I fear for the maid we did speak to, Molly ... Margaret Coley,' Carmen Pharoah explained. 'She gave information but I wonder if she was a bit naïve. What she described was frightening: very well organized, extremist politics ... young men drilling on the back lawn every Saturday ... would you believe.'

'They sound like the same sort of youths Phil Buchan described...' Hennessey observed. 'Wouldn't be the same ones, of course, those guys will be in their mid-thirties now, well past it ... but youth of the same ilk. He was frightened of them, and 'Big Phil' Buchan is not the sort of man to scare easily.'

'The British Alliance,' Hennessey said to himself as much as to those present. 'We have to find out what is known about that ...

113

how large it is ... is it nationwide or is it very small and very local despite its name? That's a job for me.' He scribbled a note on his pad.

'The meeting on Saturday, boss, the one that Molly ... Miss Coley mentioned, I think we ought to invite ourselves to it.'

'You think?' Hennessey raised an eyebrow. 'Didn't know you were active in politics, Yellich,' he added with a smile.

Yellich smiled. 'I'm not, sir, but I thought that if we take a note of the number plates of the visitors' cars, we can then identify the owners. They'll be members of the British Alliance, they'll know Audrey Aldidge and some may have known Arthur Aldidge.'

'Shadowy organization,' Ventnor offered. 'Never makes itself known, never heard of it before, British Alliance...? No one has ever stood for local or national election for that party that I can recall.'

'Me neither,' Carmen Pharoah added. 'It's the sort of thing I'd remember.'

'Yes, I too would like to know about this organization but that's for me to do, as I said.' Hennessey leaned back in his chair. 'The boss wants me more desk-bound these days with the occasional visit, just to keep my hand in, as this morning, such as to the non-threatening likes of Mrs Gentle. He's looking after my health, I think. In fact I know he is. Good of him, I suppose, not long now before I retire, he's allowing me to soft pedal.' Hennessey paused and once again glanced out of the window of his office. 'He's haunted by an incident when he was at school. I don't know whether I ought to tell you that but you may as well know ... it will help you to understand the commander. His class was taught by an able maths teacher who left the school to better himself. He achieved a head-of-department position in another school, or something like that, leaving a well-meaning but lower calibre teacher who had never taught anything but lower school maths and he was suddenly told to teach senior school maths. He was out of his depth, under stress and relieved the stress by smoking and drinking to excess ... overweight, false good humour, ruddy complexion, red nose ... so the commander told me ... all the red lights flashing ... all the danger signs. Then one day, one evening, when at home, he keeled over with a massive coronary. The commander is determined that this should not happen in his police station. So, from now on, the great majority of legwork is going to be done by you four. That's why we have been given DC Pharoah and why Ventnor and Webster joined us a little while earlier. So, now you know the reason for the background to the team's expansion, but I am in charge. I remain in charge. My hand is on the helm. Understood?'

'Yes, sir.'

'Yes, sir.'

'Yes, sir.'

'Yes, sir.'

'Right, don't do anything without clearing it with me first, that is of the utmost importance, I have to keep the overview.' He paused again. 'Now, I do think it's a very good idea to visit the house on Saturday evening, as Sergeant Yellich has suggested, note a few number plates, see where they lead us, see to whom they lead us. But that's over forty-eight hours hence. So, Yellich and DC Pharoah, this p.m. I want you to do what you can to trace Arthur Aldidge's last known steps. Mary Gentle told me that he was going to see the proprietor of the Beaconsfield Hotel, so go and interview him ... that would seem a sensible move for us to make.'

'Yes, sir.' Yellich answered for both he and Carmen Pharoah.

'And ask about a character called Dewsnap. Remember, the phone call that worried Arthur Aldidge. It'll be interesting if any of the cars this coming Saturday evening belong to a Mr Dewsnap ... He'll be well worth a visit if one does. So, we all know what we are doing?'

'Yes, sir.'

'Good ... I'm going to call on the elderly lady who is reported to have lived opposite Arthur Aldidge's office. Dare say I can do that without risking a fatal heart attack.' He grinned. 'Next debriefing and briefing here at 09.00 hours tomorrow. Right ... onwards and upwards.'

Lester Hales sat in the armchair in his living room in his small flat in Tang Hall, which was located opposite the Pike and Heron pub and which, because of its brutal, angular, brick-built appearance was known locally as the Fortress. The room in which Hales sat had matted carpets that stuck to the soles of the officers' feet, the air was musty and Ventnor for one found it particularly difficult to breathe, feeling the damp gripping his chest. Old tabloid newspapers littered the adjacent chair and settee; a varnished leg of a wooden chair burned weakly in the grate and gave off no appreciable heat. An old television sat on the corner of an equally old table.

Hales looked bewildered, as if one more impact in his life either didn't affect him, or it was the blow that would be the one to finish him. He was a short man, round of face, heavy cheeks, greasy black hair, he wore two pullovers, faded denims and heavy shoes as if, thought the officers, he felt the cold and the damp keenly. And it was still only November.

'Big Phil?' he said. 'Big Phil Buchan ... you say...?'

'Yes...'

'Haven't seen him in a while. Heard he went away for armed robbery.'

'He did. He's still inside,' Ventnor replied. 'Still tucked up.'

Lester Hales shook his head slowly. 'And he grassed me up...' Lester spoke in a flat, spiritless voice, almost a monotone, but with a strong local accent. Ventnor and Webster both had the impression that this man had once been lively and quick-witted, but life had subsequently dealt him many cudgellings and left him reeling and punch-drunk, wherein he no longer had the energy to be angry or affronted.

'He didn't want to ... I mean really didn't want to,' Ventnor explained. 'He said you were a family man. If that makes it easier for you ... but he told us your name.'

'I was ... the wife left me. Do you think a woman would let a house get into this state? A woman would be too house-proud to allow this mess.' He flicked a two-day-old copy of the *Sun* on to the carpet. 'You think this is bad? You don't need a warrant to go into my bedroom, but you do need one of them all-over suits I see on TV.'

'Biohazard suit?' Ventnor offered, thinking that Hales' observation might not be an exaggeration. He had been in cleaner homes. Much cleaner.

'Is that what they're called? Biohazard. Still it's not like "Big Phil" Buchan to grass me up, he's an old-style blagger, full of thieves' honour through and through. You know there were jobs he wouldn't do because he didn't think the person could stand the loss? He would not do violence, he was that sort ...

118

a con's con ... if he did an armed robbery the gun would be there to stop violence from starting, not to hurt people, mind that's the normal way of it ... and he'd never grass up a mate. What has he done...? He's just done that ... just gone and grassed up a mate, that's what. It's like there's no point in going on.'

'Like I said, he didn't want to do it,' Ventnor repeated. 'He was doing himself a favour though.'

'But he's done it.' Lester Hales glanced sideways, and looked longingly at the Pike and Heron, which to the officers looked grim and uninviting in the dull November townscape.

'You fancy a drink, Lester?' Webster asked.

'A bottle of vodka from the shop. I need a drink ... there's an off-licence round the back of the Fortress. I need a drink. Never thought that Big Phil would grass me up.'

'We know.'

'I like drinking vodka, you don't get no hangover from vodka. Drink a whole bottle and I mean a whole bottle, get leathered, really leathered, and you wake up the next morning like you've had a dry night. Only vodka will do that. Lovely stuff.'

'No promises but I'll see what I can do.' Webster smiled. 'Sounds like you would do with a wet.'

Hales nodded. 'I need a good drink now and then and lately it's been "then" more than it's been "now". I don't have any money ... I live on fish and chips, once each day and nowt on Sunday because the local chippie isn't open on Sunday. Sunday is a difficult day.'

'Sorry to hear that, but we're more interested in ten years ago...'

'I can remember ten years ago better than I can remember yesterday or last week ... funny that ... can't remember what I did yesterday...'

'You contacted Big Phil because he had a pickup,' Ventnor reminded Hales. 'Somebody wanted something shifting and the job paid five hundred smackers. Big Phil was in need of dosh so he agreed. Do you remember that?'

'Is that what you're interested in?' A look of relief flashed across Lester Hales' eyes. 'Is that it ... is that all?' He grinned.

'Yes ... why? Is there something else we ought to know about?'

Lester Hales shrugged. 'Perhaps ... I mean "Big Phil" Buchan could grass me up for things worse than that.' Hales reclined in the chair, as tension seemed to leave him.

'Oh, really?' Ventnor queried. 'Sounds interesting.'

'Yeah ... but you know ... least said soonest mended ... win some, lose some but always win more than you lose. Let's just say me and Phil Buchan, we was a team once, a good team, we pulled some clever jobs ... then split

120

up ... friendly like ... still mates ... but Big Phil he said the run had to stop ... and he was the man ... you know when he called out "Froggie" I went hop, hop, hop.'

'The run?'

'Of luck. We had a good run of luck ... about ten jobs.' Hales smiled as if recalling good times.

'Jobs such as?' Webster pressed him.

Lester Hales continued to smile as he tapped the side of his nose. 'If you don't ask no questions, you don't get told no lies. Anyway Big Phil said the run had gone on long enough, we was pushing our luck, we were, so we stopped before it stopped us.'

'I see,' Webster growled. 'Probably sensible of you.'

'Nobody got hurt.'

'That makes it alright, does it?' Ventnor spoke coldly. 'It hurts to come home to a burgled house ... let me tell you ... your family heirlooms lost forever.'

Hales shrugged. 'Well, we didn't murder anybody for their mobile phone like you read about these hoodies doing these days. Old time thieves like me and Phil Buchan, we respected life, and we respected property. If we did a burglary, we were straight in and out ... pick up the valuables and off ... didn't hang around to trash the place ... we had respect and we had self-respect. You can't feel good about yourself for trashing someone's home.'

'Alright, so you phoned Big Phil, someone wanted a pickup for a job that paid five hundred dump. Let's get back on track, shall we?'

'Yes.' Hales nodded. 'Yeah ... that was it. Five hundred quid. Useful money.'

'Who was that someone? Do you remember'

'Dewsnap.' Hales spoke matter-of-factly. 'Geezer called Dewsnap.'

Ventnor and Webster paused, absorbing the name, absorbing the silence. 'Who?' Ventnor tried not to sound excited.

'Mr Dewsnap. Sean Dewsnap.'

'Tell us about him,' Webster asked.

'Not a lot to tell ... I worked for him then, it was my day-time job. Easy work. He was in the used-car business. I used to clean the cars on his forecourt ... I was a bit of a gofer. One day he asked me if I knew of anyone with a pickup. Thought it was funny, I mean think about it, him in his line of work with the contacts in the motor trade he must have. I thought he'd be able to get any motor he wanted, but he asks me so I say "yes",'cos Big Phil was short of cash at that time and he had a pickup. So Dewsnap gave me an address to pass on to Big Phil and a date to take the pickup to that address.'

'And that's all you did?'

'Yes ... I earned fifty quid for the contact, Phil earned five hundred.'

'Did you know what the job was?' Webster

asked icily.

Hales paused. 'Only after, honestly, only afterwards. Big Phil came round to my house when me and our lass were still together, ranting about what I'd got him into. He was angry ... he has a temper ... told me it was a body he'd picked up with a team of really heavy guys. I swear I knew nothing about the load ... told him the same ... but he was frightened that night, never seen Big Phil frightened before.'

'So where do we find Dewsnap?'

Hales shrugged. 'Pulled the old disappearing trick, didn't he ... sold up his business and retired. He made his pot and put his feet up ... or went fishing ... there's big money in second-hand tin.'

'Alright, where was his business?'

'In Selby, it's now called Brightside Motors. Some other geezer bought the business. Guy had his own gofer, he had a full team of gofers, so I was out on me ear. It was a bit after that that our lass left me, and I began to live in a tip ... no one to clean the place you see.'

'You've helped yourself and you've helped Big Phil.' Webster took a tenner from his wallet and handed it to Hales.

'I have?' Hales took the note gently as if he did not believe he was being given it.

'Yes, you have. You have confirmed Big Phil's story ... He was not knowingly involved in the murder, even as an accessory, and

123

he was acting under duress.'

'He might escape charges altogether,' Ventnor added. 'But ... but ... but ... this investigation is far from over, we might be back ... you're not out of the loop. Neither is Big Phil. Not yet. But help us and we help you ... even if it's only another tenner for another bottle.'

Driving back to York, Thompson Ventnor said, 'He's right about vodka ... not causing a hangover.'

'Is he?' Webster glanced to one side.

'Yes ... when my wife left me I wasn't as bad as him but on my way there.' Ventnor took one hand off the steering wheel and indicated the area behind them. 'Didn't get as bad as that, nothing like it, but I did get into the vodka for that selfsame reason – blow everything out of my mind with the contents of a bottle, then get up and do a day's work without noticing any ill effects ... like he said ... I felt as fresh as if I'd had a dry night.'

'Dangerous,' Webster said softly, 'very, very dangerous.'

'Oh, yes, very, as you say ... saw the danger, talked about it with someone and he told me, he explained to me, that it's not the alcohol as such that gives you the hangover, it's the impurities in the drink. He suggested I drink a couple of bottles of red wine instead of vodka and not plan anything for two or three days after that ... it worked, believe me, it worked.' Ventor breathed deeply. 'So happened I had a weekend off so I demolished two bottles of cheap red wine on the Friday evening. I threw up in the night, and the next day I had a mouth which felt like the bottom of a birdcage and my head felt like a walnut being cracked open, and frail and weak ... hardly able to stand, took me all Saturday and Sunday to recover. Still wasn't right on the Monday but I turned up to work. A bit of self-imposed aversion therapy, after that it was and has only ever been beer for me. Unpleasant but it worked. It did the trick.'

'Close shave.' Webster glanced at him.

'Close enough.' Ventnor nodded as he slowed in response to a red light. 'Close ... close, close ... close enough ... don't ever want to be closer.'

The Beaconsfield Hotel stood close by the York racecourse; it was a modern, angular, medium-rise construction. Yellich and Pharoah parked their car in the large car park at the rear of the hotel, entered the building and walked across the ground floor to the reception desk that stood inside the front door. The young, twenty-something receptionist wore a scarlet jacket and skirt, black shoes, and had short, black hair. She smiled a brilliant, white, gleaming-teeth-and-healthy-gums smile and said, 'Can I help you?' Her nametag read: Janice. Here to help you.

'Hope so.' Yellich flashed his ID. 'We'd like to see the manager if he is available?'

'Mr Redmond? He's the manager...' She reached for a slender phone that stood on the desktop and pressed a four-digit internal number. 'Oh, hello, Mr Redmond, Janice here...' She spoke with a soft but distinct Yorkshire accent. 'Janice at reception, yes. There are two police officers here, asking to speak to the manager ... no they didn't say. Alright, thank you.' She replaced the phone and flashed another dazzling, white smile at Yellich and Pharoah. 'Mr Redmond is coming down to see you. If you'd like to take a seat?' She pointed to a leather Chesterfield style settee by the side of the door.

Yellich and Pharoah walked to the settee. Pharoah sat, causing the leather cushion to squeak, but Yellich elected to stand, looking our across the hotel's forecourt to Tadcaster Road and the racecourse beyond the road, all under a low, grey sky.

'That's where Dick Turpin was executed. Where the racecourse is now, somewhere between the stand and the first corner.'

Yellich turned. The voice belonged to a short and very well dressed man who seemed to be in his late forties.

'Police?' he asked warmly, politely and with a smile.

'Yes.' Yellich nodded. 'DS Yellich and this lady is DC Pharoah.'

'Redmond ... Tom Redmond.' He extended

his hand. 'How can I help you?'

'Just a few questions.' Yellich shook his hand. 'Won't take long, we won't take up too much of your time.'

Carmen Pharoah remained seated.

'Of course. Any way I or the hotel can help.' Redmond continued to smile. 'No trouble, I hope?'

'Not for the hotel but we do want to pick your brains ... if ... that is if you were the manager here ten years ago?'

'Ten years.' Redwood pursed his lips. 'Yes, yes, I was, I took this position twelve years ago, so yes, I was here ten years ago.'

'Good.' Yellich smiled. 'Then we do want to pick your brains. Is there somewhere we can talk?'

Redmond glanced quickly around him. 'Yes ... yes, we can go to the reception office. Please ... come this way.' Redmond led the officers to a small office which was situated behind the reception desk. The office contained just one desk and chair, which was offered to Carmen Pharoah. Yellich and Redmond stood facing each other. Yellich noted a functional office, apart from various notices and memos attached to a notice board, the walls had no decoration at all. A small iceberg behind the welcoming, brightly decorated warmth of the reception area.

'So, ten years ago,' Redmond said with a smile, a gold filling sparkling as he smiled. He wore a grey suit, expensive-looking shirt, polished black shoes, striped tie. 'What happened then that the police are so interested in?'

'Arthur Aldidge.'

Redmond paled as his brown eyes narrowed. He recovered quickly but Yellich saw the reaction, as did Carmen Pharoah who kept her eyes fixed on the man, as she had been trained to do. One officer questions in a friendly manner, the other watches closely.

'Arthur Aldidge?' He stumbled. The name clearly meant something to him.

'Yes. He disappeared.'

'Um ... yes, I know ... I remember...'

'You remember the gentleman?'

'Oh, yes, he was a financier, he was offering capital which we badly needed ... we wanted to expand, you see. We were still new then, we are still considered new and we're still in debt ... still a long way from moving into our profit. Our bank wouldn't advance the money ... too risky ... they wanted five more years of good business before they would sink any more money into us, so we turned to venture capitalists and financiers ... higher rate of interest ... but that's how they make their money, that's the nature of the game. We were in negotiations with Arthur Aldidge for a loan, and in the midst of that he disappeared. Caused some problems for us ... it was very inconvenient ... we had to look elsewhere for our money and never found any. We struggled on without the expansion we wanted.'

'I see,' Yellich replied. 'I see.'

'When was the last you saw of him?'

'Well ... ten years ago. We had a succession of meetings and by "we" I mean myself and the undermanagers, the owner's representative, and Arthur Aldidge ... about six of us round the conference table.' Redmond ran his fingers through his neatly cut hair. 'Yes ... yes ... it's all coming back to me now. He suddenly did not reply to or return phone calls ... so, yes, we had the second meeting with him, arranged a third ... then we had to postpone the third because we were all dropping like flies because of influenza and after that I phoned him and it was then that his secretary said that he was missing. Yes, that's it ... as I say, it's flooding back.'

'That's interesting,' Yellich said. 'We are trying to trace his last movements. So he did keep his second appointment with you? It was his last appointment on the day he vanished.'

'Well, he kept it. We had had one already, as I said ... then the second ... all good progress. We arranged a third to finalize the loan, one and a half million at twenty per cent ... three hundred thousand pounds he would have earned, over ten years.'

'Good return.' Yellich raised his eyebrows.

Redmond nodded. 'Yep, but high risk ... if the hotel had collapsed, I mean as a business, not as a building, he would have struggled to get his money back.' He shrugged. 'It's the risk you take. I wouldn't want to have to sleep at night having loaned that sort of money. But that's how he made his living. Anyway, we didn't get the loan because Mr Aldidge vanished. So, why the sudden interest?'

'He's re-appeared. Well, at least his body has.' Yellich paused. 'We are compiling a press release so there's no reason why you should not know.'

'Oh my ... foul play? I mean, the police wouldn't be asking questions if there wasn't ... so I assume, silly question, sorry ... I'm a bit slow on the uptake at times.'

'So he just left the hotel, after the meeting? Just drove away?'

'Not as speedily as that ... accepted our hospitality, we were doing good business ... had a few drinks, then he was driven away.'

'Oh?'

'Yes ... his chauffeur collected him.'

'Did he...?'

'She ... a female driver.'

'Mrs Aldidge?' Yellich asked.

'No ... no, I met her, just once ... it wasn't Mrs Aldidge.' Redmond replied adamantly.

'Sure?' Yellich's interest rose. This may, he thought, be very significant, very significant indeed. 'Certain?'

'As I stand here,' Redmond said with a smile. 'You see we were negotiating a loan, six-figures, in such circumstances a certain corporate hospitality is appropriate ... especially as things were proceeding very well indeed for all parties concerned.'

'Of course.' Yellich returned the smile. 'I fully understand.'

'So ... in that light, on one occasion myself, my wife, John Saunders – he was an undermanager, no longer with us, left to manage a hotel in London – we all entertained Mr and Mrs Aldidge for dinner at Bartlams.'

'Bartlams?' Yellich was impressed.

'Yes, they don't come cheap ... excellent food and for the prices they charge you'd expect nothing less ... but that was when I met Mrs Aldidge, Scandinavian bombshell ... blonde hair, blue eyes, endless legs ... my wife was insanely jealous.' He smiled. 'So, it was something of a surprise when his chauffeur appeared ... I mean, quite some surprise.'

'Are you certain she wasn't just a chauffeur?'

'No.' Redmond smiled again. 'In the hotel business you learn to read people, their relationships. She was dressed very informally, I mean in jeans and a T-shirt and sports shoes ... you know, running shoes ... and there was something between them. That look when their eyes met, the way they held each other. We helped her pour him into the back of his Bentley and she drove him off somewhere. I really doubt if she took him to his home – they were both giving off the wrong signals for that ... some little love nest would be my guess ... but that was the last time I saw him.'

'Now that really is very interesting.' Yellich glanced at Carmen Pharoah who nodded by means of reply. 'Sounds like we ought to have a chat with this young lady.'

'Well, ten years on...' Redmond shrugged. 'She'll be in her thirties now, so not so young anymore ... as indeed none of us are ... the old march of time.'

'Did you catch her name by any chance?'

'Yes.' Redmond put his hand to his forehead. 'Now, what was it? I'll remember ... Sandra ... that was her name, Sandra. It has a significance for me, the name, it's my mother's name, you see, so I tend to remember any Sandra I meet.'

'Anything else you can remember about her? Any little detail would help to trace her,' Yellich asked. 'This is really very interesting.'

'Well, unmarried ... at the time anyway ... no band or rock upon her fingers ... local accent ... a tattoo ... just here.' Redmond put his hand to his lower spine. 'A lot of young women have themselves tattooed these days, more fool them, I say. Hairdos and fashions will come and go but a tattoo you take to your grave. Hope my daughter never has one put on her body, my wife is already strongly advising her against it. But when the girl Sandra was putting Arthur Aldidge in his car she bent forward and her T-shirt rode up and

132

I glimpsed the tattoo, half-hidden by her jeans. It was a symmetrical design is all I can say, probably six inches across.'

'That helps.' Yellich nodded. 'Helps greatly. Tattoos are always useful to assist in identification.'

'They drove ... rather she drove, into York which surprised me, surprised me a lot. Handled the car expertly, by the way.'

'It surprised you ... the route she took? Why?'

'Yes, well it suggested that she wasn't going to drive him home, he lived out in the Vale you see. To get to the Vale from here, your most direct route would be on the A64 ... the York Circular ... drive away from York, left on the A64 and you're on your way to the Vale and the coast ... easy...'

'Yes.' Yellich would not disagree with Redmond on that point.

'But going into the city, I thought that was strange ... dare say she could have bulldozed her way through the city centre and out the other side as a means of getting into the Vale but that would have been clumsy. She didn't strike me as a person who would find a clumsy route ... and the way she drove away – unhesitatingly – as though she knew where she was going and was eager to get there. Ten years ago but I remember it clearly, something else which struck me as odd come to think of it.'

'Oh...?'

'Yes, Arthur Aldidge was making money but I had the impression that he was under the thumb at home. He would refer to his wife as the Long-Haired Colonel. It always reminded me that I once met a man who referred to his wife as the Gestapo.'

'Blimey!'

'Yes, it was as acid as that, but Mrs Aldidge ruled the roost, or so it did seem to me.'

'I see,' Yellich replied with increasing interest in Redmond's deposition.

'Yes, you see, after that meeting, the second one, the last one which went so well, he took out his mobile phone and pretty well asked his wife if he could stay out late ... not in so many words ... more in the manner of "I'll be a bit late ... hope that's OK", or words to that effect. Then he snapped his mobile shut and smiled as though he was embarrassed and mumbled something about his wife tending to worry a lot ... We didn't think that was truthful, it didn't seem true. It seemed to us that he was seeking permission ... or at least her approval to stay out late for a few drinks. So it really was some surprise when after he had had far too much to be able to drive safely he took out his mobile phone again, this time saying he had to phone his chauffeur. We didn't think anything of it until little Miss Sandra with the tattoo on her back arrived in a taxi, looked at him warmly like she was looking at a lover, and whisked him away into the city ... as if, as I said, to some

134

love nest somewhere.'

Yellich and Carmen Pharoah walked casually back through the ground floor of the hotel to the rear of the building without exchanging a word. They stepped out of the building as a zephyr blew a flurry of leaves across the car park and as low clouds scudded across the sky concealing and revealing the sun and blue sky beyond the clouds.

'You know,' Pharoah said softly, yet also seriously, as she and Yellich separated to go to either side of their car, 'call it a detective's nose, call it woman's intuition, call it anything you like, but you know where we are going to find Sandra, the chauffeur Sandra with the tattoo on her lower back?'

'No.' Yellich stood against the driver's door facing her across the roof of the car. 'Where are we going to find her?'

'In the missing person files.' Carmen Pharoah held eye contact with Yellich and tapped her chest. 'I know. In here, I know.' She paused. 'And the date of her disappearance will be about the same as the date that Arthur Aldidge was reported as a missing per.'

Yellich drummed his fingertips on the car roof. 'You know,' he said. 'You know, I think that you are going to be proved right.'

Hennessey, having asked the collator to find out all he could find out about the British Alliance, drove out to Arthur Aldidge's place

135

of work, now evidently once again used as it was designed to be used, as a family dwelling, as indicated by children's toys on the front lawn and children's paintings pinned to the front door. He parked the car in front of the house and, waiting for a milk float to rattle past, walked across the road to the opposite house. The garden of the opposite house was overgrown and as such, indicated, thought Hennessey, the presence of an elderly person. The lady Mrs Gentle had mentioned, might, just might, Hennessey hoped, still be numbered among the living. He walked up to the front door and pressed the doorbell which surprised him with its harsh buzzing sound. He waited. He glanced about him: middle-class suburban York in the autumn, houses with bay windows and leaves in the gutters. It could, he thought, have been anywhere in England, suburbs he had observed, having a uniformity about them. He was reluctant to press the doorbell again, reasoning that the occupant was probably elderly and he didn't want to agitate her. Eventually he heard the sound of movement within the house and stepped back from the door so as to seem less intimidating to the occupant when the door was opened. A key turned in a lock and the door opened, just an inch or two, prevented from going any further by a heavy brass security chain. The face above the chain was gaunt, drawn, with bloodshot eyes and long, silvery hair. 'Yes?'

The voice was high pitched and squeaky.

'Police, madam.' Hennessey showed his ID. 'Just a few questions. I hope you can help us.'

'Yes?' the voice whined.

'It's about the gentleman who used to live in the house opposite ... ten years ago now ... Mr Aldidge.'

'Yes?'

'You know who I am talking about?'

'Yes.'

Hennessey wondered with a growing fear if the elderly lady was fully compos mentis or whether if he asked if he was a horned toad the lady would still answer 'yes'.

'The gentleman disappeared, I believe?' Hennessey asked.

'Yes.' Again answered in a high-pitched whine.

'We wondered if you saw anything about that time?'

'Yes.'

'Did you see anything, anything that was unusual?' Hennessey was beginning to despair.

'Yes.'

'What was that?' Hennessey braced himself for another 'yes' but instead was relieved by her answer.

'They came and emptied the house ... everything was removed.'

'They?' Hennessey smiled as he felt relief flood into him.

'In a lorry ... a team of young men in those

peaked caps.'

'Baseball caps?' Hennessey suggested.

'If that's what they are called ... about six men, all very muscular, very strong looking boys, just emptied the house ... all those machines ... every desk has one these days.'

'Computers?'

'If that's what they're called ... like a television set and a bit that looks like a typewriter. They weren't gentle, they tossed them into the back of the lorry like it was rubbish ... and filing cabinets and the files ... all went in.'

'Interesting.' Hennessey turned and glanced at the house in question. 'That is interesting.'

'I thought so. She was in charge ... tall, blonde-haired woman, waving her arms, giving orders. A man was with her but the young men in baseball caps did all the work, they did it all in less than one day. Very thorough ... took it right back to the bare floorboards ... left nothing. I mean nothing.'

'You saw that?'

'Well, I went over when they had driven away and had a little peek through the window.' She smiled. 'I used to go and look at houses for sale, it was a hobby of mine, no interest in buying of course, but just liked a look round ... see how other folk live ... especially the ones in the road ... really liked doing that, it was such fun. I did it with my friend but she's gone now, and I didn't enjoy it so much when I did it alone ... no one to talk to about the houses we went in, you see, now I don't get out at all. But ten years ago, I could get out and I went across the road when they'd gone and had a peek ... they had left nothing ... nothing at all, like I said ... complete clear out.'

Hennessey smiled and doffed his hat. 'Thank you,' he said. 'That's very helpful ... really very helpful indeed.'

The elderly woman's eyes sparkled. 'Pleased to be of help ... call again if you like.'

'Paull,' Carmen Pharoah read the missing person file, 'Sandra Paull, aged twenty-one years when she was reported missing ten years ago by her parents.' She sipped her tea. 'Distinguishing marks ... would you believe a tattoo, lower back.'

'Local?' Yellich asked. 'I mean York rather than the Vale?'

'Very. Very local. Home address is Holgate. The parents' address is in York too, they notified us of the disappearance. Graham Paull, her father. Photograph here, shows a dark-haired girl, as described by Mr Redmond. Nice-looking girl ... nice look across the eyes ... there's sincerity in those eyes.'

'That'll be a visit tomorrow.' Yellich leaned back in his chair absent-mindedly straightening out a paperclip. 'The contact that family want and also the contact they've been dreading.' He glanced up and to his left at the clock on the wall. 'Well, that's it for today.' He stood and reached for his coat and scarf. 'Home time for this lucky little ferret. See you on the morrow.'

Yellich drove slowly and carefully home to Huntingdon, to his new-build house on the estate. He parked his car outside his house and walked up the drive. Jeremy burst out of the front doorway and ran towards him with open arms as Yellich braced himself for the impact. With his arm round his son's shoulders he walked into the house where he was embraced and kissed by his wife who had detached herself from the kitchen with a tea towel slung casually round her neck.

'Good day?' she asked.

'Not bad ... progress made, so yes.' He kissed her again. 'There's nothing worse than coming home with the feeling that nothing has been achieved.' He paused. 'No ... don't mean that, that came out wrong ... sorry ... sorry ... coming home is always good, it's just better when you feel you've had a productive day. That's what I meant to say. How's your day been?' He was equally interested, equally caring.

Sara grimaced. 'I'm just pleased that it's the school term ... he's hyper ... very hyper today ... only been home for an hour and already I feel run ragged. I even gave in and let him have the television on, despite bad behaviour. I know I shouldn't have ... but ... I was at my wits' end.'

'Don't worry.' He hugged her reassuringly. 'I'll get changed into something casual and take him for a walk ... give you a break.'

Somerled and Jeremy Yellich then walked side by side from their home on the estate into the old village of Huntingdon and up the path, past the church, to the meadow and the stream with birds and plants to observe.

Somerled and Sara Yellich had known the disappointment that all parents know when told that their child is less than perfect. In the event, a hitherto unknown world had opened up to them as they met and made friends with parents of similarly designated needs' children. They had also discovered the joy that their child's years of innocence were going to be prolonged and the trauma and challenge of coping with a rebellious teen-ager was something they were going to avoid. With love, stimulation, stability, it had been explained to them, then Jeremy might achieve the mental capacity of a twelve-year-old by the time he was in his twenties, and would then be able to move into a hostel with similarly vulnerable adults where, with cooking facilities, his own room, but resident staff, he could enjoy semi-independent living, possibly even obtaining approved employment with a vetted employer.

Later that evening, when Jeremy was asleep, Sara Yellich curled into her husband's arms as they sat together on the settee listening to music and sipping chilled Frascati.

'To think,' she said, 'I might have been Head of English right now in a major comprehensive school.'

'You have regrets?'

'None.' She turned and kissed him. 'None at all. You know that door marked "marriage, intelligent females for the disposal of" is not such a bad door to go through. In fact, I recommend it. Come on, let's go up ... let's have an early night.'

Reginald Webster also drove slowly home that day to his house in Selby, as usual choosing to take the quieter B122 through Naburn, Stillingfleet, Cawood and Wistow. Longer than the more direct A19 but he had always found it to be the more interesting route; much, much more interesting and it was always tolerably free of traffic, even during the rush hour. He approached his house which stood on a self-respecting housing estate and sounded the horn twice. If the sounding of the horn annoyed his good neighbours, none complained. Probably, he thought, nay, certainly understanding the reason for the noise. As he halted his car in the driveway, his slender wife opened the front door and stood there on the threshold smiling, as her dog, the lovely long-haired Alsatian romped from the house to greet him. She flicked up the perspex cover of her watch and read the hands with her fingers. 'You're early,' she called out in a warm, welcoming manner.

'Yes.' He approached and kissed her. 'Good day?'

'Quiet,' she said, feeling for the door with her right hand and shutting it behind them.

'I thought I'd do shepherd's pie tonight,' he said, once again kissing her and noticing how she had put great effort into dressing up to please him.

'Lovely,' she said with a smile, but he felt her deep disappointment, and her frustration. She had asked him, repeatedly, to be allowed to attempt to cook hot food but Webster had been adamant and had remained adamant. Cooking hot meals was just too dangerous; preparing cold suppers and salads during the summer months was acceptable and Joyce Webster excelled in such meals and she loved preparing them for her husband. But attempting to prepare hot meals was, for Reginald Webster, head of the household, wholly out of the question. 'Lovely,' he repeated, 'lovely ... lovely ... lovely.'

Webster took Toby the Alsatian to a nearby wood and let him off the lead. As with most dogs, guide dogs are happy dogs because they have a clear and defined job to do, so believed Webster. In his continued observance, dogs which are kept only as pets become frustrated and ill-tempered, but guide dogs, like all working dogs, also need off-duty time to explore woods and fields and to relax. Watching the lithe and even-tempered Alsatian, Webster could only find admiration for his wife. She had been an undergraduate, studying Fine Art at Durham University when she lost her sight in a car accident that was caused by another, drunken, driver and yet she considered herself lucky because the other three passengers in their car, her good friends, perished. The drunken driver in question escaped with a fine and a brief loss of licence following a display of guilt and remorse which, in Webster's view, may or may not have been genuine.

Webster considered himself a very lucky man. His wife was courageous, determined, warm and as beautiful on the inside as she was on the outside. He felt himself fulfilled, and appreciated the good fortune that was his life.

Thompson Ventnor went home hurriedly to what an observer might think was his modest semi-detached and neatly kept house in Bishopthorpe. He heated a ready-cooked meal purchased a day earlier from Marks & Spencer while he bathed and changed into a lightweight Italian-styled suit. After eating, he took a bus into the city and had a beer or two in The Royal Oak at the top of Good-ramgate and there enjoyed the open fire, which burns in the pub during the winter months. Later, between eight p.m. and nine, he walked to the Augusta nightclub where it was the 'over 25's night'.

'Divorced?' The woman in a tight-fitting sequined dress who sat on a stool at the bar asked, after he had bought her the expensive drink she requested. He found her age difficult to determine, but she was very definitely 'over 25'.

'Yes.' Ventnor sat on the adjacent stool. 'You?' He drank his beer.

'Yes. Twice.' She sipped her drink after saying a perfunctory 'thank you'.

'Once, for me.' He raised his voice so that it would carry over the music.

'I thought it was "second best",' the woman said as she put her drink down on the bar, 'but it wasn't true...' She shook her head slowly. 'He was worse than the first. I can pick 'em ... I really can. You'd think I'd learn from experience ... but oh, no...'

'Makes you cautious.' Ventnor ran his fingers round the rim of his beer glass.

'Not cautious enough...' She glanced at the mirror behind the bar. 'I still come here.'

And so they chatted as the club filled, they had a dance when the dance floor was full, but eventually he went home, by taxi, alone and without a telephone number to call.

It was Thursday, the fourteenth of November, 23.40 hours.

Five

Friday, 15 November,
09.00 hours – 12.17 hours

*in which more of the British Alliance is learned,
a grave concern is raised, and a man makes an
emergency call.*

'So,' Hennessey said and smiled warmly at his team, 'good progress all round, that's what I like … questions answered, questions posed. Comments…? Anyone…?'

'Interesting, I think, that Mrs Aldidge seemed to have been supervising the clearing out of her husband's place of work,' Carmen Pharoah offered. 'Particularly as she seemed to want to ensure that the computers were smashed. She seemed to be leaving nothing to chance. No stone unturned at all.'

'Yes,' Hennessey said with a nod, 'that's what I thought.' He sipped his tea and then continued, 'But making sure of what? What did she want to destroy … to hide forever?' He leaned forwards. 'I think we play this very cautiously, ultra cautiously – Mrs Aldidge is now a suspect in her husband's murder. We make that plain. I don't want to move against her until we know that we are on a firm footing, but she is definitely on the suspect list. I should also tell you that I haven't heard back from the collator yet. I asked him to dig up what he could about the British Alliance. I want us to know as much about them as possible.'

'Shall we invite ourselves to the party tomorrow night, sir?' Ventnor's voice had an eager tone. 'It was suggested that we might do that.'

'You seem keen.' Hennessey smiled.

'We all are, sir,' Carmen Pharoah said and leaned forward. 'We have talked about it ... a discreet noting of number plates will provide information about Audrey Aldidge's network ... all grist to the mill ... seems a very sensible thing to do.'

'Yes ... we'll do that, I haven't forgotten ... and yes, it will be very useful information. As you say. A sensible thing to do.'

'I am really very worried about Margaret Coley, sir,' Pharoah pressed. 'She gave us a lot of information. The other maid and the cook were clearly intimidated into not speaking to us, talking to them was like trying to draw teeth, and after what we have learned, well, I want to be reassured about her well-being. I think we should be concerned.'

'I also share DC Pharoah's concerns,' Yellich added solemnly. 'We might have made things difficult for her. If we could just call on some pretext?'

147

'Very well,' Hennessey agreed with a nod, 'but ensure your visit is about Margaret Coley ... and only Margaret Coley.'

'Yes, boss.'

'Don't alert Audrey Aldidge that she is a suspect ... I trust you two to exercise discretion there.'

'Understood, boss,' Yellich said, and then glanced at Carmen Pharoah.

'Right, when you have done that, I want you to then find out what you can about Sandra Paull. That's for you two ... Yellich and Pharoah.'

'Yes, boss.'

'Yes, sir.'

'Ventnor and Webster...'

'Sir?'

'Find Mr Dewsnap.'

'Yes, sir.' Webster answered for both he and Ventnor.

'We'll reconvene here after lunch.'

'We were worried, but she seemed happy and that was the main thing.' Mr Paull was a tall, gaunt-faced man who Yellich thought might be suffering from an internal growth. He thought the man had a dreadful look about him. He was pale and his eyes had a lost, perhaps detached look about them ... as if already resigned.

'Happy.' Mrs Paull sat opposite her infirm-looking husband.

Yellich thought her to be healthier-looking

but she too had an odd, strange, uncomfortable air of separation about her.

'She didn't live at home, we believe?' Yellich asked gently.

'No...' Mr Paull replied in a near monotone, 'she had a flat in York, paid for by that man. He put her in a little place of her own.'

'Place of her own,' Mrs Paull echoed. 'All to herself ... and for him to visit.'

'We didn't like it but she was an adult and so what could we do?'

'What could we do?' Mrs Paull glanced at the mantelpiece above the glowing coke fire. 'That's her ... middle photograph ... that's her place.'

'Yes.' Yellich smiled, pleased and somewhat relieved that Mrs Paull was capable of speaking for herself. 'Yes ... I recognize her, we have a photograph of her in the mis per file.'

'Mis per?' Mr Paull glanced at Yellich. 'What is that?'

'Sorry ... that's police speak for missing person.'

'Missing person...' Again Mrs Paull relapsed into echoing what she heard. Parrot-like, thought Yellich. Very parrot-like.

'Can you tell us what was the nature of the relationship between them?' Yellich asked.

'Well...' Mr Paull, who had given his name as Graham Paull, opened his palms. 'She said that she was his Girl Friday, that's what she described herself as ... doing this, doing that. She didn't have any office skills ... couldn't type, so she couldn't be his secretary ... but I think she said that because she didn't want to upset us. She was considerate like that, especially to me and Mrs Paull, never ever wanted to upset us.'

'Upset us.'

Yellich glanced round the room. It was, he thought, neat and well kept. It could, he reasoned, be any front room in any council house on a self-respecting estate where the family had enjoyed a regular income over the years. Too few books, he thought – there was only a line of book club editions of very popular authors and a half a dozen *Readers Digest* magazines on a shelf. The room had a cold feel about it for him solely because of the paucity of books. 'Did you ever visit the house in which she lived?'

'No, she visited us but she didn't want us to visit her. We were her parents ... it would have embarrassed her, young woman making her way in the world and all ... so we stayed away. I went there after she went missing, of course, down in Holgate, behind the railway station, down that way ... never been there before not ever ... lived in York all my life and never went into Holgate until it was time to look for our Sandra ... never been there before ... ever.'

'Never been there before.'

'It was a little black terraced house ... well, they all are in Holgate, small and black. So I

150

knocked on the door ... there was no answer ... kept knocking and then looked in the front room through the window and through the letter box. Looked neat ... sort of comfortable ... but no answer to the door knocker.'

'Comfortable. No answer. Comfortable.' Again Mrs Paull echoed her husband.

'Couldn't get in, though.'

'That was –'Yellich consulted his notepad – '22 St Swithin's Rise?'

'Aye.' Graham Paull nodded. '22 St Swithin's Rise, Holgate, York.'

'St Swithin's Rise,' Mrs Paull, who had given her name as Pearl, repeated.

'Went back again a month later.'

'Less,' said Mrs Paull, 'less ... two weeks later ... you went back two weeks later.'

'Two weeks, aye ... and it was empty, cleaned out ... down to the bare floorboards.'

'That's interesting,' Yellich sat back in the chair in which he sat. 'That is very interesting.'

'Is it?'

'Well, it could be ... it has a certain resonance for us.'

'Went back again two weeks after that and the home was up for sale.'

Yellich glanced at Carmen Pharoah, who raised her eyebrows and mouthed 'Up for sale'.

'Did your daughter, Sandra ... did Sandra seem worried about anything before she disappeared?' Yellich turned his attention back

151

to Graham Paull.

'No ... but we didn't see her for six or seven weeks before she went missing, so what happened in those weeks we wouldn't know. Last contact we had was a phone call, about a week before she went missing ... she seemed alright then.'

'A week?'

'She phoned us each week you see, every Sunday, at about nine in the evening ... so when she didn't phone the next week, we got a bit worried. We phoned her at her house that same evening ... no answer.'

'No answer.'

'Phoned all Monday ... no answer ... no answer ... all that Monday. No answer.'

'No answer ... never any answer ... all that Monday ... never any answer.'

'So I called in on her on the next day, the Tuesday, banged on the door and looked through the letter box. No one at home. No answer. It was then that I went to the police and reported our Sandra as being missing. The police contacted her employer, Mr Aldidge, and his wife, Mrs Aldidge opened the house for them ... she could have been ill upstairs, you see, but she wasn't there, she wasn't anywhere. So there was nothing else they could do. That was ten years ago ... it's been a long ten years.'

'Ten years.'

'So ... Arthur Aldidge was alive when you reported Sandra as being a missing person?

152

This is quite important.'

'Yes ... well ... we never met the man and it was his wife who opened the house. Why? Is Mr Aldidge missing ... or dead?'

'Dead ... he was missing, but his body has been found ... it was in the newspaper and on the local television news.'

'Never read the paper,' Graham Paull said with a shake of his head, 'it's always full of bad news, so we could never see the point ... don't watch much television either ... same reason ... no point.'

'No point.'

'OK.' Yellich folded his notepad and slipped his ballpoint smoothly into his jacket pocket. Carmen Pharoah, picking up the signal, reached for her handbag which she had placed on the floor at her feet. 'Well, thank you for seeing us.'

'So, you don't have any news for us?'

'No.' Yellich stood. 'It's part of another investigation. I am very sorry.'

'Oh,' Graham Paull replied flatly. 'She was our only daughter, you see ... we thought you might have some news for us ... she was our only.'

'Only daughter ... and no other children ... never wanted any more.'

'Did she have friends?' Carmen Pharoah asked suddenly, without thinking, yet immediately thought the question to be elementary.

'Just Julia ... Orr ... Julia Orr. She wed.

153

Nice girl.'

'Where might we find her?' Yellich re-opened his notebook.

'Don't know where she lives now ... but her parents live in the next street. Don't know the number. Near the bottom, yellow door. Walk past it each day when I call on my sister ... it's the only yellow door in the street.'

Driving away, Carmen Pharoah, in the passenger seat, said, 'I think I know why she left home.'

'So do I.' Yellich shook his head. 'That pair would make a saint swear.' He turned into the next street and stopped outside a yellow painted front door. 'Can't really miss it ... talk about being subtle ... and it's the only one in the street, no other yellow door that I can see.'

'Our Julie's not in any bother?' The house-holder of the property with the yellow painted door was a dark-haired, middle-aged woman of portly dimensions, who wrung her hands in worry.

'We don't think so.' Yellich and Pharoah put their IDs away. 'We need to talk to her though, it's quite important, but she has nothing to worry about.'

'Oh ... she lives within the walls with her husband. She did well, lovely house to keep. She's Mrs Baird now ... she's got little ones ... keep her at home all day ... Kym Street, 167 Kym Street.'

'Thank you,' Yellich said with a smile, 'that's very convenient, both the address and the fact she'll be at home ... very useful for us.'

'I'll phone her ... tell her to expect you.'

'Yes,' Yellich replied, 'please do, but tell her it's nothing for her to be concerned about ... all we want to do is to jog her memory, if we can ... pick her brains a little.'

'One slow day, one slow week. Saw you two and I knew you weren't customers.' The man was short, dark-haired, suited up but cheaply so. 'Haven't moved any metal for ten days ... ten whole days. Saw you two drive up ... hopes raised ... then saw you get out and walk here. Hopes dashed. Hopes raised, hopes dashed.'

'You know police officers by sight?' Ventnor asked. 'Been in trouble before, have you?'

The man held up both his hands, palms outwards. 'Clean as the driven snow, squire, clean as the driven snow.' He relaxed. 'No ... nothing like that, but the used-car trade ... the motor trade in general is like that, you rub shoulders with the bandits, particularly the used-car trade does ... the police know that and they call and quiz you. Only two types of people drive up to my little hive of industry without looking at the cars on the plot, just two types ... dissatisfied customers and the police. Never seen you two gents before, that car isn't one of my sales ... so you

155

have to be lawmen. Am I right, sir? Of course I am. Got nothing better to do than sit here sharpening pencils. Just her for company.' He glanced to his left at a calendar. Miss November, she of tumbling locks and endless legs, reclined on the bonnet of a blood red Ferrari. 'She doesn't say much, doesn't say anything really ... when you want them to talk they're dumb.' He shrugged. 'So how can I help you? Drew Farr's the name, used cars the game ... anything to help the boys in blue.'

'We are looking for a gentleman called Dewsnap.'

'The previous owner? I hoped it might have been something a little more exciting, a little more interesting ... sitting here in my little shed, watching the world go by. No visitors for ten days and when I do get a couple ... they're just after an address.' He leaned to one side and opened a drawer in his desk. 'Bought this business as a going concern from Dewsnap about five years ago now. The only thing going about it was Dewsnap. Can't say he fiddled me ... but the custom he and his books said he got just didn't seem to be there once my cheque cleared.' He extracted a notebook and turned the pages. 'Here we are ... Dewsnap ... Holmlea, 1 Dover Court, Laughton. I think that that is just outside Driffield. Quite a place to retire to ... a very nice address.'

'Thanks.' Webster scribbled the address on

his notepad. 'Appreciated.'

'Please, the gratitude is mine ... this has been a short but very pleasant interruption in my busy day. Give you a word of advice, gentlemen.'

'Oh, yes ... what's that?'

'If ever you get fed up with the police force, don't go into the used-car trade ... anything but...'

'We'll bear that in mind.' Webster smiled. 'Have a nice day.'

'They smell of warm milk and vomit and make a noise totally disproportionate to their size. I should know, I've got three.' The woman reclined on the settee and did indeed look to Yellich and Pharoah to be exhausted, though in a fulfilled and contented manner. 'My doll's house was never as chaotic as this.'

'That's the way of it.' Yellich grinned, as he found himself liking Julia Baird. 'My train set always ran on time and I never had any irate passengers to contend with.'

Julia Baird smiled. 'So, how can I help you? My mum said it wasn't anything for me to worry about.'

'It's not,' Yellich replied. 'We really want to ask you about Sandra Paull, we understand that you and she were friends.'

'Sandra...' Julia Baird put her hands to her head. 'Sandra ... yes, we were really very good friends. I haven't thought of her in a while ... been too selfishly wrapped up in my

157

domestic bliss ... but yes, Sandra and I were friends from school almost from day one. Moronic parents though, poor girl ... going home to those two and with no sibling to share the torment with. I always thought they were like a couple of toys that needed winding up.'

Carmen Pharoah smiled. She thought it an apt description of Mr and Mrs Paull. 'We particularly want to know anything you can tell us about the last four weeks of her life ... and most particularly anything you can tell us about her relationship with a man called Arthur Aldidge.'

'Whose body was found recently.' Julia Baird glanced solemnly at Carmen Pharoah. 'I watched the news on TV.'

An infant began to cry in an upstairs room. 'Sorry...' Julia Baird smiled apologetically. 'I'll be back as soon as I can ... feeding time.' She stood and left the room.

Fifteen minutes later she returned and sat, as if relieved, on the settee. 'So ... Sandra,' she said. 'She disappeared. Always think that's too awful to contemplate ... the not knowing...'

'Yes.'

'And her sugar daddy. I envied her that experience, I really did ... I had to marry to leave home. I could have done with a rich older man as a sort of interim period between home and marriage ... but I wouldn't have married like they were planning to do.'

158

'Really?' Carmen Pharoah asked.

'So she said. She was very excited about it, over the moon ... I visited her in the house he bought for her. I mean ... he owned it ... he bought it and installed her in it. So far so good, I thought ... that's what a sugar daddy is for ... set you up in a little house that doesn't cost you anything ... pays the bills ... buys you clothes ... takes you on holiday to the Mediterranean ... lets you borrow his flash car and two or three times a week he stays the night. Except in Sandra's case he stayed the afternoon ... his wife wanted him back home but he had a job which caused him to travel, so Sandra told me, so he had an excuse to be away from his office ... and two or three afternoons a week he'd spend with Sandra in the little house in Holgate. That was a sugar daddy, that is the sort of sugar daddy I would have liked ... nothing complicated ... a nice arrangement for a year or so, but marriage –' Julia Baird grimaced and shook her head – 'she was barely out of her teens ... he was forty-five, a real age gap ... something like that. Me and Michael, my husband, we are about the same age ... he's two years older than me ... that's OK. I like that, we think the same ... but a twenty-five-year gap? I would find that very difficult. You grow up in different eras ... different times ... you won't think the same, but Sandra, she didn't see it like that, she was really, really happy and looking forward to becoming Mrs

Aldidge. "He's just got to divorce her", she would say, "then it's a clear run to the coast for us".'

'Was Arthur Aldidge sincere about marriage?' Yellich asked.

Julia Baird pursed her lips. 'I think so. I only met him once but yes, I do think that he was sincere ... I was blown away by his size, he was huge ... nearly seven feet tall, a real giant. The little house in Holgate was so small, he had to crouch down to enter into it. And she was so small ... well ... by comparison to him. So I saw them together just the once ... and yes, they did seem besotted with each other. They'd play risky games sometimes ... like lovers do ... but you have to be in love to play sex games, you know take risks ... or so I have found. Michael and I used to play little games before we were married ... but with other boyfriends I didn't. If it was casual, there was no game-playing, we didn't want to play games ... if it was serious then there was. For me anyway.'

'Fair enough.' Yellich nodded, recalling his own romance with Sara. 'What sort of games?'

'Well, a couple of times he took her to his house out in the sticks ... in a village called Thaxted Green ... nice place ... picture-postcard England.'

'Yes.'

'When the long-haired colonel was away, Sandra told me, he'd sneak her in and show

160

her round with a "one day this will be yours" attitude, and she'd spend the night there ... huge four-poster bed ... so romantic. She said that you could get lost in that bed.'

'Anyone there at the time? Anyone else, I mean?'

'Just the maids, she said, but he didn't seem to be bothered about them. She said his attitude was that the domestics were there to do a job, not spy on his love life ... but it was a risk to do it because he was always a little frightened of his wife ... so Sandra said ... and that was the fun of it, so she explained. If he wasn't frightened of her then there would be no fun sneaking her in and out of the house. A bit juvenile, I thought, but she told me that he found it thrilling and so did she ... so she said.'

'How long did that last ... that state of affairs?' Yellich asked.

'Affair being the right word.' Julia Baird glanced up at the ceiling of her living room. 'Probably about a year, a year and a half ... that sort of length of time. She really was very, very happy ... she had a sparkle in her eyes for the first time ever ... and that was good to see.'

'Did you meet any of their mutual friends?'

Julia Baird shook her head vigorously. 'No ... how could I? I was the only mutual friend, just me ... she kept him well apart. I was honoured to be introduced even if it was just the one occasion. He was very nice to me, very warm, but I think he was a bit embarrassed ... or maybe he just wanted quality time with Sandra, so I left them and walked home. It was in a pub that I met him, you see.'

'I see.' Yellich tapped his notepad with his ballpoint pen. 'How long after that did you hear that she was a missing person?'

'Oh ... a few weeks, something like that. I remember there was a television item about her ... just the one ... on the regional news. They only covered her disappearance once, they didn't stay with the story for a few nights ... just the one mention ... her photograph on the screen, police appealing for information, that sort of thing, just a couple of minutes. That was a few weeks after I met him ... and about ... two weeks since I last saw her ... so happy then.' She took a deep breath. 'You just never know, do you? You never know what will be your last conversation with someone.'

'So, you had contact with her? Regular contact?'

'Oh, yes ... weekly ... two girls, you know the sort of thing ... called round with a bottle of wine and we'd just chat the afternoon away ... our plans ... well, really her plans, she had someone, I hadn't ... not then. I was happy for her but ... the age gap, like I said ... not for me, but she really was well over the moon ... though she was a bit naïve ... I confess.'

'Oh...?'

'Well, yes, I don't care what he promised her, I couldn't get round the fact that she was still his mistress ... he still employed her...'

'Employed?'

'Yes ... a sort of Girl Friday, she described herself as that, a Girl Friday. She drove him sometimes, worked through a shopping list he'd given her but it was only a few hours a week. Mostly she sat at home watching day-time TV and doing crosswords, but she was paid a full-time salary as though she was his personal assistant. She was employed by him ... on his books as an employee ... paid her salary and National Insurance contributions. It enabled her to live and live quite well, so far as I could see, all she had to do was buy her own food – no rent to pay, no travelling expenses, no clothes to buy so as to look smart at work ... just food from the sort of money a good secretary or PA could earn. She was able to save. Not bad but it just didn't seem to be going anywhere and with a man who was frightened of his wife ... and if she was such a domineering tyrant of a female, I thought that she wouldn't go with-out a fight. Sandra gave the impression that she, the wife, was going to move out with a divorce settlement and she, Sandra, was going to move in. Just like that. I never talked about it with her but I knew it wasn't going to be as easy as that. It was about a week or two after that last good natter we had in the house he had bought for her to live in, just talking about this and that, that she was reported missing. Then he was also reported missing ... a few days later. Had to be a connection, I thought ... there had to be a link.'

'And you didn't report it?'

'Report what?'

'The connection.'

'No. Sorry.' Julia Baird looked sheepishly at Yellich and then at Carmen Pharoah. 'Sorry. Didn't think to.'

'But you may have been the only person who knew they were linked.'

'No, I wasn't, her parents knew. She told them about her and Arthur Aldidge. They might not be the full shilling, either of them, but they're not brain-dead either, they could have reported it ... they should have reported it ... more than me, they should have reported it.'

'If they'd known,' Carmen Pharoah said coldly. 'They might have been too caught up in their own grief to have noticed any report about Arthur Aldidge being reported missing and they don't watch TV or read the newspapers, though you were not to know that ... in fairness. You had the only overview. A police force is only as good as the information it garners from whatever source and by whatever means ... this could have been a double murder enquiry ten years ago when the trail was still warm.'

164

'So ... what can I say? I'm sorry.' Julia Baird shrugged. 'And anyway, I had my own life to lead. I had to find a man, get married ... I wanted to get married.'

Ventnor parked the car outside the yellow painted gate of Holmlea. The house itself, the two officers observed, appeared to be a compact bungalow surrounded by a generous garden which was some ten feet below the surface of the road.

'Not my taste,' Webster remarked as he scanned the building, 'and I can tell you that a lot of work has gone into the upkeep of the garden ... too much for a retired person ... too much for a couple even.'

'Contract gardeners.' Ventnor switched off the car's engine. 'It's the business to be in these days with our aging population, more pensioners than there are people in employment, apparently. That's what Drew Farr should do ... sell his used-car business and get into garden upkeep.'

'Is that a fact?' Webster glanced at him. 'About the number of pensioners, I mean? That's a bit frightening.'

'So I believe,' Ventnor said as he continued to look at the house. 'It's remarkable what you can pick up from magazines while waiting for the terror of the drill. It's apparently a combination of a shrinking job market caused by the microchip revolution and the increase in the quality of health care and the quality of housing ... and clean air ... and stuff like that. Anyway, the fact is that folk just live an awful lot longer than they used to. The National Health Service has been a victim of its own success, anyone transported forward in time from 1900 would be astounded at the number of elderly people in the UK today.'

'Interesting.' Webster continued to look at the house. 'Frightening, but interesting.'

'It is, isn't it? Anyway, contract gardening, that's the number to be in ... all that fresh air, all those elderly people that can't manage their gardens any more. It's a job I could cope with. It's a mistake that last fella made, like I said ... a lot healthier in mind and body than trying to make a living by selling used tin. Anyway, let's earn our money our way, let's go and meet Mr Dewsnap, see what he had against Arthur Aldidge.'

The wood and glass door of the bungalow was opened by a slender woman who appeared to the officers to be in her late fifties. She had short auburn hair and wore a yellow cardigan that matched the yellow of the house, the doors, the window frames as well as the gate, and a light-coloured tweed skirt, the hem of which hung between her knees and ankles. Brown sensible shoes encased her feet. She casually inclined her head to one side, showed no fear of the two strange men who had rung her doorbell and said, 'Yes?'

'Police.' Ventnor showed his ID, as did Webster.

'Yes?' The woman said again. 'How can I help you?'

'We'd like to talk to Mr Dewsnap, please.'

'He's in the back garden, burning leaves, it's that time of year, as you know ... I'll go and get him for you. If you don't mind, I'll shut the door to keep the central heating in.' She closed the door on the officers and did so in a rude and dismissive manner.

Webster glanced at Ventnor. 'Please come in and take a seat...'

Ventnor grinned. 'Hostile to the law ... suits me ... suits me down to the ground ... I like to know where I stand with folk.'

'Better get her name and numbers for a criminal record check. As you say, hostile, she's got a history –' Webster put his ID back in his wallet – 'definite history here ... and we have to know about it ... it may be relevant ... very relevant indeed.'

Webster and Ventnor remained standing in silence until the front door was reopened. The man who stood there in the doorway was mid-fifties, grey, receding hair, tall, slender-framed but with a large, beer drinkers' stomach. He was dressed in an old sports jacket and green army-style pullover and brown corduroy trousers. He wore socks but no shoes upon his feet, soiled gardening shoes or boots evidently having been removed prior to walking through the house. 'Yes?'

'Police.'

'Yes, my wife told me. What's this about?'

'We have a few questions, Mr Dewsnap.'

'About?'

'Arthur Aldidge.'

'Oh, yes ... I heard that his body had been found, and yes, I did know him ... quite a turn up for the books.'

'Can we come in?' Ventnor asked. 'It would stop your central heating escaping.'

Dewsnap smiled and stepped aside. 'We'd better go into the lounge.' He led the officers into a large room that both officers thought was comfortably furnished in pastel shades of yellow, it clearly being 'the' colour for the Dewsnaps. Three settees encircled a heavy coffee table on which were copies of *Country Life* and *Yorkshire Ridings*. 'Take a pew,' Dewsnap said as he indicated the settees. He sat on one of them which caused his back to be towards the window which looked out on a large expanse of grass, surrounded by a herbaceous border, all encased in wood fencing. A brazier containing a pile of smouldering leaves stood in the bottom corner of the garden. Another pile of leaves had been gathered, clearly awaiting consignment to the flames, and which lay beside the brazier.

Ventnor sat on the settee facing Dewsnap, Webster sat on the third settee, adjacent to the man.

'Have to excuse Mrs Dewsnap...' Mr Dewsnap looked embarrassed and uncomfortable.

'Oh?' Ventnor's attention was drawn to a framed painting of a hunting scene that hung above the fireplace.

'Yes ... her brother was wrongfully convicted of a very serious offence. One of those cases that the police like to be seen to solve, a high profile murder of a man who had many friends ... a sort of local celebrity. The evidence against my brother-in-law was weak, the defence team poor – was poor, even to my untrained eye – and my brother-in-law gave a bad impression of himself during the trial, shouting and arguing. It was just the way he reacted to stress but it looked bad, sounded bad, and did not endear the jury to him ... and some previous conviction for acts of violence didn't help his case. The jury found against him and he collected life. He served nearly twenty years before he was paroled.'

'You have to admit guilt before being paroled,' Ventnor argued.

'Yes, I know ... he did eventually admit guilt in order to get out, but he still protests his innocence and frankly I believe him. I've read the reports of the case. It does still seem to me like a knee-jerk decision by the jury, even allowing for my partiality – popular victim, no motive for the attack and a man who gave a bad impression of himself. He, my brother-in-law, came across as aggressive

169

and ill-tempered ... but that's still a long way from being evidence of guilt.' He paused and forced a smile. 'So, that's a long-winded way of explaining why I doubt you'll be offered coffee by my wife.'

'I see.' Ventnor smiled. 'Not to worry. What case was that?'

'*Regina* versus Richardson, Newcastle Crown Court. Why? Do you know the case? You seem a little young to remember it...?'

'Just interested.' Webster saw Ventnor scribbling on his notepad. 'Might look it up when I get a minute. You know, contrary to what you and Mrs Dewsnap might think, we are not comfortable with unsafe convictions. They might appear to wrap things up at the time but it's a short-term fix ... they won't lie down and sleep ... they come back to haunt us. That is never comfortable ... apart from the fact that the guilty person escaped conviction.'

'Well, Charlotte would be gratified to hear that, I am sure ... she feels betrayed by the police. This was up in Northumberland, where she comes from, the murder of a magistrate in Alnwick. Didn't help that Charlotte's brother had been before that beak previously and was sent down by him and the other two magistrates. The police tried to make that the motive.' He leaned forward and rested his elbows on his knees. 'Well ... you have not called about that ... but about Aldidge ... the late Arthur...'

170

'Yes.'

'What would you like to know?'

'We understand you knew him?'

'Professionally. I was a used-car salesman. What a waste of a life ... the money is there but very little personal satisfaction. We had a business deal, Arthur and I, it went pear-shaped ... he betrayed me ... I lost money.'

'Much?' Webster queried.

'Enough–' Dewsnap shook his head – 'enough ... I lost enough. Let's leave it at that.'

'What happened?'

'We were going to open a pub ... we had our eyes on the site, central York. It was going to cost over a million pounds ... purchase, development ... we'd be in debt for a few years, but we thought we'd be in profit within five years. The vendor wanted a non-refundable deposit of two hundred thousand pounds.'

'Non-refundable?' Webster repeated.

'Yes.'

'Unusual?'

'Well, that was the deal they offered, they were clear about that from the start, didn't want people to back out and demand their money back. It's not that unusual and it's fair if the product or the property is free of hidden defects. It's a bit unfair to ask for non-refundable deposits on a building that you know is going to fall down within ten years or for a company that isn't as healthy as

171

its order book appears to indicate, but if all is above board and shipshape and Bristol fashion ... if the premises or company are exactly what they are said to be, then a non-refundable deposit, even for that amount, is ... well, acceptable in business practice and not uncommon. Not widespread either, but not uncommon.'

'I see.' Webster sat back into the settee. 'That's quite interesting.'

'Well ... this is where we ... where I went wrong –' he shook his head – 'and to think I had been self-employed since I left school ... even started generating an income when I was still at school, but that was theft...' Dewsnap smiled.

'Theft?' Webster stiffened.

'Yes ... doubt you'll arrest me though. I had a paper round you see, when I was a lad, and the owner of the shop was a young man who had a girlfriend. Each morning he used to go away in his sports car to deliver his girl-friend's newspaper, leaving the shop to the paperboys who were packing their papers, silly man. So, we'd nick stuff ... magazines, cigarettes ... but we were clever, we were cautious, we harvested rather than plundered so the theft wasn't obvious ... one glossy magazine and one packet of twenty cigarettes for each boy, each day. We sold the magazines and cigarettes at school for half their retail price. We made more doing that than from the money we earned for the paper round. I was fourteen and I was wealthy, I was selling seven magazines and 140 cigarettes a week.' He paused. 'Anyway, me and Aldidge ... we ... I made the fatal mistake of not forming our company before we paid the deposit.'

'Ah...' Ventnor anticipated him. 'Not clever ... a bit of risk.'

'You see where I am going, young man?' Dewsnap smiled at Ventnor.

'I think so, sir.'

'We agreed to pay one hundred thousand each to the vendor and once we were joint owners, we would form the company, turn the building into licensed premises ... make it work itself into profit. That was the plan. I paid my money and as soon as my cheque had cleared, Aldidge got cold feet, he backed out ... so I lost my loot. The whole lot ... one hundred thousand. This was over ten years ago now, so in today's terms I lost about quarter of a million ... that money would be very handy right about now. The house ... the garden might appear to be comfortable and impressive, but Mrs Dewsnap and I don't have a lot of capital. We are still too young to qualify for the state pension but when we do qualify, we'll be grateful for it ... that's our position.' He spoke apologetically. 'There is little substance behind the image.'

'I see.'

'We bought this house from the sale of my used-car business. The business itself wasn't worth very much, just the value of the metal

173

for sale and the value of the land. I didn't have an order book like a manufacturing company would have ... not really the sort of value you could call retirement money.'

'So you had reason to be angry with Arthur Aldidge?'

'Angry! I was livid!' Dewsnap's chest expanded. 'I don't mind admitting it.'

'Enough to hurt him?' Webster probed.

'Hurt him? I would cheerfully have wrung his neck if I had the opportunity.'

'Did you harm him?'

'No...' Dewsnap's face flushed red. 'Sadly I never experienced that satisfaction.'

'He was murdered.'

'Good.'

'About the time he reneged on his agreement with you.'

'So I believe,' Dewsnap spoke angrily, 'but if that puts me in the frame as I believe you say, then all I can say is that you are wasting your time. I had the motivation to kill him ... I had the passion ... and if I had had the opportunity ... well ... anyway, I didn't.'

'I see.' Ventnor sat back in the settee, which he found luxuriously comfortable. 'Do you know Mrs Aldidge?'

'Yes, we ... Mrs Dewsnap and I were friends of Arthur and Audrey Aldidge, we knew each other socially ... and that was another mistake, going into business with someone who was a brief acquaintance. Had we been good friends who had known each

174

other for years, then Aldidge might not have pulled out of the deal, but going into business with people you hardly know ... fatal. And to think I have been doing business all my life and I make a mistake like that!'

'How did you know them?' Ventnor pressed. 'How did you meet? How did your paths cross?'

'At a social evening at a mutual friend's house, I believe. Yes, that was it. He was younger than me but we seemed to click as businessmen ... spoke the same language ... walked the same walk.'

'What do you know of an organization called the British Alliance?' Webster asked suddenly.

'Nothing!' Dewsnap's response was rapid, too rapid for either officer to believe that he was being truthful. His eyes also dilated with surprise. The name meant something to him, clearly so. 'The British Alliance?' Dewsnap shook his head, making a futile attempt to recover his composure. 'What is it? A pressure group? A cultural exchange organization?'

'We don't know ourselves. The name cropped up in the course of this inquiry.' Webster softened his voice, he didn't want Dewsnap to go too much on the defensive, he didn't want him to be too guarded. 'We have not heard of it before ... whatever it is ... the name cropped up a few times in connection with Arthur Aldidge.'

'I see.' Dewsnap seemed to relax. 'Sorry, I can't help you there.'

'You were asked to provide a pickup truck,' Webster stated. 'Can you tell us about that?'

'Oh, this is all going back a few years, but I remember Mrs Aldidge asked me. I hadn't got one – only dealt in cars. I passed the request on to a man who worked for me. A man called Hayes who I knew had contacts in the building trade and who might have access to such a vehicle. I never asked her why she needed one.'

'So,' Ventnor began, 'going back to Arthur Aldidge...'

'Yes.' Dewsnap responded with what both officers felt was clear and evident relief. He had obviously been made to feel uncomfortable by the mention of the British Alliance. 'Aldidge ... can't say I am sorry he's no longer with us.'

'You knew Mr and Mrs Aldidge socially?'

'Yes ... I just told you ... but not very well. We didn't exchange cards at Christmas.'

'Then you moved into a business relationship with Arthur Aldidge?'

'Yes.' Dewsnap nodded. He looked intently at Ventnor. 'Where is this going?'

'So you would, I assume, have met him a few times?'

'I met him to discuss business, of course. Face to face is better than over the phone.'

'Just you and he?'

'Yes,' Dewsnap replied in a guarded manner.

'Did you find out anything about his life outside his marriage?'

'Outside his marriage?' Dewsnap raised his eyebrows.

'Yes, things that Audrey Aldidge might not have known about?'

'I don't think so.' Dewsnap shook his head. 'We met on occasions, he didn't like people to call at his office, he was an "outworker" in that sense.'

'Outworker?'

'Preferred to meet on neutral territory to talk business ... a quiet pub. His favourite...' Dewsnap's voice faltered as if he regretted saying what he just had. 'But he never spoke about his social life.'

'His favourite?' Webster asked.

'Well, nothing really...' Dewsnap looked uncomfortable.

'No,' Webster spoke firmly, 'tell us ... his favourite...?'

'We'll be visiting it,' Ventnor added. 'And if the publican doesn't remember him, we'll be back to obtain the name of the real pub.'

'This is a murder inquiry.' Ventnor also spoke firmly. 'In fact, it's a double murder, so don't invite suspicion on yourself. So let's have it. The name of Arthur Aldidge's favourite pub in which to do business.'

Dewsnap looked uncomfortable.

'The pub!' Webster leaned forward. 'Or be

177

charged with obstruction.'

Dewsnap groaned. 'It's called the Vine.'

'The Vine,' Ventnor repeated as he wrote on his pad. 'Lovely pub in Dorset I know by that name ... real ale from the wood ... but I doubt...'

'It's in Hale St Andrews, sort of that direction.' Dewsnap indicated the area behind him, towards the window that looked out on to the lawn with the brazier of smouldering leaves. 'East of here.'

'You mean Poland or Latvia ... or a bit nearer than that.'

'It's north of Hull, between Hull and Beverley.'

Webster glanced at his watch and smiled. 'Just opening for lunchtime trade.'

Hennessey listened to Webster, clearly speaking from within a moving car and agreed to his request to check criminal records for Charlotte Dewsnap, neé Richardson, and Sean Dewsnap, and also ask the collator for any documents relating to *Regina versus Richardson* heard at Newcastle Crown Court about twenty years earlier. He also approved of Webster's suggestion that he and Ventnor proceed to the Vine at Hale St Andrews. He replaced the phone and, as soon as he did so, it warbled again. He let it ring twice before picking it up.

'DCI Hennessey.' He spoke with a soft but authoritative voice.

178

'Collator, sir.'

'Ah ... I was about to phone you.' He allowed his smile to be heard down the phone.

'Oh ... how can I help you, sir?'

'C.R. checks on Charlotte Dewsnap, neé Richardson, and her husband Sean Dewsnap, of Holmlea, 1 Dover Court in Laughton. Both in their fifties. Can't be many Dewsnaps ... not a common name. Also, anything we might have on the case of *Regina v Richardson* of about twenty years ago. '

'Very good, sir, I'll get on to it.' The voice was male, young, enthusiastic. 'What I have for you, sir, is something on the British Alliance as you requested.'

'Ah ... excellent ... good man.'

'Yes ... very little on file, I'm afraid ... in fact nothing on our files, I had to phone other forces and search the web ... very little.'

'Yes ... yes...' Hennessey reached for his notepad. 'What do you have?'

'Well, really the goods came up via the collators' network. No website in its name at all. I phoned the collators in neighbouring forces, as I said, and they phoned collators in other forces.'

'I see ... well done.' Hennessey raised his eyebrows. Youthful enthusiasm, he found, tended to tire him on occasions.

'Well, it's a shadowy organization by all accounts, sir, it's an extreme right-wing political party ... and very secretive ... and it further seems to draw its membership from

179

the professional and business class of the community, the sort of people who could lose a lot if they were to be exposed as having dealings with extreme politics. Hence no website of its own ... but mention of it on the websites of the more vocal extreme parties, where it is not by all accounts wholly popular.'

'Really?'

'So far as I have been able to gather, sir. It seems that whilst it is a far-right group, it holds itself aloof from other Neo-Nazi groups because of their street thug images. The British Alliance, so far as I can tell, seems to see itself as providing the officer class of far-right politics when and if such parties can take office.'

'God forbid.' Hennessey sighed.

'Indeed, sir ... a frightening prospect.'

'Reports we have had talk of youths in baseball caps drilling like soldiers in the grounds of a house belonging to someone in the British Alliance. That sounds a bit street thug like to me.'

'Can't comment, sir. I have no information about military-style activities but I'll keep checking.'

'Good man.' He replaced the phone gently, and wrote the information just provided by the eager collator into the growing file on the murder of Arthur Aldidge, now cross-referenced to the missing person file of Sandra Paull. That done, he glanced at the clock on his office wall: 12.10. He stood slowly, climbed into his overcoat, wound a woollen scarf round his neck, twisted his fedora on to his head and strolled into York for lunch at the fish restaurant in Lendal.

'Gone!' Carmen Pharoah did not disguise her hostility. 'What do you mean, she has gone?'

'Exactly what I said. Gone. No longer here. You do understand English?' Audrey Aldidge stood in the doorway of the house. She seemed calm and collected and more than a little defiant. 'Gone,' she repeated, 'she is no longer resident in this house, no longer in my employment. Gone ... where to I know not.'

'She wouldn't go just like that.' Carmen Pharoah raised her voice.

'She did. I assure you.' Audrey Aldidge contained her own voice to conversational level.

'She had been here for a long time,' Carmen Pharoah protested. 'She had no one, no relatives ... nothing. She was isolated. Totally on her own. She said it was here or the Salvation Army shelter.'

'Then perhaps that's where you'll find her.' Audrey Aldidge smiled smugly.

'What reason did she give for leaving?'

'None!' Audrey Aldidge stepped back one pace and slammed her door on Carmen Pharoah and Somerled Yellich.

Later, at her desk, in Micklegate Bar police

station, feeling distressed but concealing her emotion, Carmen Pharoah gently put the handset of her telephone down. 'Not there.' She shook her head. 'That's the last place ... Salvation Army, Women's Aid Hostel, York District Accident and Emergency ... not known anywhere.'

'We'd better report her as a mis per.' Yellich rested on Ventnor's vacant desk. 'It's all you can do now but we'd better add our suspicions to the recording in the file.'

'Yes.' Carmen Pharoah nodded slowly. 'We better had. I'll do that. In fact I want to do it.'

'Do I know Arthur Aldidge?' The publican smiled, though the smile was not a smile of humour. 'I'll say I do ... or I did.'

'You did?' Ventnor raised his eyebrows.

'Yes –' the publican laid two meaty and well-manicured hands on the bar – 'he was my brother.'

'Ah ... we are sorry,' Ventnor replied. 'In that case, please accept our sympathy.'

'Thank you. Appreciated. I am Derek Aldidge.'

He was, thought the two officers, smartly dressed in an expensive-looking blue shirt and matching tie, cavalry twill trousers. He was thin-faced with neatly cut black hair and cold-looking eyes. He had what Ventnor and Webster took to be the usual superficially affable manner of a publican, which could turn sour in an instant, though, at that moment, the mention of his late brother had evidently subdued his attitude. 'I heard about his body being discovered just yesterday when my sister-in-law deigned to phone me ... I missed the news bulletins you see.'

'Only yesterday?' Webster did not attempt to conceal his surprise.

'Yes ... well that's my sister-in-law for you, she sits on news like that for a day or two, then she decides that she has a moment to spare in which to tell me that my brother's body has been found ... after ten years, mind. Anyway, how can I help you?'

'Any information you can give,' Webster replied. 'Anything you think could help us.'

'Alright ... well, let's go and sit over there, shall we?' Derek Aldidge pointed to the far corner of the saloon bar, which, at that moment, was empty of patrons and smelled strongly of furniture polish. 'I'll join you in a minute or two.'

Webster and Ventnor walked across the heavily patterned red carpet, weaving between circular tables with shiny beaten brass surfaces and small wooden chairs and sat in the corner on a bench seat beneath gleaming horse brasses and prints of nineteenth-century hunting scenes. Moments later, Derek Aldidge joined them. A slender man, tall as was his brother, with an erect posture and a leisured, unhurried gait. A man in charge, clearly so.

'I've ordered coffee and a round of sandwiches for us.' He sat on a chair opposite the officers and leaned forward. 'Thought you could use it ... it's lunchtime anyway.'

'Thank you.' Webster smiled. 'It will be well received. We are getting a little hungry.'

'Well, you are doing what you can to bring my brother's killers to justice, a cup of coffee and a sandwich is the least I can do in return and you've come a long way ... no matter that you are just doing your job ... I still appreciate it.'

'You said killers,' Ventnor queried suddenly.

'Yes, my brother was nearly seven feet tall, you must know that, you'll have read his missing person file ... I am not as tall as he was but I am over six feet ... we learned to fight when we were young men.'

'I am surprised.' Webster smiled and glanced at Ventnor who nodded his head as if to say, 'me too'.

'Well, just as small guys get picked on, so there's always some hard man with a chip on his shoulder, usually about being short, that wants to fell the likes of me and my late brother ... so Arthur could handle himself. It would have taken more than one man to put him down ... unless he was at a disadvantage ... asleep when he was attacked ... or something like that, but I have always assumed attackers in the plural.'

'I see. Well, that we have yet to find out.'

'We understand your brother, Arthur, came to meet here to do business with other businessmen?'

'Yes. That's just Arthur, it meant nothing, he could have conducted it at his house ... you'll have visited it?'

'Yes.'

'Well, plenty of room there, but I think his wife didn't want him around all day. That suited Arthur because he liked to work away from home anyway. He could always and easily talk business with his clients in the house he used as an office, but he liked to meet them here.' Derek Aldidge pointed to the floor. 'This very corner was his preferred seat in the pub and when he came he'd come at this time, about midday, so as to be assured of this corner ... Arthur's corner, King Arthur's seat as we called it. Ah...' Derek Aldidge stopped talking and leaned slightly backwards as a slender, blonde-haired girl of about twenty placed a tray of coffee on the table.

'Sandwiches on their way,' she said as she smiled warmly.

'Thanks, Helena.' Aldidge smiled and waited until the girl was out of earshot. 'Life is basically unfair.' He reached for the coffee pot. 'My brother murdered when he still had many good and productive years to live and a lot of money still to generate, and that girl, Helena, has everything. Not only has she got supermodel good looks without having to starve herself, she eats sensibly, as you have seen she has looks that could blow ninety per cent of women out of the water, but she has brains as well ... she's a PhD student at Hull. In a couple of years' time her title will be Doctor ... she just has everything. She could be so aloof, so haughty and get away with it but in fact she is a modest, unspoiled, sweet-natured gem of a girl ... it's as if some flaw is missing that would make her real.'

A few moments later Helena glided back across the carpet holding a generous plate of sandwiches, which she placed gently on the table top, smiling a sweet smile as she did so and then withdrew.

'I always thought that women like that only existed in my dreams.' Derek Aldidge poured the coffee. 'Then who, but who, should respond to my ad for part-time bar staff but Miss Too Good To Be True. Well, tuck in, gents.'

'Well ... were you close to your brother?' Ventnor took his notepad out and laid it on the table. He reached for a ham and pickle sandwich.

'I think we were close ... there was only ever just the two of us, both parents now deceased. Sadly, Arthur predeceased them, as you may know ... or was reported missing, I should say, but we had to accept the inevitable and we did so after only a few days. Our father was a very pragmatic man, Merchant Navy retired; it was he who said that Arthur

186

was dead and that we had to accept that. He said people like Arthur just don't disappear, he wasn't some old down-and-out or drug-addicted youth who lays down and dies in thick shrubbery, and Arthur was too well integrated to fake his disappearance and start a new life somewhere ... And my mother too, she was of the same down-to-earth attitude, after some years in the women's armed services, so we knew he was no longer with us, with just the how and where is his body to haunt us.'

'Difficult,' Webster conceded. 'We've said that ... the not knowing is worse ... that's difficult.'

'Very, exceedingly so ... not knowing, as you say, that's the worst.' He took a sand-wich. 'Each day brings hope, each dusk disappointment. It eventually wore away at my parents and something was lost from them. They were not particularly old ... in their sixties, not old at all ... still plenty of life, as had Arthur.'

'Your brother's marriage?'

'Strained ... he soon referred to his wife as the long-haired colonel. Her hair was longer in those days than it is now. Now she wears it short.'

'So we have heard, about the name he called her, I mean. They were not married for very long before he disappeared?'

'About three years ... suspiciously short ... and I can tell you that she moved like greased lightning to obtain power of attorney.'

'What was the marriage like?' Ventnor helped himself to another sandwich.

'Well, apart from him calling her what he called her very early on –' Derek Aldidge shrugged – 'it was evidently unhealthy enough for him to take a mistress of tender years...'

'Miss Paull?'

'Yes.' Derek Aldidge nodded. 'Yes ... I met her a few times, she chauffeured him here. A very pleasant girl.'

'He liked being driven?' Webster asked. 'Unusual for a man.'

'Yes, but not in an arrogant self-important sort of way as if driving was beneath him; in fact, he enjoyed driving he once told me, but having someone to drive him freed up time for him to sit in the rear seat going over documents and such before or after a business meeting.'

'I see,' Webster said. 'I can understand that.'

'So, what do you know about Miss Paull?' Ventnor asked.

'They were very happy together, he was happier with her than when he was with Audrey ... in fact, I thought a separation might well be on the cards. I would rather have fancied Sandra as my sister-in-law despite the age gap, they just seemed so well suited, I was happy for Arthur ... a hand in a glove, you could say. I understand that she also disappeared?'

'Yes, about the time that your brother disappeared, but her body remains to be discovered.' Ventnor sipped his coffee.

'You think she was murdered too?' Derek Aldridge inclined his head to one side.

'Yes,' Ventnor spoke frankly, 'we are thinking along those lines.'

'Only line to think along if you ask me, that is if she disappeared ten years ago.' Derek Aldidge calmly reached for another sandwich. 'Dad was correct, I am sure ... Arthur not only is no more but he died at the hands of another ... or others ... but Sandra's disappearance at the same time is more than a coincidence ... so it's the only line to think along, so it seems to me.'

'Who would benefit from your brother's death?' Webster queried.

'His wife ... who else? His will was opened when he had been missing for two years as is normal in such circumstances. He was a wealthy man; he had made a real success of his life, financially speaking. It seemed empty in an emotional sense but lovely Sandra Paull filled that gap, admirably.'

'So there was a real relationship there?' Webster sought clarification.

'I think so –' Derek Aldidge nodded affirmatively – 'despite the age gap, like I said. Anyway, the will ... Arthur left me a lot of money, bought a very nice house that my wife and children love ... and we put the rest

189

in a safe place, it is accumulating interest nicely ... but the substantial amount of Arthur's estate went to his wife, as you may expect. She owns that house in Thaxted Green, it was theirs, now she owns it outright, and other property besides ... and she bought horses and long holidays in the winter. Stays in England for Christmas but as soon as January is upon us she is off to the Mediterranean as she and Arthur used to do. She has a villa in Malta ... she bought that with Arthur's money. Marry for money, get rid of the husband, keep the dosh...'

'So you think Mrs Aldidge, Mrs Arthur Aldidge is behind all this?'

'Yes, whether a major player or a small part player, but I think she's in there somewhere. She's a cog. Whether large or small, I don't know ... but she's a cog in there somewhere. Do either of you gents want the last sandwich?'

'No, thank you.'

'No, thank you.' Ventnor slowly tapped his pen on his notepad. 'So, tell us about the British Alliance? We have never heard of the organization before we began this inquiry.'

'Well, Arthur and I were brothers but we did not always see eye to eye and his political leanings were too far right for me. I mean way, way too far right. I am Conservative ... most people in the licensed retail trade are. In fact I haven't met a licensee that isn't a true blue. It's a business you see, driven by

190

the profit motive and like most businessmen, we are Conservative in our political leanings. But Arthur leaned a bit too far ... and joined the British Alliance. It's a far-right party ... suicide businesswise to go there, not literally, but if his name was linked ... I didn't approve and I didn't want to know anything about it and I told him so. I made my views known. I still don't want to know either ... I mean, don't these people learn anything from history?'

'No, I'm not giving my name, you stupid or something...? I got form. I don't like the law and I know you're taping this...' The man gripped the phone and looked around him anxiously. 'But near here there's a lane ... called Laughing Water Road ... yes ... go down there about half a mile, old cottage on the right ... it's a ruin ... what's the word? Covered in ivy – no roof. Derelict. It's derelict, nobody ever goes there, not even the local kids, it's unsafe ... so ... I use it to stash stuff, stuff I nicked and I don't want to be found in my house ... so just go and look in the derelict cottage. I'm doing you a favour. I phoned 999 because it's important but it's not an emergency. She's well dead. I mean very well dead ... she's danced her last jig, she has.'

It was Friday, the fifteenth of November, 12.17 hours.

191

Six

Friday, 15 November, 13.45 hours
– Sunday, 17 November, 01.47 hours

*in which a second and possibly a third body
are discovered and the good Detective Chief
Inspector is at home to the gentle reader.*

George Hennessey looked at the corpse with
horrific fascination. Even as an experienced
police officer the sight of this particular
corpse caused him to feel distressed. Terror
seemed to be frozen on the face and that, he
thought, was perhaps the worst. The arms
and legs were rising with rigor. He then
looked upwards through the hole in the roof
at the blue sky with low scudding clouds and
then around the cottage. There was a small,
single room on the ground floor with what
remained of a kitchen in the back of the
property, and upstairs was once just a single
small bedroom, the floor of which had long
since rotted and collapsed, as had the roof
above. The rotted timbers had long since
been removed, possibly, Hennessey thought,
as the first stage of a subsequently abandon-
ed renovation project, leaving only a roofless,

empty shell. At the further side of the floor to where the corpse lay, was a pile of rubble which had been roughly bonded by cement. It was, he guessed, about six feet long and angled towards the wall and had, he thought, a sinister quality. He glanced at Sergeant Yellich with a wide-eyed and tight-lipped expression.

'Yes, I confess, I thought the same thing, sir.'

'Well, first things first.' Hennessey glanced again at the corpse. 'There was nobody about when the constables arrived?'

'They didn't see anybody, sir. They went initially to the phone box, which is in the village, where they found the phone resting off the hook, and not a soul to be seen. So they followed the directions. This is the only derelict building around ... and ... here we are.'

'Here we are,' Hennessey echoed, glancing at Yellich. 'Here we are.'

'Carmen Pharoah was right to be worried about her.' Yellich added, a little needlessly thought Hennessey.

'Seems so.' Once again Hennessey looked at the corpse of Margaret Coley. 'No obvious injuries.'

'Clothes are soaking,' Yellich observed. 'Hasn't rained in the last couple of days but the temperature has been low, normal for November, but low enough to prevent the clothes from drying.'

'Immersed, you think?' Hennessey raised his eyebrows and looked at him. 'Death by drowning...? Confess that is one of my fears.'

'It's a guess, sir. I've seen that look on a drowning victim before ... accidental in that case ... but the fear of the victim's certain and imminent death is frozen on the face ... it's unmistakable.'

'Well, Dr D'Acre will doubtless tell us. You have...?'

'Yes, sir.' Yellich smiled. 'She's on her way.'

'Alright, we'll let SOCO take their photographs. You can invite them in now...'

'Yes, sir.' Yellich turned and left the derelict cottage and walked briskly to where two Scene of Crime Officers stood, a reverential distance from the building, waiting to be asked to take photographs so as to record the scene. Hennessey followed Yellich out of the building, holding his hat on his head, and with the wind flapping his coat collar, he walked over to where Carmen Pharoah stood still and silently, facing away from the cottage, head slightly bowed.

'We should have pulled her out of there,' she said softly when Hennessey stood by her side. 'I should have been more insistent ... should have ... should have ... another should have to add to all the "should have's" on my "should have" pile.' He glanced at her and saw that she appeared to have been weeping. 'We could have saved her,' Carmen Pharoah spoke softly. 'We should have saved her.'

'You were not to know...'

'Weren't we?' Carmen Pharoah turned on Hennessey with anger in her eyes. 'She gave us good information before she could be intimidated like the other two domestics. There's dead bodies all over this case ... all over it. It's like a battlefield. There's reports of Neo-Nazi skinhead thugs drilling like soldiers on Audrey Aldidge's back lawn, we've discovered an outfit called the British Alliance and we left her in the middle of that. We should not have left her there, despite what she said.' She shook her head. 'I will blame myself for ever...'

'Well, some good may have come out of this...' Hennessey's eye was caught by the sight of a red and white Riley RMA circa 1947 drawing to a stop behind the mortuary van and at the sight he felt his chest seem to expand with pride and passion.

'Oh ... what good?' Carmen Pharoah's voice was cold and angry. 'What good can possibly come out of abandoning a helpless, isolated woman to her death?'

'The discovery of Sandra Paull's body,' Hennessey said quietly. 'That will bring some closure for Mr and Mrs Paull.'

Carmen Pharoah's jaw sagged. 'The rubble...?' She bent slightly forward. 'I saw it but never ... I just didn't think.'

Hennessey nodded. 'The rubble. Somebody in this inquiry likes burying bodies

195

under rubble ... loose or cemented.'

'Oh...'

'Well, it's body-sized.' Hennessey spoke calmly. 'We'll have to check it, but it's the correct size ... in just the right sort of location.'

'You mean that in a few days' time Margaret Coley's body would have been covered in stone, bricks and stuff and then cemented over?'

'Possibly. In fact probably, I'd say. That pile of rubble might not contain anything at all but it's difficult to see what purpose it does serve if not to conceal something ... sarcophagus-like.'

'It is, isn't it?' Carmen Pharoah's voice tailed away. 'I would never have thought...'

'Nor would I when I was a twenty-something detective constable, but when you are in your fifties and your pension is calling your name, and you look back more than you look forward, then you will make observations like that. It's only experience that makes it possible to make observations like that.'

Carmen Pharoah smiled. 'Thank you for saying that, sir. I appreciate it.'

'Look, we are well covered here, we have all the people we need, there's nothing you can do ... I'd like you to go back to York.'

'Yes, sir.'

'Consult the Land Registry.'

'Yes, sir.' She smiled eagerly as if pleased to

196

be escaping this particular crime scene.

'Find out who owns this property.' He nodded at the derelict cottage. 'The voice that tells me that the pile of rubble in the cottage contains a body, possibly that of Sandra Paull, is the same voice that tells me this little ruin is owned by Audrey Aldidge.'

'We'll be bringing her in then, sir?' There was enthusiasm in her voice.

'Yes, I think so, I do think so, but not yet, she's not going anywhere and I like to be sure of my footing ... softly, softly ... that's the ticket, as the thieves say ... "softlee, softlee catchee monkey" ... don't go charging at your quarry.'

'I'll remember that, sir. I plan to make a career out of this.'

'Not going to give it up for a family?'

She shook her head. 'Can't see it, sir ... no one could replace my dead husband. If I can't be with him, I don't want to be with anyone. I may feel differently in time, but right now that's what I feel ... that's my attitude.'

'I can understand that ... So, close your quarry with ever and slowly decreasing circles. That way he ... or she ... doesn't bolt, doesn't make a run for it. So, we need to know who owns this cottage.'

'Right, sir, I'm on it.' She turned and walked to where she and Yellich had parked their car.

Hennessey also turned and walked towards

the approaching Dr D'Acre, scanning the low, flat autumn landscape behind her as he did so. 'Thank you for coming,' he said when they were within earshot.

'The obligations of office, Detective Chief Inspector. I hardly had any say in the matter.'

'In the ruin, ma'am.' Hennessey indicated the cottage.

'Messy,' she sighed, 'to end one's days in a ruined cottage. If indeed she did end them here ... that remains to be determined.'

'Interesting that you say that, ma'am.' Hennessey walked half a pace behind her. 'My sergeant thinks she was drowned.'

'Does he indeed.' Dr D'Acre glanced at Hennessey. 'That's interesting.'

'Yes, ma'am. Not treading on your toes, of course...'

'I'm so pleased,' she said dryly. 'On what basis does he make his observation?'

Hennessey told her.

'Well...' Dr D'Acre paused at the threshold of the cottage. 'Let us see what we see ... let us see if he is correct.' She stepped into the cottage, the SOCOs moving respectfully to one side for her.

Hennessey halted and turned at the threshold. Knowing how cramped it was within the four walls of the cottage, he decided it politic to remain outside. The cottage, he noted, could not be overlooked. Possibly, he thought, possibly very significant, in the distance, some three large, flat and tilled fields

198

away were the red-tiled rooftops of the village of Great Easton from where, from a public call box, the emergency call was made which alerted the police to the location of Margaret Coley's corpse. He could, however, see no windows from which a person could look directly at the cottage, the village appearing to occupy a natural hollow in the landscape. In all other directions the rich fields that surrounded the cottage gave way to dense woodland. But, he further reasoned, this was the country – rural England, the Vale of York – where, as everywhere else in the world, the fields have eyes, as the ancient proverb has it, and the woods have ears. The police activity, with the marked cars, the sinister and ominous-looking mortuary van, black and windowless, could not have escaped attention, but it was still comfortably distant from Thaxted Green and the home of Audrey Aldidge, so that the news of the discovery and subsequent recovery of the corpse of Margaret Coley might not reach her. Unless ... unless ... she had a useful British Alliance contact in Great Easton or perhaps a personal friend, who was at that very moment phoning her. It was a chance Hennessey decided to take. He would not issue a press release. If there was just half a chance that Audrey Aldidge did not know of this development, then Hennessey wanted very much to keep it like that.

Softlee, softlee, catchee monkey.

Dr D'Acre emerged from the cottage and stood next to Hennessey, her coat being buffeted by the wind. 'Blue sky, white clouds, plenty of light,' she observed, 'you could model swimwear on a day like today and it would look like the height of summer in the photograph, yet this wind could chill you to the bone.'

'Indeed,' Hennessey agreed and nodded. 'Cameras, they can be made to mislead.'

'They can be made to issue forth great falsehoods,' Dr D'Acre said, smiling in agreement. 'Cameras are useful, with a potentially dangerous underside, like a horse with a vicious kick. But that aside, I can say that your sergeant ... being Sergeant Yellich, I assume?'

'Yes, ma'am.'

'Your sergeant may very well be correct ... drowning is already emerging as the likely cause.'

'Really?'

'Yes, really ... well ... the police surgeon confirmed life extinct...?'

'Yes, ma'am. I am advised he had a suspicious death in Selby otherwise he would have remained to hand over to you as a professional courtesy.'

'Yes, Dr Mann would.' Dr D'Acre inclined her head. 'He is a gentleman ... I have always found him very easy to deal with.'

'Indeed, ma'am.'

'Well, I have taken rectal temperatures and

made and noted initial observations but there are clear indications that she is a victim of drowning, as I said. The body may be conveyed to York District without delay.'

'Good. Good.' Hennessey smiled. 'I want us to vacate this particular scene as soon as possible; our presence can't fail to have been noticed, and I don't want it noticed more than is necessary. We believe we know who is responsible for this ... we don't want to tip them off that we have found the body, if we can avoid doing so.'

'They were just going to leave it like that?'

'No.' Hennessey held eye contact with her, and unusually, very unusually, she allowed it. 'They were most likely going to cover it with a rubble and concrete overcoat. Exactly like the other corpse that is almost certainly concealed in there.'

'Oh ... that mound against the opposite wall?' She looked away, as if back to the cottage.

'Yes, but if that mound contains who we think it contains, then she has been there for ten years. We'll return in our own good time, and on our own terms to excavate it. The priority now is to spirit this corpse to the hospital as rapidly as possible.'

'I'll precede you, Chief Inspector.' Dr D'Acre fumbled in her pocket for her car keys. 'Will you be observing the post-mortem for the police?'

'Yes.' Hennessey nodded. 'Yes, I will.'

Carmen Pharoah evidently could not conceal her surprise because the official at the Land Registry grinned and said, 'Not what you expected, madam?'

'No.' Carmen Pharoah smiled at the man whom she saw as being short, bespectacled, dressed as well as a limited budget would allow, the very epitome, she thought, of the status of 'clerk', but yet who was clearly efficient and eager. 'No,' she repeated, by any means what I expected, but very, very interesting.' She tapped her notepad. 'Very interesting indeed. Many thanks.'

Dr D'Acre adjusted the microphone which was attached to a stainless steel anglepoise arm and which in turn was bolted into the ceiling, so that it was poised just above and in front of her. 'The body is that of a well nourished Afro-Caribbean female of early middle years and is believed to be one Margaret Coley.' Dr D'Acre glanced at Hennessey who stood against the wall, wearing green disposable coveralls, hat, jacket, trousers and slippers.

'Yes ... it is Margaret Coley,' he confirmed with a nod. 'She was identified by one of my officers this morning.'

'That is confirmed, Susan,' Dr D'Acre said turning her attention once again to the corpse, 'Margaret Coley and please give this a reference number.' She looked at the corpse, which lay face up on the leftmost table, from Hennessey's vantage point, of the four tables in the pathology laboratory. A starched white towel had been placed over her genitals. 'Older than many,' Dr D'Acre observed, more to herself than anyone else, 'but still too young to be in here. No sign of injury recent or otherwise is noted but the eyes are open and seem to be protruding which might suggest an expression of fear frozen into the face. This is quite rare but not at all unknown.' She took a scalpel from the instrument trolley and drove an incision down the chest towards the abdomen. 'I am performing a standard midline incision.' She spoke calmly as she did so. From the abdomen Dr D'Acre confidently cut the flesh down to the right thigh and then similarly down to the left thigh so that to Hennessey, the incision over the stomach looked like an inverted letter Y. Dr D'Acre then peeled the flesh backwards in three separate folds. 'My patients don't feel pain,' she said with a smile at Hennessey, 'and neither do they complain ... both exceedingly useful and helpful.'

'Indeed,' Hennessey replied for want of something to say and noted that Eric Filey, the slightly overweight but always good-humoured assistant to Dr D'Acre, was well mannered enough to smile at the joke, even though he, like Hennessey had heard it numerous times before.

'The suggestion and indications are that this lady drowned, so that is where we'll look first.' Dr D'Acre took an electrically powered handheld circular saw and sawed with a high-pitched whine down the rib cage at the side of the corpse, removing the ribs one by one until the right-hand-side lung was exposed. Laying the saw on the instrument trolley she took a large knife and cut into the lung, slicing it in half. 'And the guess ... the observation made by Sergeant Yellich was quite correct,' she announced, 'the lungs are observed to be waterlogged. This lady drowned, or was drowned. The left lung will be the same.' She stepped back from the table. 'I can take a sample of water from the lungs. It may be possible to match it to a specific water source. The diatoms will also be a good indicator.'

'Diatoms?'

'Wee beasties that get from the water into the long bones of drowning victims.'

'Into the bones!' Hennessey could not hide his surprise.

'Into the bone marrow to be specific. They are silica-covered organisms ... microscopic in terms of size. They will be found in both the lungs and the bone marrow. They can possibly be used to match the water in which Mrs Coley was drowned ... a specific stream or river, for example, or they will show whether she was drowned in a bath filled with tap water. But you'll need a sample of

204

said river or stream or tap water for comparison in order to determine the exact location of her drowning.'

'Of course.'

'I'll take a sample of the water from the lungs and a sample of marrow, that will provide the diatom signature. We'll get them off to the forensic science laboratory at Wetherby as soon as possible.'

'Appreciated,' Hennessey said with a nod, 'much appreciated.'

George Hennessey walked at a gentle pace from York District Hospital back to Micklegate Bar police station, not via the walls, being his usual pattern, but through the city, by the Minster and up Micklegate. He felt it made a change and the walls, whilst quicker, as any resident of the city knows, make dull walking: more to see at street level he reasoned, especially for a police officer. Upon arriving at the police station and signing as being 'in', he checked his pigeonhole and found nothing more than routine circulars. He walked into the CID corridor, to his office, and wrote up the verbal feedback he had received from Dr D'Acre in the still thin file on the disappearance, but now murder, of Margaret Coley and which had been cross-referenced to the file on the murder of Arthur Aldidge.

He then drove home to Easingwold, leaving earlier than usual, and thus managing to avoid the rush-hour traffic. He drove slowly and carefully through Easingwold and shortly after leaving the town on the Thirsk Road, he turned into the driveway of a solid-looking detached house, his car tyres crunching the gravel and causing a dog to bark excitedly from within the house. He entered the house and man and dog greeted each other warmly.

'Strange case,' he said softly when a few moments later he stood on the patio at the rear of his house, holding a mug of steaming tea and watching Oscar criss-cross the lawn, having picked up a scent. 'Started oddly enough with information given by a young fella trying to do himself a favour after he was arrested for stealing suitcases from passenger trains ... bit prolific and we're lucky to have arrested him but talk about a can of worms. Anyway, as I told you yesterday, he reported another felon who was given to boasting about assisting in disposal of a body, a corpse. Things moved fairly quickly and we met the widow who is now under deep suspicion and indeed appears to be the kingpin of a shady political organization ... at least lets the local chapter of same and said organization use her house for meetings and her back lawn for the drilling of young men, military style ... Confusing that...' Hennessey sipped his tea, noting again how different, pleasantly so, tea always seems to taste when taken out of doors. 'You see the early information we have about the British Alliance is that it distances itself from Neo-Nazi thuggery, it holds itself aloof, so to speak, but our information is incomplete and spartan. Anyway, today we found the maid who was reported missing from Audrey Aldidge's house ... the poor woman had drowned ... possibly been drowned or else why should her body have been concealed as if prior to being encased in cement? DS Yellich was right, he said that she had been drowned, the damp clothing, the facial expression of fear. Well observed, I thought, and he is probably right about the pile of concrete, which lay opposite to where we found the body of Margaret Coley. It's just the correct size to contain an adult human body, which will very probably be that of Sandra Paull. You remember she was the youthful mistress – or indeed youthful lover – of Arthur Aldidge? But if it is, well then, she's not going anywhere soon or in a hurry. We don't want to alert Audrey Aldidge to the discovery so we spirited the body of Margaret Coley away as speedily as we could. That is because we really want the party to go ahead. You remember I told you? The British Alliance are having a meeting at Audrey Aldidge's house tomorrow evening, that is information that Margaret Coley gave, I want that to go ahead as planned. Thompson Ventnor's idea is to let it go ahead so we can note down a few number plates ... see who is in the British

Alliance, Vale of York chapter … that should be interesting, potentially very interesting indeed.'

He paused, sipped his tea, and enjoyed the evening.

'Charles is doing well, father of two now,' Hennessey continued, 'expects to take silk soon … probably end his working days as a judge. I am so proud of him, and you would be so too. I do wish you could see him in his wig and gown; it makes my chest expand so much that pride just isn't the word. My lady friend and I are very happy with each other but I think we are both content to keep things as they are. We won't merge house-holds … we are a bit like two ships on each other's horizon, but keeping company with each other, keeping in perfect station as they would say in the navy and closing with each other on a frequent and regular basis … then moving away again … a bit like that, sorry, just the way my mind works … I'm always thinking in images. I have done so for as long as I can remember. Well…' He drained his mug of tea and returned into his house, leaving Oscar, by then contentedly exploring the orchard, which lay in bronzed and autumnal stillness beyond the lawn.

When George and Jennifer Hennessey, newly married, had moved into their home the rear garden was a dull, flat expanse of grass, not unlike a football pitch as he recalled, and so Jennifer, by then heavily pregnant, had spent one evening redesigning the rear garden. The lawn, she decided, would be divided widthways by a privet hedge of about six feet in height, the remainder of the lawn would be turned into an orchard, save for the very bottom of the garden which would be allowed to revert to a natural state, to look after itself, and in which a pond could be dug and amphibians introduced. Two garden sheds, to house garden tools and potted plants, would be placed in the orchard close to the privet.

Then tragedy had struck and had done so for the second time in George Hennessey's life. One unexpected bereavement is bad enough for any person, so might the gentle reader believe, but two within ten years had left George Hennessey feeling singled out and persecuted over and above his sense of loss and sorrow. It had been one hot summer's day, when their son was just three months old, Jennifer had been walking in Easingwold, a young wife and mother with all her life and its joys and occasional tribulations ahead of her, shopping for her family, when she collapsed. People rushed to her aid assuming that she had fainted but no pulse could be found and S.D.S., Sudden Death Syndrome, was entered on her death certificate, the dreadful diagnosis being as close as medical knowledge can offer in order to explain, as best it can, why it is that young, healthy adults should suddenly stop living, in an instant, like the switching off of a light. Jennifer had been cremated and Hennessey had scattered her ashes in the back garden of their home which he had then set about landscaping in accordance with her design. It was fully five years before he had deemed the task to have been completed. It had then become his enjoyable custom upon his return home each evening to tell her of his day. Recently, earlier that year, in the height of the summer, he had told her of a new love in his life and as he did so, he felt a sense of warmth wrap about him that could not be explained by the sun's rays alone.

Later that evening, after eating a wholesome casserole, which he had prepared the previous evening and then reheated, he settled down to read a recently acquired book to add to his impressively large collection of military history. It was a newly reissued memoir of a Yorkshireman's war on the Western Front from 1915 to 1917, when the author was wounded and considered himself one of the lucky ones to have sustained a 'blighty' and could thus retire from the terror with honour. The piece did not tell Hennessey anything he did not already know but he loved the honest, simple, fresh, crisp style of the clearly under-educated but very intelligent author and the immediacy of the observations.

Later still, having fed Oscar, he and the brown mongrel strolled out amid swaying trees to a field fifteen minutes' walk away, where Oscar was slipped from the lead while Hennessey walked slowly round the perimeter of said field before man and dog returned home, content in each other's company. Yet later still, Hennessey, snug in an overcoat and scarf and fedora, walked into Easingwold for a pint of brown and mild at the Dove Inn, just one, before last orders were called.

'Saturday?' Philip 'Big Phil' Buchan leaned back in the metal framed chair in the agents' room in Full Sutton gaol. 'I thought you liked your weekends?'

'We do,' Yellich replied. 'We do like them ... we appreciate them.'

'Very much,' said Carmen Pharoah, 'but working weekends is part of the deal, it comes with the territory ... and we both came into this work with our eyes open.'

'Crime doesn't stop at five p.m. on Friday afternoons and neither do we.' Yellich leaned forwards and took a packet of cigarettes from his jacket pocket. He opened the packet and offered one to Buchan. 'Smoke, Phil?'

Buchan snatched the cigarette greedily. 'Run out,' he said, holding it to his lips as Yellich flicked his disposable lighter. 'Smoked my ounce a few days ago. An ounce a week ... you get through that in a day in here. Half a day sometimes.'

'So, have you thought at all about what

myself and Mr Hennessey said when we visited last Tuesday?'

'Big Phil' Buchan nodded, drew deeply and lovingly on the cigarette, stroked his fiery red beard and said, 'Yes ... yes, I have been thinking about it and the answer's still the same, though I reckon I have worked out which big mouth grassed me up. Little fella called Gunn ... Tommy Gunn. Imagine being called Tommy Gunn ... it's like being called Chieftain Tank ... Anyway he is known as Gunny. Yes?'

'Can't tell you.' Yellich remained stone-faced. 'You know I can't.'

'I know it was him, had to be...' Buchan inhaled deeply. 'This is good. This fag is good.'

'Just calling to let you know of developments, Phil.'

'Oh yes?' Buchan exhaled through his nostrils. 'Very good.'

'Yes ... dug into the rubble, the bloke was murdered ... had his head smashed in.'

'Unlucky.' Buchan inclined his head to one side and flicked the cigarette ash into a Bakelite ashtray, which lay on the table top.

'You could say that, but it was no accident.'

Buchan shrugged.

'It's time to re-think the offer, Phil, we're rapidly closing in on his killers. Getting very close now.'

'Good for you,' Buchan sneered.

'Tell me about Sandra Paull,' Yellich asked

212

suddenly.

Buchan's eyes narrowed. The name clearly meant something to him.

'Who?'

'Sandra Paull.'

'Never heard of her ... don't know that name. Sorry.'

'Yes, you have,' Carmen Pharoah spoke icily, 'your eyes narrowed at the mention of her name ... dead give away.'

'Dead,' added Yellich, 'dead give away.'

'Dead in the real sense,' Carmen Pharoah pressed. 'She was the lady friend of Arthur Aldidge, deceased. Did you ever visit the Aldidge house?'

'Nope...'

'The house where the two domestics are black like me, Afro-Caribbean?'

'No ... never went there ... I mean I should know if I ever went to a house or not, shouldn't I?'

'So you never met Margaret Coley, from Jamaica, who worked there as a maid because it was better than living in the Salvation Army hostel?'

'Never had the pleasure.' Buchan dragged on the cigarette but he seemed to the officers to look increasingly worried. 'Never, ever had the pleasure.'

'We mention her name because she too was murdered,' Carmen Pharoah continued. 'Don't know how yet...'

'Drowned.' Yellich turned to her. 'I read the

213

chief's recording before I went home last night ... she was drowned. I thought she might have been. Turned out I was right.'

'Drowned!' Carmen Pharoah looked at Yellich.

'Yes. They can apparently identify the water she drowned in ... I mean, if we can find it, the white coats at Wetherby can confirm it was there that she was drowned. Match the water to the water in her lungs and long bones ... by means of things called diatoms.'

'So,' Carmen Pharoah said as she turned back to Buchan, 'you see, Phil ... you don't mind if I call you Phil?'

'No.' His voice shook nervously.

'So you see, Phil, the body count is climbing...'

'Well, I have an alibi for the black maid.' Buchan forced a smile. 'Margaret, whatever.'

'Coley.' Carmen Pharoah spoke calmly, but icily. 'She was quite alone in the world, she had no one ... she gave us some very useful information and now she's dead. Drowned as you have just heard. No accident, because her body was concealed.'

'You see –' Buchan crushed the cigarette stub into the Bakelite ashtray, 'you see, that's exactly what happens when you grass ... and you want me to grass. Just proved my point, haven't you? Cough to nowt and don't grass up your mates. Tommy Gunn is going to get what's coming to him.'

'Any assault on Tom Gunn can now be
214

linked to you ... so ... think twice.' Yellich eyed Buchan coldly. 'Think twice ... you made the threat in front of two police officers.'

Buchan shrugged again.

'But we mention Margaret Coley,' Carmen Pharoah continued soberly, 'not because it's one more murder in this case of many murders, one more murder linked to the Aldidge household, but because of where her body was found.'

'In a derelict cottage,' Yellich added. 'Out in the sticks.'

Again Buchan's eyes narrowed. The officers saw that they were clearly reaching him.

'Also in the cottage was a mound of rubble ... not loose rubble like the mound that had covered Arthur Aldidge's body these ten years past, but concreted.' Carmen Pharoah leaned forward. 'Very suspicious, we think.'

'We'll be attacking it with pneumatic drills in a day or two ... no desperate hurry, whatever is in there won't be going anywhere, but we are going to find a body in there, aren't we? It's the right shape ... the right size to conceal an adult human body.' Yellich reached for his packet of cigarettes. 'Another?'

Buchan slowly took the cigarette and put it in his shirt pocket. 'For later,' he said softly. 'I have to ration myself. I've learned that in here.'

'We'll find the body of Sandra Paull, won't we?' Yellich pressed.

Buchan remained silent and avoided eye contact. For Yellich and Pharoah it was as good as 'yes'.

'Every contact leaves a trace,' Carmen Pharoah said. 'DNA will have been nicely preserved in all that concrete and we have your DNA on file, you having being convicted of a recordable offence ... many recordable offences in fact ... otherwise you wouldn't be here, would you?'

'You see our thinking?' Yellich pointed at Buchan. 'You have been fingered as being an accessory after the fact in relation to the murder of Arthur Aldidge ... which you deny but your denials do not ring true, they ring hollow, very hollow ... and the name Sandra Paull meant something to you as my colleague said. Sandra Paull was involved with Arthur Aldidge at the time he disappeared and Sandra also disappeared at about the same time. She was murdered, we are certain of that, and the murders were ... in fact they still are, linked. If you were part of the crew that disposed of Arthur Aldidge's body then you are also likely to be part of the crew that disposed of Sandra Paull's body.' Yellich paused. 'Just the slightest microscopic trace of your DNA on her body will leave you with a little explaining to do.' Again Yellich fell silent. 'And you said yourself that no one can survive more than ten years in maximum security ... and you could be looking at twenty years. How old are you now ... fifties?

Be in your seventies before you breathe free air.'

'Or go into a pub for a beer,' Carmen Pharoah added.

'Take a stroll by the coast, enjoying sea air.' Yellich raised his eyebrows. 'It's these little things that mean so much, little things that so many people take for granted that you miss when you're banged up. Things like that which won't be yours for another ten, fifteen, twenty years...'

'And here's you sitting in your cell confidently counting off the days until you are released and here we are, telling you that you might not be going anywhere after all ... not for a bit, well not for a long time,' Carmen Pharoah added.

'Except possibly the Grey House.'

'The Grey House...' Buchan's voice faltered. 'Me in the Grey House...?'

'Depending on what we find when we start digging into the concrete ... in a few days time.' Yellich smiled. 'Give you a chance to do some hard thinking, Phil ... as we often say in these situations ... you can work for yourself or work against yourself ... the decision is yours.'

Buchan's jaw sagged. He looked sideways at the floor of the agent's room.

Yellich stood, as did Pharoah.

'Oh.' Pharoah turned to the door. 'We know who owns the derelict cottage. I can tell you that that discovery came as quite a surprise. We'll be revisiting him quite soon, very soon in fact. Does he know you? Will he start to help himself, I wonder, before you start to help yourself? You know where we are if you want to talk … it's a bit like a race now,' she added. 'The first one to talk will be doing himself a huge favour. A very huge favour. Think about it Phil.'

'I really am quite disappointed, thought that they would at least mount a guard.' Yellich sat in the driver's seat of the vehicle which he had parked on the road outside the Aldidge house in Thaxted Green. 'I mean, with the reports of soldier boys marching up and down the back lawn and the closed nature of extremist groups … but nothing, not even a single, solitary sentry … nothing evident any-way. Not even a dog … and a handler. Not even a dog by itself.'

'It is strange.' Hennessey sitting in the front passenger seat glanced at the house, all lights were burning in the building yet it still seemed to him to possess a sinister, disturb-ing quality and in his mind he was instantly transported back to a holiday he and Jennifer had had before they were married, in what he privately called his 'golden summer', when everything, everything was good, so very good, and when he had known true happi-ness. They had hired, he recalled, a small blue and white pleasure craft for a week on the River Shannon and had, at the close of their second day on the river, tied up for the night at a concrete jetty in a rural location about a quarter of a mile from a small town. After eating they had walked into the town while it was still light and had seen no one during the walk, not one car drove past them on the road and not a single bird was heard singing. And all about them was still. Too still. The town itself was of a dull, grey stone and was also utterly silent, not one person was to be seen, not one noise was to be heard either natural or man-made. He remembered clearly a grim-looking building with an arched entry in a cobbled courtyard with a workhouse-like appearance and which seemed to him to be defying him to enter. He and Jennifer glanced at each other and, without a word passing between them, had turned and walked back to the jetty, and to the river, and to the boat. After locking out Ireland, they had settled down and had an early night. The following morning they had left, thankfully.

Hennessey never found the name of the town, nor did he recognize the concrete jetty in the rural location on the return trip up river, and had it not been for Jennifer's presence, he would have had difficulty convincing himself that the silent, utterly silent walk into an utterly silent and still town one summer's evening had not all along been a vivid dream. But it had been real, and whilst nothing had been out of place and there had been no evident source of threat, the sense of danger had been overwhelming. He now felt that selfsame sense of danger when looking at the Aldidge's house under the cloudless, starlit sky. He glanced upwards and searched for the Plough, always having been seven stars, now it was six and a half as one of the pointers to the Pole Star having begun to flicker in its death throes. He located the Pole Star and then Orion and then looked at the house again. Behind them in a second vehicle, Ventnor and Webster waited, patiently.

'Nothing evident, as you say,' Hennessey whispered. 'Alright, tell Ventnor and Webster to go and collect car numbers ... you and I will take a stroll round the rear.'

'Is that wise, boss?' Yellich glanced at him. 'I mean if there are Rottweilers there we can't show them our IDs and say, "Stop, police".'

'I know, but the drive is gravel ... we'll deliberately crunch it heavily as we walk ... that will definitely start dogs barking if there are any dogs to bark.'

'OK.' Yellich reached for the door handle. 'Confess I didn't notice any dogs when we called, on either occasion, and Margaret Coley never mentioned any guard dogs.' He stepped out of the car and beckoned Webster and Ventnor to join him. Hennessey also left the vehicle, his breath evaporating as it met the cold night air.

The four officers stood looking intently at

the house, at the wide U-shaped gravel-surfaced drive with its separate exit and entrance from the road, and the line of cars drawn up, all prestigious makes, Bentley, Mercedes, Audi, Saab, Volvo.

'Alright,' Hennessey spoke softly, 'let's do it.' He walked across the road and stepped confidently on to the gravel, followed by Yellich, Webster and Ventnor with Yellich and Hennessey crunching the gravel particularly loudly.

'Dogs,' Yellich hissed in response to Ventnor's questioning and alarmed glance.

The four officers then stood in silence. No dogs barked. The lights in the house continued to burn, but no response came from within.

'Alright,' Hennessey spoke quietly, 'from now on we tread very softly, very softly indeed, use the grass verge as much as you can, avoid walking on the gravel if possible. We'll rendezvous back at the cars, that is our cars, not these cars in the drive, in thirty minutes' time.'

Hennessey and Yellich walked in single file along the verge beside the parked cars towards the house. At the side of the house they found a stone-flagged pathway, which led directly to the rear of the house and which they followed. The evening was starlit and moonlit and the expanse of lawn, about half the size of a football pitch, and surrounded by rhododendron bushes, was plain to see. Also plain to see was a springboard and stainless steel handgrips of ladders at the edge of a tiled area.

'Got anything to hold water on you?' Hennessey hissed, as he fumbled in his pockets.

Yellich did the same and then said, 'Just this.' He held up a ballpoint pen. 'I can extract the nib and ink reservoir, it will leave me with a hollow tube. I can screw the top back on and hold my finger over the other end.'

'It'll do, it'll do very nicely indeed – we'll get an official sample later if the results are what I think they'll be,' Hennessey said with a smile, 'because just as I know in my waters that the body of Sandra Paull will be found in the concrete mound within the derelict cottage, so I also know that swimming pool will be where Margaret Coley was drowned. An old copper's waters ... rarely wrong.' He tapped the side of his nose with his index finger.

Hennessey and Yellich walked silently across the lawn towards the swimming pool with Yellich dismantling the ballpoint pen as they went. At the poolside, Yellich knelt and scooped up water with the now hollow outer tube of the pen. He screwed the top back on and held it upright. 'Is that it, boss?' he whispered. 'Have we got what we want?'

'Yes.' Hennessey nodded. 'In fact more that what we want ... I didn't expect to find a

222

swimming pool. That was pleasantly convenient.'

'What did you expect to find?' Yellich fell into step with Hennessey as they walked quietly back across the lawn.

'Oh ... I dunno...' Hennessey smiled. 'Just wanted to look at the grounds of the house, just getting to know my quarry. Softlee, softlee, remember. And I also wanted to get out where the action is ... so that's one in the eye for the commander.' He grinned. 'Put that water in the fridge at the nick, find some way of sealing it ... then send it by courier to Wetherby on Monday, first thing. Attach a note asking for priority to be put on it.'

'Yes, skipper.'

'Did you read Carmen Pharoah's recording following her visit to the Land Registry?'

'Yes.' Yellich glanced to his left, at the house, curtains shut, all lights burning, but still no sound or sign of activity. 'Astounding. Who would have thought?'

'Who, indeed?' Hennessey echoed. 'Who indeed?'

Back at the cars, Hennessey and Yellich approached Ventnor and Webster who were waiting for them. 'Success?' Hennessey asked.

'Got them all, boss ... all fifteen.'

'Good, well done. We'll see who they are on Monday.'

'Monday?' Webster sounded surprised. 'You're not following this up tomorrow, sir?'

'Nope. Though I appreciate your enthusiasm, Webster, I know that we burn the candle at both ends, but even we deserve a day off now and again ... and it is Sunday. No ... nobody is at risk ... nobody is going anywhere. We'll pick this up on Monday.' He turned to Yellich. 'Let me carry that water, sergeant ... you know how much I dislike driving.'

It was Saturday, the sixteenth of November, 22.47 hours.

The demon, his other awful, terrible demon, came later that same night, utterly uninvited when for some reason, after what had been a very long and exhausting day, sleep evaded George Hennessey. The demons, his demons, haunted him, visited unbidden, often when he could not sleep, and it was for that reason that he consistently pursued the policy of retiring for the night only when he felt sleep weighing heavily upon him, not so much to get the most out of his waking hours but to prevent the demons from invading. It was still and quiet, after midnight, he slept in the back bedroom which looked out across the back garden to the fields beyond and so was little disturbed by the occasional late night car that passed the front of his house. An owl hooted and the sound of a distant railway locomotive's two-tone horn carried a long way in the still, crisp air over the hard ground. He groaned and turned to one side because Graham came to mind. Lovely, lovely, Graham.

He thought of his childhood home in Greenwich, on Colomb Street, close to the junction with Trafalgar Road, at the fashionable 'bottom end' of the borough, the terrace house which almost abutted the pavement. Two steps would take a pedestrian to their front door, where the young George Hennessey would sit whilst Graham would lovingly polish his beloved motorbike. If the weather was good, Graham would take young George Hennessey for a spin into London, across the river at Tower Bridge and back over the water by Westminster Bridge, returning home in time for Sunday lunch.

Lying abed, as the owl hooted, he was forced to re-live that terrible night. Listening in his bedroom as Graham kicked the silver Triumph into life, listening as he roared away down Trafalgar Road, climbing through the gears until the sound of the machine died and was replaced by other sounds in and of the night, the drunk making his way up Colomb Street, reciting his Hail Mary's, the sound of the ships on the river and then later, later that terrible knock on the door, the classic police officer's knock: tap, tap ... tap. The muffled voices, his mother's wailing and his father stumbling up the stairs, coming up to his room to tell the eight-year-old George that his elder brother, his father's beloved first born, had ridden his motorcycle

225

to heaven, 'to save a place for us'. He learned later that no other vehicle was involved, that Graham was not being reckless, but had lost control of the bike when he skidded on a patch of oil.

The funeral, painful at any time, was doubly painful because, like Jennifer, some eighteen short years later, Graham had died in the summer months and Hennessey felt there was just something wrong, something alien, something deeply unfair about dying young during the height of the foliage, and amid the birdsong and the flitting of butterflies. How it seemed so wrong that his brother's coffin should have been lowered into the ground to the sound of 'Greensleeves' chiming gaily from a close by, but unseen, ice-cream van. Summer is for weddings, he believed, and winter for funerals and he felt some compensation in the appropriateness of his father's coffin being lowered into rock-hard ground amid a snow flurry, and after a long life, well lived.

He wondered what sort of man Graham would have become, recalling how he had worried their parents by announcing his intention to resign from the bank and go to art college to study photography. Not for Graham would be the sleazy slick world of photographing stick-like models in swimwear, but for him would have been the world of photojournalism, in which one photograph can shift world opinion. That, he felt that would have been Graham Hennessey. The gap he always felt to be ahead of him, would have been filled by such a person, a good father to his own children and a good uncle to Charles Hennessey, barrister-at-law.

Hennessey lay awake, thinking and listening, until sleep in all its goodness and mercy, visited him.

It was Sunday, the seventeenth of November, 01.47 hours.

Seven

Monday, 18 November,
09.10 hours – 12.10 hours

*in which a freelance journalist provides
useful information.*

Hennessey sat quietly at his desk reading the list of names that the collator had acquired for him. Yellich, Ventnor, Webster and Pharoah sat in front of his desk, each with a copy of the list of names, each also silently studying the list.

'Interesting,' Ventnor murmured softly. 'Interesting.'

'What is?' Hennessey glanced up at him over the top of the sheet of paper he was holding. 'What has caught your eye?'

'The names ... none of them known to us, so all squeaky clean and the addresses ... very posh ... very high end ... it's difficult to see folk like this conspiring to murder someone and do so more than once.'

'What did you expect?' Webster turned to Ventnor. 'You saw the cars ... being outside that house was like being in a hotel car park in Monaco.'

'That means nothing.' Ventnor shook his head. 'Means nothing at all. Not these days. Walked round an estate once, not long ago really, used to be a high amenity council estate, they sold off the houses into private ownership a few years ago. Now the houses have shiny Mercedes Benz and Volvos outside ... still looks like a council estate ... small houses, small gardens but flash motors everywhere.'

'Alright!' Hennessey growled. 'Save the argument for the pub. Any names, any addresses spring out at you ... at anyone? Despite them not being our usual sort of customers?'

'I am most intrigued by the address here, the one in Sunk Island,' Carmen Pharoah pointed out. 'That's a long way to come. All the others are local but Sunk Island...'

'Yes, I also saw the name. It also caught my eye.' Hennessey read the address. 'Intriguing name. Where on earth is Sunk Island?'

'HU12,' Carmen Pharoah read the postcode. 'That's the Hull area and HU12 would be well east of the city centre.'

'East of Hull?' Hennessey queried. 'Is there anything east of Hull but sea?'

'Yes, quite a lot of land,' Carmen Pharoah said with a smile. 'Hull isn't a coastal city, though when the wind is from the east you'd think you were standing on Spurn Point, the easterly cuts like a knife, it's a real biter ... but there really is quite a bit of land between

Hull and the coast; it's an inland port on an estuary, you see. I have friends there. Even before I came to York I had friends in Hull ... I have visited often.'

'I see ... well ... as you have pointed out, all the other addresses are obviously local, the York chapter of the British Alliance is clearly well heeled ... but Sunk Island ... East of Hull ... doesn't the British Alliance have a Hull chapter, I wonder? We'll have to call on all the names, it really is time to start rattling a few cages, time we were getting a little proactive in this inquiry, see if we can start someone running in circles.' Hennessey paused. 'Two, possibly three murders are associated with the Aldidge household, which is the base of the so called British Alliance in this area, so it's high time we started to lean on people. Let's see ... we're waiting for feedback from Wetherby about the water taken from the swimming pool. If they come back as speedily as they can we still won't hear from them before the end of their working day today, so we can't yet link Margaret Coley's death to the Aldidge household. So ... alright, DC Pharoah, since, for your sins, you know Hull, I want you to team up with DC Webster ... go and have a chat to the gentleman who lives in the astounding and intriguing sounding Sunk Island, Mr –' Hennessey glanced at the sheet of paper – 'Mr Fenty, Mr Franklin Fenty. Yellich and Ventnor ... a sergeant, half a dozen constables and a pneumatic drill, see if your intuition about that concrete mound is correct.'

'Very good, sir.' Yellich smiled and nodded.

'If you are right, as you will be, notify me, I want to witness the body before it is removed. I am not going to be as hands off as Commander Sharkey wants me to be. I rediscovered my taste for hands-on police work on Saturday evening.'

'Understood, sir.' Yellich stood.

'And Pharoah and Webster, back to you two, since you're in the Hull area, there's a very interesting character with a lot of explaining to do who lives out that way. Mr Derek Aldidge, publican, who claims to frown upon the British Alliance yet whose expensive car was at his sister-in-law's house on Saturday evening last ... and especially strange when he claimed to dislike her so much.'

'Very especially strange since he owns the derelict cottage in which Margaret Coley's body was found,' Carmen Pharoah remarked and also stood, 'and in which Sandra Paull's body is likely to be found.'

'Indeed.' Hennessey smiled. 'But Franklin Fenty beforehand.'

'Well, that depends on who you are. It depends who I am talking to.' Franklin Fenty stood squarely in the doorway of his house. Phaorah and Webster both thought him

231

defensive, agitated, fearful.

'Police,' Webster repeated calmly. 'We told you.' He continued to hold up his ID.

'Well, anyone can say they're from the police.' Fenty closely scrutinized Webster's card making no attempt to take if from Webster's hand, as if he was fully aware of the 'look but do not touch' rule. 'But you seem alright.' He stepped aside and beckoned Pharoah and Webster into his house, glancing anxiously around him as he did so, scanning the flat, lush fields.

'You seem very anxious, Mr Fenty.' Webster accepted Fenty's invitation to sit and chose a comfortable-looking armchair.

'I do?' Fenty also sat in a similar armchair.

'Yes.' Pharoah smiled as she sat on the settee and took her notepad from her large leather handbag. 'Yes, you do.' She thought the room was a little musty and in need of ventilation.

'Well, I may have reason.' Fenty glanced out of the window.

'Really?' Webster settled into the armchair and read the room, books, quality newspapers, unwashed coffee mugs, photographs of a springer spaniel on the wall. A bookish, dog-loving bachelor, a strangely young man, Webster thought, for such a remote house. Sunk Island had revealed itself to be a crossroads in the middle of rich fields to the east of Hull, close to both the bank and to the mouth of the River Humber. The only

232

buildings at the crossroads were a church and a church hall; beyond that was a farmhouse and outbuildings. Fenty's cottage was between the farmhouse and the village of Ottringham along a straight road lined with closely planted beech trees.

'Remote.' Webster observed.

'Here?' Fenty queried. 'You mean this house is remote?'

'Yes,' Webster said with a smile. 'It must be enjoyable if you like solitude.'

Fenty shrugged. 'Possibly, but I can walk into the village in twenty minutes, quite pleasant in the summer. Winters are bad, though ... the east wind, it's worse than the northern wind. Straight off the North Sea, cuts through your clothing like a knife, you really need your thermals in this part of the UK.'

'Not local?'

'No,' Fenty said as he shook his head, 'unforgivably in this part of the world I'm from Lancashire, though I tell folk I'm from West Yorkshire, otherwise I'd never get acceptance. It helps that I don't have a Mancunian accent to hide.'

'Lived here long?'

'About ten years. I began to get acceptance after about six years. Every day for six years me and one of the local farmers passed each other as I walked into the village, every day he walked straight past me on the opposite side of the road as though I was invisible.

233

Then one day he glanced at me and said, "Alright?" and I was in, accepted ... took six years.' Fenty reclined in the armchair and smiled. 'So now, how can I help you?'

'The British Alliance.' Webster spoke quietly.

Fenty paled. 'What about them?'

'You seem frightened of them,' Webster probed. 'Is that who you are frightened of?'

'Yes ... yes, it is. Heavy boys. Very heavy boys. How did you find me?'

'You attended a social meeting of the Alliance on Saturday last at a house in Thaxted Green.'

'Yes ... how did you know?'

'We were not invited, so we invited ourselves.' Webster smiled. 'Not to the party, of course, just to the house ... really to the outside of same, noted down the car registration numbers ... fed them into our computer.'

'I see, and mine was the little blue VW, the least expensive car there.'

'Forgive me,' Pharoah said as she leaned backwards into the settee, 'but you don't seem to be of that ... that ... persuasion.'

'I am not, most definitely not, but what makes you say that?'

'The books, the newspapers of the informed press...'

'I am a freelance journalist, I am trying to expose the Alliance ... to name and shame.'

'Dangerous.' Carmen Pharoah held eye

contact with Fenty.

'Very.' Fenty nodded. 'It isn't clever to play with hidden cameras, especially with these people, their enemies tend to disappear.'

'You have evidence?' Webster's voice hardened.

'Not enough to bring to you, not yet but ... I know the rules. Once I do have evidence I'll go directly to the police.'

'Good.'

'Just hearsay thus far,' Fenty said. 'That's all I have so far.'

'What sparked your interest?'

'A chance remark. I visited their website, expressed an interest, then they visited me ... here ... some months ago. Fortunately they gave me a little notice of their coming. I had enough time to prepare ... cleared the shelves of books and hid the left of centre news-papers, kept the right of centre ones. They looked around, but didn't search as such, chatted to me and went home happy. I told them I was an unemployed economist, you see, which is partially true. I have a degree in economics so I can speak the economist speak – law of diminishing returns, and so on ... but of course I kept my real occupation a secret because I am trying to make a docu-mentary ... to name and shame, like I said.'

'What have you found out that might interest us?' Webster asked.

'That their enemies disappear, like I said, but no proof, like I also said. It is going to be difficult, it was always going to be difficult. Only recently have I begun to realize just how difficult. And how dangerous ... also how dangerous ... how extremely dangerous.' Fenty was a tall but slightly built man, clean-shaven, apart from a pencil-line moustache. Webster felt that he would not be able to give a good account of himself in a fight, and would have much to fear from the thugs who were reportedly drilled, military style, on the rear lawn of Audrey Aldidge's house. 'The difficulty, and from their point of view the clever thing, is that they don't get their hands dirty. They contract out the dirty work. They are very cautious in that respect.'

'Oh?'

'Yes. What do you know about them?' Fenty asked.

Webster glanced at Carmen Pharoah being unused to having questions asked of him. 'What do we know? We know only that they see themselves as aloof from other ultra right political parties.'

'Yes,' Fenty agreed and nodded, 'that is essentially their ethos. If Britain voted in an ultra-right government, the British Alliance would see themselves as providing the cabinet, the front bench in the House. That is their fantasy.'

'So, tell us about the youths who are drilled on the back lawn. Who are they?'

'That lot!' Fenty raised his nose in a gesture of contempt. 'The BA holds itself aloof, but not separate. It has links with the other right-wing parties and especially with the York branch of the Defenders of St George.'

'We have heard of them,' Webster sighed. 'Have heard of them...'

'Oh, we all have,' Fenty replied. 'They have no discreet place to march about so Mrs Aldidge allows them to use her rear lawn and if some foolhardy investigative journalist should get too close to the British Alliance, York chapter, then a phone call will ensure said investigative journalist will have his skull cracked open, or worse, by some of the good boys of the Defenders of St George, York chapter, and it will happen while each member of the British Alliance, York chapter, will be establishing cast-iron alibis. You scratch my back, I'll spill your enemies' blood, and smile as I do so.'

'Why travel so far?' Webster asked. 'Is there no chapter in Hull? This is something we wondered about.'

'No ... no, there is no local branch of the Alliance in Hull ... plenty of support for the Defenders of St George and other right-wing, close-cropped, clean-shaven thugs, but Hull as a city is just too working class to provide enough extreme right-wing professional business types, so the York chapter it is for me and another couple of guys from this far east.'

'I see,' Webster said. 'Thank you. That has

explained something.'

'So, what are you interested in?' Fenty seemed to be getting more relaxed; Webster noted easier breathing, more eye contact. 'If I may ask.'

'The death of Arthur Aldidge.'

'Yes, I read of his body being found after ten years. There's a story there alright.'

'And the death of Margaret Coley,' Carmen Pharoah added.

'Who's she?' Fenty turned to Carmen Pharoah with interest.

'One of the domestics in the Aldidge household.'

'Oh, the black ladies.' Fenty nodded. 'You see, that is the British Alliance for you. Openly encourages its members to employ only black servants, not to help black people obtain employment but rather as a gesture of white supremacy, that's their motivation.'

'I assumed as much,' Pharoah said, 'or rather, we assumed as much.'

'Fairly obvious if you ask me,' Fenty replied. 'Nothing much to assume. I've been to other houses owned by members of the Alliance ... black maids, cooks, chauffeurs ... it's a clear policy, got some lovely footage. That's my problem, too much footage of the same sort of thing. I was getting careless, and thankfully I have learned to listen to my intuition.'

'Oh?'

'Yes.' Fenty took a deep breath and exhaled

238

slowly. 'I was wired up with a small camera in my jacket, lens in the buttonhole to record whatever I was able to record at the social evening you invited yourselves to and when I was driving there, almost at the house in fact, a voice in my head seemed to be saying, "Don't do it, don't do it, don't do it".'

'I have also heard such a voice.' Carmen Pharoah nodded. 'I have learned to listen to it.'

'Yes.' Fenty looked at her. 'It's almost always in the negative, "don't do it", or "don't say it" ... but you are right to listen to it.'

'Yes.'

'Anyway, I pulled over, a lay-by appeared just at the right time, as if by providence ... seemed to be significant ... as though it was there for a purpose and so I stopped, took the camera from my jacket and hid it in my car. Then I went to the party and for the first time ever, I was asked to submit to a search. I protested, of course, but eventually capitulated, trying not to overact. In fact I was done very thoroughly by a couple of heavies from the Defenders of St George, you know, the British Alliance lackeys. They didn't find anything because by then there was nothing to find and so I was allowed back to the party. Fortunately they didn't search the car but I am definitely under suspicion. These people, I tell you ... paranoid is just not the word. I have been attending their meetings for a few months but things are now getting too uncomfortable.' Again he glanced out of the window. 'I haven't got nearly enough for the hour-long documentary I was planning. For an hour-long documentary I will need about two hundred hours of footage. If I pull out I will live, but with nothing to show for months of work. If I don't make the film, I don't eat. I'm self-funding you see, living on the profits from the previous film.'

'What are you going to do, do you think?'

'Pull out.' Fenty laughed. 'I have to. I want to live. It's my only option.'

'Sensible.'

'Yes ... I just didn't realize how heavy these people are, which explains why very few, in fact none of them, is professional in the real sense of the word. They don't seem to belong to the professions ... I have met no doctors, lawyers or accountants, for example. They all tend to be middle class by birth and upbringing but all are self-employed, or are just wealthy like Audrey Aldidge having inherited a nice bit of dosh. They have nothing better to do than sit and dream of running Britain as a fascist state.'

'So their ambitions go beyond parliamentary democracy?' Webster asked.

'Depends on whom you talk to,' Fenty replied, 'but they're all crackpot anyway, politically speaking. They're just fantasists when it comes to wanting to assume real political power, but it's their attitude to individuals which makes them so very dangerous. Like I said, their enemies disappear. Now you are telling me a maid has been murdered?'

'Drowned, we believe,' Pharoah explained.

'Oh...' Fenty's hand went up to his head. 'Poor woman. Thank God I took the camera from my jacket. I wouldn't be here now ... this is going to haunt me ... it's definitely going to go on to my haunting list.' Fenty briefly closed his eyes. 'I have enough to make me toss and turn all night as it is. I might be unscathed but it's going to be a difficult memory to live with. One more scar inside my head. What could have happened but didn't is still very difficult to live with, so I have found, like putting your head into the jaws of death and withdrawing it again, but only after, so I have found, leaving it there for plenty long enough for said jaws to snap shut. I have a few such memories and this is going to be one more.' He paused. 'Thank God I stopped. Thank God I listened to that voice in my head.'

'So, Mrs Aldidge?'

'The boss.'

'Is she?'

'Yes, she heads up the York Branch of the BA, very forceful, gets her own way. She likes her own way and she gets it. Always gets whatever she wants.'

'What have you heard about her that might be of interest to us?'

'Well, nothing about the maid, Margaret Coley, but Audrey Aldidge did say once, "Arthur didn't toe the line, so he had to go".'

'She said that?' Carmen Pharoah sat up. 'She said that?'

'Yes,' Fenty said as he nodded. 'I had only just met her and didn't know to whom she was referring. It was only subsequently that I learned that she was referring to her late husband. And I didn't realize she meant he'd been topped ... she said it so calmly, so matter-of-factly that I thought she meant she had dismissed an employee.'

'"Arthur didn't toe the line, so he had to go",' Carmen Pharoah repeated as she scribbled on her notepad. 'Did you find out what line she meant?'

'I got the distinct impression that it was her line, the Audrey Aldidge line, not the party line. He offended her, not the British Alliance, but the deed would have been done by thugs hired from the Defenders of St George.'

'Any names mentioned?' Webster asked.

'Not to me, and of course I didn't ask. I had to be careful not to give myself away and nothing raises suspicion like too many questions.'

'Ever heard of Philip Buchan?' Webster suggested. 'Also known as Big Phil?'

'Big Phil?' Fenty nodded again. 'Come to think of it ... yes. Described as a "useful man", and "one who got his silly self locked

242

up, useful when he gets out", comments like that. So yes, that name rings a bell.'

'Who said that?'

'That was said by a man called ... called ... called ... Burnell. Foreign first name, he has an Italian mother, or so I later learned ... Bruno ... that's it, Bruno Burnell. He, for example, is very typical of the membership of the British Alliance.'

'Really? In what way?' Pharoah kept her pen poised. 'How so?'

'Well, yes, he claims blood line links to the Italian fascists of the 1930s and that gives him kudos in the BA. Quite some prestige in fact. Comes from money, private schools and all that, but is now self-employed as a second-hand car dealer ... no education beyond school. I find him a bit dim in fact.'

'Oh...?'

'But he only deals in quality cars which he insists on calling "horseless carriages", Rolls Royce, Bentleys ... class cars. He apparently only ever has two or three vehicles for sale at any one time, not like the usual second-hand car dealers who have acreages of metal for sale. He advertises only in specialist car magazines and has his business premises in a village outside York. His customers come to him, you see, or so he likes to say, he doesn't need a main road premises ... but he is typical of them, typical of the Alliance, monied but not a learned, educated man, not a member of the professions just a bit toffee-nosed and values Anglo Saxon Britain which is a bit rich since his mother was Italian, and he is of Mediterranean appearance ... you know, olive skinned. But it was he who mentioned Big Phil.'

'You sure?' Pharoah pressed. 'This is quite important.'

'I have it on film,' Fenty said with a smile. 'One of my earliest forays into the BA. He was chatting to another member called Holmes ... he seemed to know Big Phil as well come to think of it. It's all on videotape. What was his name ... Nigel Holmes ... he's a photographer. Again, like Burnell, he only has posh clients ... society weddings, that sort of thing. He has a studio in York, I think it's central. Now he worried me ... Holmes caused me worry.'

'Why?'

'I thought if I was going to be rumbled, then it would most likely be by him because he is a photographer, he would have been able to recognize my lens for what it was.' Fenty fell silent as if realizing something. 'Maybe he did, maybe it was he who tipped off Audrey Aldidge ... it could have been she who had me searched? In fact, I bet you that was what happened. Holmes saw my lens...'

'We'd like to look at your film?'

'You're welcome to it. In fact I'm not safe until it's all out of this house ... either in your custody or incinerated.' He stood. 'I'll get the tapes for you.'

244

Sandra Paull's father stood and handed the gold pendant to his wife. 'It's our Sandra's alright.' He spoke in a monotone.

'Our Sandra's,' his wife echoed. 'Our Sandra's alright.'

'I'm very sorry,' Yellich said.

'What's the grit on it?' Mr Paull returned to his chair and seemed to Yellich to sink into it, rather than sit in a controlled manner.

'Cement.' Yellich felt awkward, breaking bad news was something he never found easy. He found it very hard to do it as sensitively as he wished.

'Cement?'

'I'm sorry ... yes ... Sandra's body was encased in cement.'

Mrs Paull seemed to him to be fighting back tears and so he spoke to Mr Paull. 'The post-mortem is being conducted at the moment. I really am very sorry.'

'Post-mortem?' He looked at Yellich with an appealing expression. 'Is that when they cut open the body?'

'Yes, afraid so ... but after ten years...'

'There's not much of her body left ... I can understand.' He seemed to gaze into the middle distance. 'But this is good news in a sense, I mean, we can bury her now, give her somewhere to rest. We can have a grave to visit.'

'We won't know for certain that it is Sandra until we have checked the dental records,'

Yellich explained. 'Dentists have to keep records for eleven years, so we are still within that time span. Who, can I ask, was her dentist?'

'Mr Hillyard, we have always gone to Mr Hillyard, he has a surgery in the city, on Gillygate.'

'Thank you.' Yellich wrote the name on his notepad

'He's a good dentist, we are lucky to have him. He mentions Sandra sometimes. He remembers her.'

'Failing that we could confirm her identity with DNA samples.'

'It'll be her, her grandmother gave her that pendant, she loved it, it was so precious to her.' Mr Paull looked at the pendant being held by his wife. 'She wouldn't sell it or give it away and it's not worth much ... not worth enough to steal, anyone can see that. It's Sandra's and the body will be Sandra's. When can we have her to bury?'

'Very soon,' Yellich said as he stood, 'as soon as the PM is completed. That's being carried out now. I am really very, very sorry.'

Ventnor had been surprised by the amount of flesh still on the body; he mustered the confidence to comment on it.

'Being encased in the cement did that.' Dr D'Acre surveyed the corpse. 'It kept it airtight you see. Some decay is inevitable, as you see, but not to the extent that would

246

have been the case had she been left in the open for ten years. She's also too young to be in here.' Dr D'Acre adjusted the microphone attached to the anglepoise arm which in turn was attached to the ceiling between two perspex covered filament bulbs. 'I mean, many are too young to be in here, very few people are laid on these tables unless they have expired before nature intended them to expire, even the older ones, but some ... like you, pet, some are laid here cruelly early.' She paused. 'Do we have her name?'

'Believed to be Sandra Paull, ma'am, aged twenty-one years when she was reported missing.' Ventnor stood at the edge of the post-mortem laboratory, dressed head to foot in green paper disposable coveralls.

'Well, the age appears consistent, if she died about the time she disappeared.' Dr D'Acre was similarly dressed in green coveralls, as was Eric Filey the pathology laboratory assistant. 'Please give this a file number, Susan.' Dr D'Acre spoke to the microphone. 'And give the name as Sandra Paull, aged twenty-one.' She turned to Ventnor. 'You're new, I think, recently joined Mr Hennessey's team?'

'Yes, ma'am. DC Ventnor, Thompson Ventnor.'

She smiled. 'What a lovely name ... in fact, two interesting sounding names. I haven't heard either used as names ... Thompson?'

'Yes, ma'am, it's unusual but not unknown,

it's a northern England variation of Thomas.'

'I see.'

'I am in fact Thompson Ventnor the third, an older cousin and my grandfather were also Thompson Ventnor.'

'And Ventnor is a resort on the Isle of Wight?'

'Yes, ma'am, no idea how we acquired that, it might be a corruption of a foreign name that sounded a little like Ventnor and so it might have been changed to Anglicize it ... so as to help a refugee gain acceptance in times gone by.'

'Yes, it is a pity that that had to happen.'

'Yes, indeed.'

'And it was the case that surnames like Ruby and Diamond appeared in the nineteenth century because custom officials who couldn't pronounce Slavic names took it upon themselves to rename individuals from the jewellery they were wearing. Well, nice to meet you anyway, Mr Hennessey did mention that his team was being expanded and that he will be spending more time behind his desk. Not sure he was happy about that ... there was a noticeable lack of enthusiasm about him when he told me he was acquiring new people.'

'I think he has mixed feelings, ma'am, likes the extra manpower but I think he's going to miss the hands-on approach. Mr Hennessey likes being in the field.'

'Yes, I have gained that impression. Not too

happy behind a desk all the time.'

Dr D'Acre then turned her attention to the corpse, probed the skull beneath the mass of hair. 'Fracture,' she said, 'massive fracture ... no other signs of injury on the body.' She took a scalpel and described an incision round the circumference of the skull above the ears. Laying the scalpel in the instrument tray she peeled the flesh away from the top of the skull. 'Ah, yes,' she observed, 'quite sufficient to have caused death ... a linear object.' She turned to Ventnor. 'I understand that this case is linked to the death of the man found under a pile of rubble last week, isn't it? What was his name? Made quite a splash in the local press, the nationals even carried it on the inside pages ... dare say it was somewhat newsworthy.'

'Mr Aldidge, ma'am, Arthur Aldidge.'

'Yes. That's it.'

'And yes,' Ventnor confirmed, 'the two murders are believed to be connected. Mr Aldidge and Miss Paull were involved with each other, romantically so, we believe, and both disappeared at the same time.'

'I see, well, they shared the same form of death. They probably didn't want to have that in common but unfortunately for them they got to have it in common anyway. Both met their deaths in similar ways, banged over the head with a very solid linear object ... a golf club, a wooden stave ... like a pickaxe handle, that sort of thing but not a hammer

249

which would have caused a different fracturing. I'll have the body X-rayed in case there are other injuries but I am sure it will be negative.' Dr D'Acre took a stainless steel rod and placed it in the mouth, forcing it to open with a loud crack. 'The jaw has seized solid,' she explained with a smile. 'Let's see what ... oh ... what have we here?' She delicately probed the mouth with latex encased fingers and carefully extracted a small object. 'Production bag, please, Eric.'

Eric Filey efficiently and speedily handed her a small self-sealing cellophane sachet into which she dropped the item.

'One for you,' she said and smiled again at Ventnor. 'It is nothing medical ... it seems to be a small locket of some description, it seems to be gold and it appears that it has an inscription.'

Eric Filey crossed the floor of the pathology laboratory and handed the sachet reverentially to Ventnor.

'Thank you, I'll get this up to the forensic science laboratory at Wetherby,' Ventnor examined the locket. 'We'll see what they can tell us about it.'

'I'll bet my pound to your penny that that was Miss Paull leaving a present for you,' Dr D'Acre mused, 'not that that is my field, of course.'

'I wouldn't take that bet.' Ventnor turned the locket over, closely examining it. 'I think you're right, ma'am, either that or perhaps

250

someone put it in her mouth ... either way, we were clearly intended to find it. I do hope it was put there by someone else.'

'Oh?' Dr D'Acre examined the teeth. 'Why so...?'

'Yes, well you see if she put it there herself, it meant she knew her life was in danger ... the terror of knowing that your life is over at such a young age, yet still having the presence of mind to leave something for the police to find. So for her sake, I hope it was put there.'

'I see what you mean, Mr Ventnor, terrifying indeed ... well ... we'll see what it tells you. The teeth show signs of dentistry, British dentistry, so there will be dental records somewhere.'

'Sergeant Yellich is with the family now, ma'am, he'll be obtaining the information.'

'I see ... we'll use dental records to determine identity ... much, much less intrusive for the family. I can't think of anything worse than having to give a sample of my DNA to verify that a corpse is that of one of my children.' She paused. 'I can remove the jaw, we'll send it to Wetherby, they will be able to match the lower teeth to dental records, that way we don't have to involve the parents. They have enough to cope with, I imagine.'

'Understood, ma'am.'

Dr D'Acre picked up the scalpel and then drew a long deep incision across the surface of the stomach so as to expose the contents.

'Quite a small stomach,' she noted. 'A strange organ, the stomach, you know, you can't tell how large it is from the outside, even in respect of very slender women, the sort that can lay a ruler from hip to hip can have large stomachs, and can drink a pint of beer in one go ... but not m'lady ... no ... she would have sipped her beer and eaten little, yet still not felt hungry. There is sadly and alarmingly no sign of any food in the stomach. Even after this length of time some food would have been identifiable had she eaten a few hours before death.' She drummed her fingers on the rim of the stainless steel table. 'Slight discolouration to the left wrist is noted,' she said softly. 'It is difficult to tell, but that could very well be bruising. A pattern seems to emerge: she was perhaps restrained by a device which was fastened sufficiently tightly round her left wrist that it caused bruising during which time she was starved of food and then she was murdered by a blow to the head with a linear instrument. Perhaps.' Again she took the scalpel and forced it into the upper arm. 'I am looking for a vein,' she explained. 'Ah ... closed up ... no sign of a trace of blood. Eric, can you take the feet please?' Dr D'Acre took hold of the shoulders and said, 'Clockwise from your point ... after three...' And with practised ease, the corpse was turned to rest on its anterior aspect. 'Again, we have shaded areas on the shoulders, buttocks and

252

legs ... that,' she explained, 'is the remnants of lividity. She was laid upon her back immediately after she was killed, and the blood, still fluid, settled according to gravity. That could have happened where she was found, but somehow I doubt it ... too open ... too near the village. I would have thought it much more likely that she would have been allowed to cool and stiffen where she would not be found and then, when it was safe to do so, her body was conveyed to the derelict cottage and encased in concrete.'

'Yet somehow,' Ventnor mused, 'somehow managed to escape or evade capture long enough to put a present in her mouth for us to find.'

'Or, as we agreed, and indeed we both hope someone put it there after she was murdered for us to find.' Dr D'Acre looked down at the corpse. 'What did happen to you, little one?' She paused. 'Well, I will have my report written up and faxed to you, for the attention of DCI Hennessey or yourself, Mr Ventnor?'

'Oh, to Mr Hennessey, please.' Ventnor smiled. 'He's the boss, he keeps the overview.'

'Very well, I'll send the jaw to the forensic science laboratory at Wetherby, they can easily confirm ID via dental records. I'll X-ray the body and also send a tissue sample to Wetherby asking them to test for poison. I doubt they'll find any and only heavy poisons like arsenic will be detectable after this

253

length of time, but I'll do it anyway for the sake of thoroughness. She died, like her lover, from a massive blow to the head but, unlike her lover, appeared to have been held captive and deprived of food for a significant amount of time prior to death.'

'So, arrest me!' Derek Aldidge suddenly revealed an aggressive streak in his personality which was not uncommon amongst publicans, in Webster's experience. Often, very often, he had come across a publican who seemed warm, friendly, chatty but who could turn deeply unpleasant and do so in an instant. 'I mean, if you suspect something ... arrest me ... then we both know where we stand.'

'No reason yet to arrest you.' Webster sat motionless in the chair and glanced around him at the pub beginning that day's business. Isolated, elderly patrons in the main, he noted. 'You are not going to go anywhere.'

'You think?' Aldidge sneered. 'How do you know?'

'It's a fairly safe bet,' Webster said with a shrug of his shoulders. 'You are not a member of the underworld that we know of, you have no contacts that can hide you and keep you hidden, provide you with a false ID, no one in the BA is a criminal, that's the nature of the organization, so we have found ... everything is legal and above board, no one has a criminal record.'

254

'You use other people to do your dirty work, such as thugs from the Defenders of St George, folk who like violence,' Carmen Pharoah added. 'That's very clever of you.'

Aldidge remained silent, but glowered at Carmen Pharoah.

'Being the owner of a building in which a dead body is found is not a crime –' Carmen Pharoah eyed him intently, she was not at all intimidated by his angry stare – 'especially when the building is derelict and entry is unrestricted. Not a crime at all. But we do wonder if you knew anything about the body being in there, and again, especially since you have or did have some connection with the deceased.'

'I do? I did?'

'You do,' Webster replied with a serious-toned voice. 'Your sister-in-law. She is or was the connection. Technically, I suppose Mrs Aldidge is still your sister-in-law despite your brother's death ... your sister-in-law employed the deceased. Margaret Coley was a maid in your sister-in-law's house. That is a clear link. A clear connection.'

Aldidge seemed to flush with anger.

'You see the reason for our suspicion?' Carmen Pharoah pressed. 'We are also concerned about a little discrepancy, something you can help clear up.'

Webster leaned forward. 'It has nagged at us.'

'Oh?' Aldidge replied coldly. 'What might

255

that be...?'

'Yes ... well, a few days ago, when myself and my other colleague DS Ventnor visited you here at the pub...'

'Yes?'

'You made a very clear statement distancing yourself from the British Alliance, yet you attended the British Alliance's social function at Audrey Aldidge's house on Saturday last, in the evening.'

Derek Aldidge paled.

'We were there too,' Carmen Pharoah explained. 'As our boss says, we were not invited, so we invited ourselves. We noted the registration numbers of the guests' cars.'

'Can you do that?'

'We did anyway. But that's not the point. Please be clear ... what is your attitude to the BA? What is your relationship with Mrs Aldidge?'

'The answer to the first is confidential.'

'Fair enough.' Pharoah smiled. 'I can accept that ... we can accept that. But the second question? That's much more pertinent, that has to be answered.'

Aldidge remained silent.

'Margaret Coley drowned,' Webster pressed. 'Any idea where that might have occurred?'

Aldidge shrugged. 'None at all.'

'No?' Webster held eye contact with Aldidge. 'I mean, if we can identify the stream or lake ... or similar, where she drowned, and

256

if said stream or lake is connected to a suspect...'

'Suspect?' Aldidge gasped.

'Yes,' Carmen Pharoah replied and nodded calmly. 'We are at that mature stage in the investigation of talking about suspects. And we are looking at two murders ... possibly three.'

'Three?'

'Three. We are looking closely at the disappearance of Sandra Paull again and we are doing so in a fresh light. She disappeared at the same time as your brother Mr Arthur Aldidge, and we also now know that they were romantically involved with each other. So, three murders. Possibly. I mean, this is Premier Division crime, quite rich for people who want to be the officer class of an extreme right-wing Britain. The ruling elite cannot be criminal, hence, I dare say, the usefulness of the boys of the Defenders of St George.'

Carmen Pharoah sat slowly back in her chair. She noticed and enjoyed the smell of the interior of the pub: furniture polish and air freshener. She further noticed that the clean and pleasant aroma did not prevent Derek Aldidge from looking very ill at ease. 'What will Bruno Burnell and Nigel Holmes be able to tell us?'

'Bruno ... Nigel...' Aldidge gasped. 'You know them?'

'Two names that were helpfully given to us

as being of possible interest to the police.'

'Who by?' Aldidge snapped. 'Who told you?'

'Confidential source,' Webster said, 'but it's interesting that you should refer to them by their first names. They were also at the party on Saturday.'

'It wasn't a party ... a few drinks, conversation ... hardly a party.'

'So, your attendance wasn't a coincidence?'

Again Aldidge remained silent. The silence lasted fully thirty seconds. It was eventually broken by Carmen Pharoah. 'You see, Derek ... you don't mind if I call you Derek?'

Derek Aldidge shrugged, he seemed to Pharoah to be close to despair, as if wishing himself a long way from where he presently sat. 'You see, we largely think that Mrs Audrey Aldidge was instrumental in her husband's murder, and instrumental in the murder of his lover, Sandra Paull. We also think that Mrs Aldidge orchestrated the murder by drowning of Margaret Coley as retribution for giving us a lot of information. I personally spoke to Margaret, a lovely lady, and I can tell you that she gave us some very useful information, she pointed us in the right direction, but when we tried to talk to the cook and the other maid ... well, they wouldn't say anything. By that time, Audrey Aldidge had got to them and had intimidated them. But Margaret had done damage and so she had to be silenced, perhaps as an example, perhaps to prevent more damage being done ... but silenced nonetheless.'

'Fortunately for her, she did not live in Colombia,' Webster added.

'Why so?'

'Because there, in Colombia, any police informant has their throat slashed and their tongue pulled down the throat and out via the incision in the neck. It's apparently called a Colombian necktie.'

'Drowning is neater,' Carmen Pharoah said with a smile, 'and it serves the same end ... transmits the same message.'

'A seller of quality cars, a society photographer ... like you, they are not going anywhere soon. We don't want to start the clock before we have to. So we won't be arresting you ... not just yet anyway ... and the one person who can disappear because he is a felon with felonious contacts is safely tucked up in prison, so he's not going anywhere either.'

'Who's that?' Aldidge asked wearily.

'Fella by the name of Buchan. Big Phil Buchan ... know him?'

Derek Aldidge's jaw sagged.

'He's beginning to talk, you may as well know that, he sees a bargain in it for himself.' Webster smiled, then paused. 'You see, Mr Aldidge, it's like this ... I've said this many times before ... not to you, of course, but to other people in other investigations, but I'll say it to you now ... you are a man who is

259

standing at the side of a road...'

'I am?' Aldidge looked puzzled.

'You are,' Webster spoke solemnly. 'You are feeling very cold and very isolated, and very alone in the world. A bus is coming but there is something hugely important about this particular bus ... it's the last bus. You can put up your hand to stop it, climb aboard it, where it is dry and safe, or you can let it go past you, leaving you in the cold and the wet ... and in a state of dreadful isolation.' Webster paused then pointed to Carmen Pharoah and then to himself, then back to Carmen Pharoah. 'We,' he said, 'we are the bus ... we are the last bus.'

'And we'll be making the same offer to Audrey Aldidge, Phil Buchan, Bruno Burnell, Nigel Holmes, in fact anybody and everybody who is involved in these murders,' Carmen Pharoah added. 'We're closing down on you now, all of you ... the first one to cough will be doing himself a huge, very huge favour.'

Carmen Pharoah and Reginald Webster stood and walked out of the Vine.

It was Monday, the eighteenth November, 12.10 hours.

Eight

*in which another used-car dealer, a photo-
grapher and an elderly criminal are met, and
are met most profitably.*

Hennessey carefully turned over the locket
which he held in his hand and which had
been presented to him by Thompson Ventnor. 'Have you opened it?'

'No, sir.' Thompson Ventnor sat stiffly in a
chair opposite Hennessey's desk. 'I brought
it straight to you.'

'But you have logged it in as evidence ...
you've done that, I hope?'

'Yes, sir, then I brought it straight to you.'

'Good...' Hennessey doggedly attempted
to open the locket but eventually conceded
that he had failed. He handed it to Ventnor.
'Younger, more nimble fingers required,
methinks.'

Thompson Ventnor also struggled with the
locket but eventually succeeded to open it. It
did not, as both he and Hennessey expected,
spring open, but opened loosely, casually,

261

almost reluctantly. Ventnor handed it immediately back to Hennessey who mumbled his thanks and opened it fully. 'It was indeed Sandra leaving us a present,' he said softly. 'There's an inscription, clear as day: "To Audrey, all my love Arthur".'

'Audrey Aldidge's locket.' Ventnor also spoke softly as if a reverence had descended upon the office. 'And found in Sandra Paull's mouth. She was indeed leaving us a present. She must have known she was going to be murdered. Such courage, such presence of mind ... it's humbling to think about.'

'Yes,' Hennessey said as he looked closely at the locket, examining it carefully, 'and we owe it to her not to betray the trust she had in us that the leaving of this gift implies. This puts her in the Aldidge household ... I mean deep within it. Where would a woman keep such a locket when not wearing it?'

'On her dressing table, I would think, sir, or one of the drawers therein.'

'That would be my guess.' Hennessey nodded in agreement.

'Time to bring Audrey Aldidge in?' Ventnor spoke eagerly.

Hennessey paused. 'Not yet ... not yet. Let's let her stew for a while yet. She knows we are sniffing around, with any luck she might trip herself up. I want very much to search that house ... I need a warrant ... she won't co-operate.'

'The maid's murder, sir,' Ventnor suggested. 'She was resident in the house, surely that's sufficient, and the locket found in the mouth of the dead girl ... that is more than sufficient I would have thought.'

'Possibly, I'll see what CPS say, but I think I know what their views will be ... nothing to connect the murder of Margaret Coley with the house because she was found well away from it, and Sandra Paull may have stolen the locket and removed it from the house at a much earlier date. I suppose she did steal it in a sense, but her motivation wasn't criminal. No, we need more in order to belt and bracer it ... Carmen Pharoah and Reginald Webster are presently interviewing two interesting sounding characters in the British Alliance, names that were fed to them by a nervous undercover reporter who seemed frightened for his life, so they have told me.'

'Interesting ... they sound promising.'

'Oh, yes ... these are serious players alright. Pharoah and Webster said that Derek Aldidge was shaken by their visit but gave nothing away. People are closing their mouths as tightly as this locket has been closed for the last ten years. We need to get someone talking. Pharoah and Webster apparently left Derek Aldidge thinking about the last bus...'

'The last bus?' Ventnor queried. 'Sorry, I don't follow.'

'It's an image that we've employed before.

263

You can catch it and do yourself a really huge favour or you can let it go by and stay out in the cold.'

'Being the wrong side of the law?'

'Yes. That's it. Catching the bus won't necessarily bring you on to the right side of the law but you'll be doing yourself a very big favour, as I said. We have planted the same notion in Big Phil Buchan's head, he was looking forward to getting out quite soon but now he's already looking at accessory to murder after the fact. He might be ready to cough. Go and see him again.'

'Yes, sir.' Ventnor stood.

'See what he has to say.'

'I think it would be well for Sergeant Yellich and myself to pay a call on Audrey Aldidge, when he returns ... just a friendly chat ... talk to the other maid and the cook.'

Pharoah and Webster found Bruno Burnell's business to be just as Franklin Fenty had described. It was a small business in terms of the size of the premises and seemed to Pharoah and Webster to be sitting with a certain aloof smugness in the centre of the village of Lower Rise, with the village post office on one side and on the other side was a small patch of closely cut green with a highly varnished wooden bench upon it; behind the bench stood a beech tree, which at that time of the year, was an orb of brilliant bronze glowing in the sun, against a blue sky. The sign above the showroom read: 'Bruno Burnell, Purveyor of Horseless Carriages'. In the showroom window was a gleaming maroon Rolls Royce Silver Shadow, probably about thirty years old, thought Webster, who cast a covetous eye over the machine as he and Carmen Pharoah left their much more modest car at the kerb and walked up to the showroom. Webster pushed open the door, causing a bell to sound and he and Pharoah then stood waiting by the Rolls Royce.

'Not a man who feels the need to be attentive to his customers,' Webster growled after he and Pharoah had been waiting for a full minute. 'Would you buy a used car from this man?'

'Doubt if he'd sell to me anyway,' Carmen Pharoah said with a smile. 'He'd be drummed out of the British Alliance for selling a Rolls to a black, and a black woman at that.'

Webster's chest heaved with suppressed laughter and then he and Pharoah stood waiting calmly for a further two minutes before they, as potential customers, received any attention.

The man who made an appearance, by opening a door at the rear of the showroom, was tall and slender, his short hair was plastered down on to his skull, above a pencil line moustache. He was dressed in a loudly chequered sports jacket, a yellow waistcoat and cream cavalry twill trousers. His feet

265

were encased in highly polished brogues. He coldly glanced at Carmen Pharoah and stopped walking. His eyes narrowed with evident anger and distaste. 'Mr Hunter?' He addressed Webster.

'No.' Webster shook his head. 'Detective Constable Webster. This is my colleague, Detective Constable Pharoah, Micklegate Bar police station, York.'

'Oh ... I was expecting a customer you see, by the name of Hunter. He's a little overdue.'

'You didn't seem particularly anxious to greet him.'

'If he had been on time I wouldn't have kept him waiting,' Burnell sniffed. 'But I can be discourteous as well. I can remain, and indeed do remain, in a good way of business without having to treat my customers like royalty. My customers live throughout the world ... throughout the western orbit of nations at least. I do not allow my cars to go to the Middle East, India, Eastern Europe, the former Soviet Union, only the Republic of South Africa in that continent. I also do not sell to the Far East.'

'Doing yourself out of good business.' Webster observed.

'I am a man of principle, Mr Webster. I love the cars I sell. I lavish great care on them when I am bringing them up to resale condition. I care where they go. I only sell where I know they will be cared for, where there are proper and fully qualified mechanics to offer

266

the service they need. So I sell within the UK, Ireland, Western Europe, North America and Australia and New Zealand. I sell one car at a time, and sell ten or twelve a year. I make a good living. I provide for my own.'

'Only Rolls Royces?'

'And Bentleys. I also sell Bentleys. So, how can I help you?'

'Some information,' Webster said. 'We were told you could be of help in that way. Rather not say who told us. But we do need information.'

'Such as?'

'Arthur and Audrey Aldidge, such as Derek Aldidge, such as Nigel Holmes,' Carmen Pharoah spoke with an edge to her voice. 'Twenty-three Ash Lane, Thaxted Green, such as the British Alliance. Information like that, about people and places like that. You are Bruno Burnell?'

'Yes...' Burnell's voice faltered. He was indeed olive skinned but his voice was perfect received pronunciation. He recovered quickly and replied, 'I am he.'

'And the names I mentioned?'

'People I know ... I don't deny knowing them.'

'And the British Alliance?'

'It is an above board political party. And yes, I am a member, I am proud of it.' He addressed Webster despite the questions coming from Pharoah. 'I believe what I believe. I just don't like the way England is going. I don't like it at all. I don't like multi-cultural-ism. I don't like illegal immigrants. I like Europe for Europeans. I am Italian English. On my Italian side I am distantly related to Benito Mussolini, of which I am also proud. Very proud, in fact. He did much for Italy.'

'Well, we'll save the history lesson for a later date,' Webster growled. 'But what can you tell us about Audrey Aldidge?'

'A lovely lady, a fine lady.' Burnell smiled. 'A real leader, just what we need ... charismatic, strong, powerful...'

'We?'

'The British Alliance of course. She was voted the leader of the Yorkshire chapter of the BA. Any rivals she had were minnows by comparison. She is headed for national office within the party.'

'Did you know Arthur Aldidge?' Webster asked.

'Yes ... and I know his body has been found. I read the newspapers and watch the TV news. I dare say that that is why you are here?'

'Yes.' Webster held eye contact with Burnell. 'That is why we are here.'

'Sold him his last car, in fact, a Bentley. Nice car. I let him have it cheap. Cheap for a Bentley, cheap for one of my cars.'

'What do you know of his murder?'

'Nothing,' Burnell replied clearly, defiantly. 'Nothing at all.'

'What did you hear? You were close to the Aldidges ... part of the British Alliance ... selling him classic cars at a discounted price. What rumours did you hear? You must have heard something.'

'Rumours are evidence?' Burnell smiled. 'That is news to me.'

'No,' Carmen Pharoah said icily, 'but they often point us in the right direction ... rumours can and have been very useful.'

'What did you hear?' Webster pressed.

'I have a customer due...' Burnell glanced at his wristwatch.

'You were going to let him wait. If he arrives, he'll have to wait a little longer,' Pharoah said firmly.

'Let me ... let us put it to you like this,' Webster said as he eyed Burnell coldly. 'We are talking about three murders, Mr Arthur Aldidge, his younger lover, Miss Sandra Paull, and very recently the murder of the maid Margaret Coley. Any involvement in any of those murders means serious trouble. Clear?'

'Crystal,' Burnell replied in a confident sounding manner, but he seemed nervous, so thought Carmen Pharoah.

'You knew Mr and Mrs Aldidge, and you sold Arthur Aldidge his last car at a discounted price ... you have just said so ... so you were part of their social circle at the time of the disappearance of Arthur Aldidge and Sandra Paull. So what did you hear?

269

What was the gossip?'

Burnell shrugged. 'Well, they had vanished.'

'Yes...'

'It was assumed that they had run away
together, if you must know.'

'That is interesting,' Webster replied, 'and
yes, we must know.'

'It seemed obvious, why should it be interesting? It happens all the time ... rich older
man, his young mistress.'

'Who thought they had run off together?'

'Pretty well everybody I spoke to ... everybody in the York chapter of the Alliance, that
is ... you know ... other people who also knew
them.'

'Yes, I see, so, Nigel Holmes, whom we are
about to call upon, he thought the same?'

'Yes ... yes, he did.'

'Franklin Fenty ... that's another name we
know of?'

'No, he wasn't around then, he joined only
recently.'

'So, who else thought they had run away
together?'

'Jack Stanford.'

'That's a name we don't know, who is he?'

'He ... he's a farmer in the Vale, out by
Pickering ... a village called Tibberton. His is
the farm in the area, you'll get directions
easily enough.'

'Who else thought they had run away?'

Burnell shrugged. 'Well, Audrey, of course,

and I can tell you that she was spitting nails into oak trees ... calling her "a little tart" and hoping that they didn't come back. Believe me, it didn't do to be in the same room as Audrey when she found out that Arthur and Sandra had run away together.'

Carmen Pharoah smiled. 'You see, it's that, that makes it interesting, not the fact that they may have run away together to start a new life. What makes it interesting is that Audrey Aldidge knew of her husband's infidelity, that she knew about Sandra Paull.'

Brunell's jaw sagged.

'That's motive,' Webster explained. 'People have murdered for a lot lesser motive than infidelity. And you have described a fiery tempered female of the species. She sounds like she has her own way of going about things, in fact she gave us that very same impression when we met her.'

'She does.' Burnell nodded. 'And she gets it. Always gets what she wants.'

'Would you say that she was a self-centred personality?'

'Possibly.' Burnell began to look uncomfortable.

'Again, that's interesting,' Webster continued, 'because, you see, some years ago now, I once passed a few minutes with an eminent QC in the corridors of York Crown Court, and this venerable and learned gentlemen told me that he had been pleading in murder trials by then for twenty years and in his experience murders are always committed by people who think the sun shines just for them, and that, he said, includes the so-called crimes of passion. People like Audrey Aldidge, for example, she sounds like she believes that the sun shines just for her.'

'I only heard the gossip ... that's all I heard ... rumour and gossip.'

'Then you have nothing to fear. But if your name is linked in any way...' Carmen Pharoah raised an eyebrow. 'And you still could link yourself, even now...'

'I could?' Burnell gasped. 'How ... ten years on? I can't be linked.'

'Yes, you could, a phone call to Audrey Aldidge, telling her of our visit ... tipping her off ... that would be perverting the course of justice.'

'Not good for a member of the British Alliance,' Webster added. 'No problem for the Defenders of St George, they have a good police record to gain street cred, one more offence is all grist to the mill for them.'

'The Defenders,' Burnell again gasped. 'You know about them as well.'

'Oh, yes, we've done our homework, the British Alliance provides the officer corps, the Defenders of St George is the infantry ... the foot soldiers, if you like.'

'Well, that's one way of putting it, I suppose.' Burnell leaned on the Rolls Royce, then straightened himself up and wiped the bodywork with a handkerchief where he had touched it.

'So the Defenders do the dirty work?'

Burnell remained silent.

'Arthur Aldidge was a man of towering presence, nearly seven feet tall, he would have needed some weight to bring him down,' Webster spoke calmly. 'Nobody we have met in the Alliance seems to have had the strength, even his brother who is of similar build, or the criminal inclination.'

Burnell held up his hand. 'Look, I didn't know anything about the murder until I read that his body had been found. For the last ten years I have assumed that he and Sandra were sunning it up in the Seychelles, or some similar romantic place, basking in the sun and in each other's company.'

'So you knew Sandra Paull?'

Burnell sighed. 'Knew of her ... met her once or twice but I can't say I knew her. Arthur wasn't discreet, he put her in a little love nest in York and made no secret of his visits ... employed her as his chauffeur ... he was a financier.'

'So we understand.'

'I think some money also disappeared at the time, that was another rumour that flitted to and fro and that also angered Audrey.'

'Big money?'

'Seven figures, so I was told, but such rumours have a way of growing each time they are told, so I don't know the exact

273

amount, even if money was taken out at all ... but you can't live on thin air, so I assumed some had been removed, enough for them to live on in luxury.'

'Luxury?'

'Well, Sandra might have come from the wrong side of the tracks but Arthur liked the finer things in life and he would have needed to attract Sandra. So if Arthur was going to disappear, he'd take some money with him ... he'd take enough to see himself out, and also to enable him to provide for Sandra.'

'I see.'

'But now we know he didn't disappear,' Burnell mused. 'Well, well, quite a turn up for the books.'

'Yes. So what is Audrey Aldidge's source of income?'

'You'd have to ask her that, I'm sorry. She doesn't work, that I know but money is coming in, that is plain ... that house, those clothes, the servants, the cars...'

'Do you know how much she knew about her husband's business dealings?'

'A lot, I think,' Burnell replied. 'That's the reason that Arthur bought the house in York, so he told me, to use as his office, because she kept breathing down his neck, you see.'

'How did she react to the move?'

'His move out?' Burnell pursed his lips. 'Arthur said that she didn't like it but if she wanted money coming in, he had to work. Simple as that.'

'How long after he moved out did he disappear?' Pharoah asked.

'Not long, as I recall ... about a year, I think.'

'How long was Sandra Paull involved with Arthur Aldidge?'

'Between a year and eighteen months, I think. Don't know the exact start date, of course, but I first met her about a year before they disappeared.'

Webster glanced at Carmen Pharoah. 'I think that about wraps if up.'

'Yes.' Pharoah nodded. 'But to advise you, Mr Burnell, we can access phone records, landline and mobile ... keep out of this for your own sake. Any phone call from you to Mrs Aldidge from this moment on –' she glanced at her watch – '2.47 p.m. and we will assume you are attempting to pervert the course of justice.'

'Understood.' He paused. 'I appreciate the warning. Thank you.'

'How do we contact the Defenders of St George, the local chapter?' Webster asked.

'You're going to see Nigel Holmes, you said?'

'We did and we are.'

'He's the contact person. All contact between the Alliance and the Defenders goes through Nigel. Convenient for you.'

'So he'll know all the jobs they were asked to do ... all the dirty work.'

'Not all,' Burnell replied in a snappy,

defensive manner.

'Oh?' Pharoah asked. 'What do you mean "not all"?'

'Private arrangements have been known to be made.'

'Really?'

'Yes, Jack Stanford for instance ... he had major trouble with travellers on his land, the caravans and litter ... making a right mess. Police wouldn't or couldn't do anything, so Jack got rid of them in his own way ... said he asked the Defenders for some help in persuading them to move on. He would have paid good money into the Defenders' funds but it was a job the Defenders enjoyed doing.'

'I remember that ... a few years ago ... the caravans were burnt and travellers hospitalized.'

'Yes ... travellers are on the list, you see, we have it all planned.'

'The list?' Webster pressed.

'The list –' Burnell smiled and indicated Carmen Pharoah – 'the list that she is on and you are not. That list. The travellers didn't come back so that was a very nice result but Nigel Holmes knew nothing about that ... that was a private arrangement between Jack Stanford and the Defenders. There have been other, similar arrangements. Just a bit of mutual back scratching. So Nigel knows much, but not all.'

'I quite like being on their list.' Carmen

Pharoah smiled as she and Webster walked back to the car. It makes me feel all warm and good inside.'

'Yes, it's my locket, alright, no mistake, Arthur gave it to me when we were married.' She turned it over in her fingers. 'Can I take it out of this plastic bag?'

'No,' Hennessey spoke softly but with clear finality. 'It is evidence, so sorry but we cannot return it to you just yet.'

'I can't have it back?' Audrey Aldidge seemed indignant.

'Not yet,' Hennessey repeated again with finality.

'Oh...' Audrey Aldidge remained calm, poised, elegantly dressed in a blue dress with a black leather belt about her middle, and matching blue shoes. She sat on the settee in the drawing room of her house. 'Where did you find it? Where has it been all this time? I thought I would never see it again.'

'It was found on the person of Sandra Paull. I can tell you that.'

'On her person? How on earth did it get there?'

'That's what we would like to know. What do you know of Sandra Paull?'

'Very little.' Audrey Aldidge raised her eyebrows and glanced round the room. 'I knew more of her after she disappeared than when she was ... well, not disappeared, present. First of all, all sorts of horrible, really horrible rumours started flying round, really awful stuff, I didn't believe them at first ... linking Arthur's name with hers ... people said that they were an item. I mean, how preposterous, Arthur would never do anything like that, so I thought. How wrong I was. You need this back?'

'Yes.' Hennessey stood from his chair and crossed the floor and received the locket as Audrey Aldidge, who, imperiously in Hennessey's opinion, remained seated, proffered it. 'Thank you.' Hennessey resumed his seat. 'We understand that you cleared your late husband's office? Removed all the computers ... all the files?'

'Yes, and I gave his secretary the sack. Told her that her services were no longer required. Gave her some money, all that I had in my purse, and told her to go. Just like that. I was livid.'

'So why did you clear your husband's office so thoroughly?'

'I felt deserted. I heard other rumours, you see, about him and his little tart ... rumours like they were not just seeing each other behind my back but that they were jetting off together. Then I found he had really gone and so had she. I was a woman scorned, you know ... Hell hath no fury ... I destroyed everything, I mean everything, not just at his office but here also ... everything ... his clothes ... everything he left behind I threw out. Everything. It all went to the charity shops.'

'Alright, we'll leave that for the moment.' Hennessey was aware of Sergeant Yellich looking intently at Audrey Aldidge, searching for any giveaway sign, any nervous look in a particular direction, any giveaway body movement. 'So what can you tell us about Margaret Coley's murder?'

'Nothing.'

'Nothing?' Hennessey queried. 'That seems strange.'

'Nothing at all. I mean that, nothing at all. The girl was here one day and gone the next. It was her right. She can ... she could have walked out at any time, the same as the other two.'

'They are?'

'Belinda Sweet ... she's the cook.' Audrey Aldidge smiled. 'Apt name for a cook, don't your think ... Sweet?'

Hennessey smiled. 'I knew a cook called Bacon once. Harry Bacon, but that's a long time ago.'

'Yes, apt ... and Prudence McVey. She's the other maid. Have to find a replacement for Margaret now. I need a minimum of two maids and a cook.'

'So you are saying that Margaret just walked out?'

'Yes,' she held eye contact as she replied. 'Just like that. She walked out. I warned her that she was vulnerable, and in danger.'

'Where? Who from?'

'Out there.' Audrey Aldidge pointed to the huge windows of the room. 'Out there ... in the world. There is great danger out there for people who have no one to turn to, and little or no money. In here she is ... she was safe, my employees are safe in here, they have the protection of my house. So what happens? She leaves, crossed the path of the wrong man and look what happens ... dead ... she's killed, silly girl, but it has served to do some good.'

'Oh ... it has?'

'Yes ... the other two, Belinda and Prudence, it's scared sense into them,' she said with a smile, 'they won't be leaving in a hurry. So, are you going to tell me what happened to Sandra Paull, my husband's ... my late husband's little toy? You said that the locket was found on her person ... that, I think, suggests some measure of incapacity on her part. Does it not? If something is found on someone's person then surely that person is deceased, unconscious or has been apprehended and searched.'

It was, thought Hennessey, a fair observation. 'Sandra Paull is deceased,' he said flatly.

'Deceased?' Audrey Aldidge's surprise seemed genuine, so genuine that both Hennessey and Yellich thought her a consummate actress. 'How?'

'Can't tell you that ... sorry.'

'When?'

'Not at liberty to tell you that either, I am

280

sorry.'

'What can you tell me?' Again Audrey Aldidge revealed an indignant aspect to her personality. 'You are wasting my time, I have a house to run.'

'It's for you to tell us things, Mrs Aldidge, not the other way round, and it is our time that is the issue here, not yours.'

'Well!' Audrey Aldidge flushed with anger. 'Well!'

'So, tell us, Mrs Aldidge, you say that you have a house to run?'

'Yes!' She waved her hand, indicating the room in which they sat. 'This is just one room of a large house. It takes time and effort to keep on top of it.'

'So what is your source of income?'

'That is private ... it is no concern of yours.'

'It is of relevance. It is of concern to the police.'

'How so?'

'Because three people have been murdered,' Hennessey spoke sternly, 'all were connected with this house, and two were very closely connected. In such circumstances everything to do with this house is relevant, including the source of income which keeps it going, or running, as you seem to prefer to say.'

'But I have already told you, when you visited a few days ago. I told you then.'

'Remind me,' Hennessey growled. 'I tend to forget some details.'

'I was able to obtain power of attorney, accessed my late husband's account,' Audrey Aldidge explained with a show of forced patience. 'He didn't take all his money with him, and I also sold the house he used as an office.'

'Kept you afloat for ten years?' Hennessey queried.

'He must have left quite a lot,' Yellich added.

'Not really, not as much as a good divorce settlement would have given me, but the house is paid for and I have few outgoings ... few for one of my station in life.'

'Very well,' Hennessey said as he stood, 'that clears up a few questions, a few outstanding queries.'

Audrey Aldidge smiled. Yellich also stood.

'We would like to talk to Belinda Sweet and Prudence McVey.'

'You would?'

'Yes, we would, but not here, at the police station.'

Again Audrey Aldidge flushed with barely contained anger. 'They are both very busy.'

'We won't keep them long. They'll be back shortly. Very soon. You won't miss them. If you could go and get them, please.'

'Bruno said you'd be calling.' Holmes stood as Webster and Pharoah entered his office.

'He did?' Webster asked a little angrily.

'Yes.' Nigel Holmes patted the telephone

on his desk. He was a large, well-built man, smartly, but casually dressed, so the officers observed, with a cravat rather than a tie, shirt cuffs held together with cufflinks. A very large and very expensive-looking framed photograph of Malham Tarn hung on the wall behind Holmes.

'We advised him not to make phone calls,' Carmen Pharoah spoke similarly with a disapproving and angry tone. 'He could be making things very difficult for himself.'

'He said you said that.' Holmes sank slowly into the chair behind his desk and gestured to the two chairs in front of his desk. 'Please, do take a pew.'

Pharoah and Webster sat on the upright chairs. Pharoah took her notepad and ball-point from her handbag.

'I don't think he has harmed himself, Bruno is too clever for that.' Holmes sat back and looked up at the ornate plasterwork on the ceiling, as if, thought Webster, lost, or puzzled, as if disorder had suddenly entered his very ordered life. 'He told me not to phone Audrey Aldidge as he wasn't going to, advised me to co-operate as much as I could.'

'Sensible,' Webster said quietly.

'Well, I confess I didn't realize how close to home the murder of Arthur Aldidge might be ... this could wreck the Alliance, not just the York chapter but the Alliance nationally speaking. The entire party. Very few people know about us, and that's how we like it. We don't seek publicity and this case, this murder, is likely to generate exactly the sort of publicity we don't need. So, how can I help you?'

'Tell us all you know about the murder of Arthur Aldidge, the murder of Sandra Paull and the murder of Margaret Coley.'

'Who is Margaret Coley?' Holmes glanced at Webster and then at Pharoah.

'She was a maid at Mrs Aldidge's house,' Carmen Pharoah explained. 'She isn't anything any more.'

'The third name, Margaret Coley,' Holmes protested. 'I haven't heard of that name at all. I didn't know a maid of Audrey's had been murdered. That is sad news.'

'It hasn't been announced. We are keeping it under wraps.' Pharoah held her pen poised over her notepad.

'The other two names?' Webster probed.

'Well, they do both mean something to me, of course, but only as a couple who disappeared. Tell me the old, old story, henpecked husband takes up with a younger woman and they head for the hills. I assumed Arthur took all the money he needed ... he had offshore accounts you know.'

'He did?'

'Oh yes, the Alliance prides itself on being law abiding, it is a law and order party, amongst other things.'

'Such as white supremacy,' Pharoah growled, 'other things like that?'

'If you like, but really it's racial separation that we advocate, you see we value the Anglo Saxon race ... it's about preservation rather than supremacy for us. That is the issue. But above all, we are law-abiding.'

'Jack Stanford wasn't very law-abiding when he turned the Defenders of St George on the travellers.' Carmen Pharoah eyed him coldly.

Holmes held up a slender, cautionary finger. 'Listen ... point one ... those people, and I am being most generous and most kind calling them people, those people not only occupied his land unlawfully, they trashed it. Such a mess they made. You wouldn't believe what they dumped on his field ... what in terms of content, and what in terms of quantity ... it was impossible to believe what they did. Getting them off was just the first step; the big problem was the clear up. The clear up cost Jack a lot of money, he had to dig deep into his own pocket ... the insurers said it was not insurable damage. Having stuff dumped on your land doesn't amount to an act of God, nor can it apparently be construed as damage. Point two: they looked like they were getting comfortable. That was the worrying thing, it was shaping up to be a permanent site for those people. Property values in the village just fell, burglaries increased ... and point three, you people couldn't or wouldn't do anything about it.'

'Couldn't,' Webster explained. 'The issue was civil not criminal. It had to be resolved through civil procedures.'

'Which takes time, and a lot of money, and the travellers knew that. They are not stupid. Whatever else they might be they are not stupid. Jack is not an unreasonable man but these people wouldn't listen to reason ... so he made an arrangement with the Defenders, made a contribution to their funds, and they did a favour for him one night ... burnt the caravans, put a few travellers in hospital, they didn't return, the travellers, I mean ... Jack had cleared his land.'

'Alright, we won't pursue that.' Webster glanced round the room, neat, orderly, smelling of air freshener and furniture polish. The small window to one side of Holmes' desk offered a view of the Minster standing proudly above the low, medieval rooftops of the ancient city. 'Bruno Burnell told us that you were the contact point between the British Alliance and the Defenders of St George. Is that the case?'

'Yes,' Holmes agreed with a nod. 'That is the case. I won't deny it.'

'For what purpose are the two movements linked?'

'That we share the same goal. It's as simple as that. We value right-wing politics ... the Defenders are, shall we say, a little more ... direct in their action. Yes ... I'll say that. They favour the direct approach.'

'Thugs?' Carmen Pharoah offered. 'Muscular, clean-shaven, short-haired men in baseball caps.'

'Thugs is not a word I would use. It has unfair implications of criminality.'

'But the local chapter drills military style on the back lawn of Audrey Aldidge's house?'

'Yes, yes they do. That doesn't make them thugs. But they do need leadership. The Alliance offers that. But any violence is outside our policy. If the Defenders do a favour for someone it's a private arrangement and it doesn't have to be done through me. Anyone can pick up a phone ... meet in a pub, hand over a brown paper envelope ... happens all the time.'

'Alright ... so who would anyone phone if they wanted a favour doing?'

Holmes paused. 'This is all about damage limitation now, I suppose?' He seemed to be thinking aloud. 'If we are going to come through this with our credibility intact we have to be seen to co-operate with the police.'

'Yes,' Pharoah agreed and nodded, 'that's a very sensible way of looking at it.'

'Well in that case you should talk to a man called Gunn. You'll know him, he's done his rite of passage in half the prisons in England. Henry Gunn ... a man in his late forties. He lives here in York. I phone him when necessary. He comes here to discuss matters.'

'Here?' Webster was surprised. 'That's surprisingly open of you.'

'Yes ... but always after hours. I have some very prestigious clients, I am a society photographer so it wouldn't do for Henry Gunn to be seen by my clients ... so, after hours ... usually about five thirty p.m. on Fridays, we close early on Fridays. I have a receptionist, whom you have met ... and assistants ... we finish early on Fridays, at four p.m. instead of the usual five p.m. So there is a full ninety-minute buffer zone between the last client and my staff leaving and Mr Gunn arriving. So if the Defenders were involved in Arthur's murder, which is what you seem to be implying, if a brown envelope was passed across a table one evening, then Henry Gunn will know about it ... but he's a criminal ... he has a code of honour ... getting him to talk is another matter.'

'Let us worry about that. How do we find him?'

Hennessey smiled and said, 'Thank you, thank you, very much.' He gently replaced the phone. 'That was Wetherby. The water from the pool matches the water in Margaret Coley's lungs. So, the question now is did she drown or was she drowned?'

'I think we both know the answer to that, skipper.' Yellich was stone-faced. 'Let's see if we can get enough for a warrant to take a lawful sample.' Hennessey leaned back in his chair. 'Then milady will have some explain-

288

ing to do. As will her brother-in-law.'

'Yes.' Hennessey reclined further in his chair and pyramided his fingers. 'We could bring them in now really, lean on them, see how far we get, but let's see what Prudence and Belinda can tell us. I like to be forewarned and well armed with information.'

'We are getting there.' Ventnor smiled as he handed Big Phil Buchan a cigarette. 'We are really getting there ... and nicely so.'

'Oh yeah?' Buchan grabbed the cigarette and held it steady in his lips while Ventnor flicked his yellow lighter and held the flame to the top of the cigarette.

'Yes ... knew we would.' Ventnor lit a cigarette for himself.

'So why this call?' Buchan inhaled deeply. 'I can't see how I can help you.'

'Just a social call.' Ventnor glanced round the agents' room, tiled walls, opaque glass set high, near the ceiling. 'Just a chat while passing.'

'You don't make social calls.' Buchan again dragged on the cigarette, deeply, desperately.

'Well ... dare say that's true, so let's just say this call is more social than it could be ... more social than formal, more social than official.'

'You're still fishing,' Buchan sneered, 'otherwise you wouldn't be here. I've been round the block ... you forget that ... I know how you work.'

Ventnor drew on his own cigarette. 'Yes ... it's true ... we are still fishing and when we started the pond was vast, and very still, and we didn't know what was beneath the surface ... but over the last few days the pond has got smaller ... and smaller and smaller ... as though it is being drained and the fish are beginning to jump, and I mean jump as if they are scared of something or looking for an escape route, and some fish are jumping higher than others as though they are anxious to do a deal ... they are anxious to help themselves.'

'Deal?' Buchan's brows furrowed. 'What do you mean?'

'Turn Queen's evidence.' Ventnor flicked the ash from his cigarette into the ashtray.

Buchan paled and glanced sideways and downwards.

'The first two to talk will be doing themselves a huge favour. It's all falling apart at the seams, Phil. A confession on your part now...' Ventnor opened his palms. 'Well...'

Buchan shook his head. 'Nothing to say.'

'OK. So, tell me, were you a member of the Defenders of St George?'

Buchan looked at Ventnor. The name evidently meant something to him.

'Probably a bit too old to be a foot soldier ... a bit too old for thuggery,' Ventnor probed, 'but we were all young once. I saw that look in your eyes, you couldn't hide it: the name has a significance for you.'

290

'So ... I was once ... still am.'

'You are?'

'Yes, I am not ashamed of it.' Buchan relaxed once again. 'I am not on the active service list anymore ... too old now ... but I am still a member, it is a lifelong commitment. I can't leave. No one can.'

'What happens if you want to leave? What happens if you want to change your political allegiance and become a wet liberal?'

'You'll likely disappear ... but no one wants to leave ... after years of good service you go on the reserve list. I am on the reserve list. When I'm not in here I help raise funds, set out chairs in halls prior to conferences, drive folk, do what I can to help, but I am not in the frontline any more. Still part of the crew, though.'

'I see,' Ventnor murmured.

'It's like a brotherhood, like a family ... looking out for each other.'

'Ah...'

'White is right, keep the Anglo Saxon way of things ... keeping the race pure. I am proud of what I believe in.'

'Evidently.' Ventnor drew on his cigarette. 'But fish are jumping all around you, Phil, and the pond is getting shallower by the day, by the hour, by the minute, even by the second. Soon all the fish we need will be flapping about on a patch of mud and we'll just wade in and pick 'em up and toss 'em in a basket. And you were one of the frontline

291

members of the Defenders of St George … and that was about the time that Arthur Aldidge and Sandra Paull were murdered … interesting. You're involvement was much, much deeper than you claimed it to be, wasn't it, Phil?'

'But Mrs Aldidge is very good to us.' Prudence McVey sat upright in the chair, handbag perched on her lap in a very institutionalized manner, thought Hennessey. 'We don't want to say anything against her.'

'Very good,' Belinda Sweet repeated as she nodded her head vigorously. 'We couldn't survive out there … we need her to provide for us.'

'Out there?'

'In the city. At Mrs Aldidge's house we have our own room and all the food we can eat. We're safe.'

'Safe,' echoed Prudence McVey, 'safe. Mrs Aldidge keeps us safe.'

'How long have you been working for Mrs Aldidge?' Hennessey asked.

'Fifteen years.'

'Seven in my case,' Belinda Sweet said eagerly. 'We have no complaints.'

'No complaints,' Hennessey echoed.

'No … better than a hostel … no complaints at all.'

'Much better,' Prudence McVey agreed, also with distinct eagerness.

'She's really got to you, hasn't she?' Hennessey sighed.

'Who?' Belinda Sweet asked, 'Who has got to us?'

'Audrey Aldidge ... filled your heads full of nonsense about being unable to survive,' Hennessey replied angrily, 'the only alternative to her house is a hostel for homeless people, indeed. What nonsense. Ever heard about council accommodation?'

'Council accommodation?'

'Property owned by the city and let to people ... rented. There are some very nice council house estates in York.'

'Very nice,' Yellich echoed. 'The city wouldn't put you where you'd be at risk, and we could offer protection. And she can't reach you in here.'

'We're not under arrest?' Prudence McVey seemed genuinely surprised.

'No.' Hennessey smiled reassuringly. 'You haven't committed a crime, have you?'

'No, sir.'

'No, sir.'

'Alright ... so tell me what happened to Margaret Coley.'

'She went back to Jamaica, sir. She has family there.'

'She did? Really?' Hennessey inclined his head to one side.

'Yes.'

'How do you know?' Hennessey pressed. 'How do you know?'

'Mrs Aldidge said so,' Prudence McVey

said. 'She told us Margaret had returned home.'

'Did she say goodbye to you? Did you see her leave the house?'

'No ... she just wasn't there one morning, at breakfast.'

'You didn't think that a little strange?' Yellich leaned back in his chair. The two women were clearly nervous. He didn't want to intimidate them.

'This hasn't been made public,' Hennessey spoke softly, 'but I regret that I have to tell you ... with deep sadness, that Margaret Coley is no longer with us.'

The two women gasped. Prudence McVey struggled to fight back tears.

Hennessey continued after a pause. 'I can tell you that she drowned in the swimming pool in Mrs Aldidge's garden. We think she was drowned. In other words she was murdered. So, let us know what you know. You are safe here.'

'Among friends,' Yellich added.

'And clearly at risk out there, and by "out there" I don't mean in a hostel, I mean at Twenty-three Ash Lane, Thaxted Green. Margaret gave some good information to us and it cost her her life. That is how Mrs Aldidge looks after her staff, that is how she protects her employees. So what did Audrey Aldidge say to you when Margaret was talking to Mr Yellich and DC Pharoah? Did she warn you, as we believe she did, not to

294

say anything?'

'Yes,' Prudence McVey sobbed, 'she said we owed it to her ... she said terrible, bad things happen to those who betray her.'

'She said that?' Yellich sat forward. 'That is a clear threat, clear intimidation.'

'Yes.' Belinda Sweet similarly started to sob. 'That's what she told us.'

'So would Margaret have walked near the swimming pool?'

'No, she was a maid in the house and so has to keep inside the house even when off duty. The garden is tended by contractors, the pool is full of leaves now, it's going to get drained soon for the winter.'

Hennessey and Yellich glanced at each other.

'Better hurry this,' Yellich said. 'Better crack on with this.'

Hennessey nodded and turned to Belinda Sweet and Prudence McVey. 'So, to help us to help Margaret ... to help get justice for Margaret ... did either of you see or hear anything on the night before Margaret wasn't at breakfast?'

The two women looked at each other, then Prudence McVey said, 'We heard screaming.'

Hennessey and Yellich once again glanced at each other.

'Good enough?' Yellich raised his eyebrows. 'I think that's all we needed.'

'I think so. I think so too. You do that, warrant to search the house and grounds and

295

take an official sample of water from the swimming pool.'

'Very good, sir. I'm on it.'

'You two ladies, you'll remain here ... certainly overnight ... but right now we need a statement from each of you.'

Hennessey listened intently to Webster and Pharoah's account of their visits to Bruno Burnell and Nigel Holmes. 'Right,' he said, 'right that's all very useful. I doubt we'll get anything more on the attack on the travellers a few years ago ... write it up anyway and cross-reference it to the file on the incident.'

'Yes, sir.'

'But I do want to talk to Henry Gunn ... and I want you with me on that, Webster.'

'Yes, sir.'

'DC Pharoah, if you could make yourself available to DS Yellich, he and a van load of uniforms are going to turn over the Aldidge house.'

'Yes, sir.'

'Don't know what you are looking for ... anything you find of relevance. But do remind Sergeant Yellich about the swimming pool.'

'The swimming pool, sir?'

'The swimming pool, Pharoah, the swimming pool. Just say I told you to say "swimming pool" to him. He'll understand.'

'Very good, sir,' Pharoah replied with enthusiasm. 'The swimming pool.'

★ ★ ★

'You people were always all the same, and are always going to be the same.' Henry Gunn drew heavily on the cigarette. 'Never leave a fella alone. Once your old claws are in a geezer, they stay in. So I did a few stupid things once ... and you still hound me.'

'Not hounding you, Henry.' Reginald Webster sat opposite Gunn and glanced round him, a small, stuffy, poorly ventilated room in a council house, faded blue wallpaper with a flower pattern, old, inexpensive furniture, threadbare carpet, a few sticks of wood in the hearth being licked by an indifferent flame. 'We are looking for help.'

'Me?' Gunn pressed a fleshy thumb into his chest. 'You want me to help you?' He moved his head from left to right and back again.

'Yes, in a word.'

'Last time I went down, it was for something I didn't do. I know they all say that but in my case it was true. Still is. Wrongful conviction. It happens.'

'So, what about all the things you did do and got away with?' Webster argued.

'That's not the point,' Gunn protested strongly.

'It's very much the point, Henry, you've been making a living by breaking the rules, then someone breaks the rules at your expense, you scream injustice ... play the game.'

'This is my house!' Gunn raised his voice. 'You want favours, and you insult me ... and in my house.'

'The Defenders of St George?' Webster moved the conversation on, he had to concede that Gunn had an arguable point and he, Webster, had been tactless, he wanted the man's co-operation.

'What about them?'

'We were told you were the man to talk to? I mean *the* man.'

'Who said that and about what?'

'Our sources are always guarded and this source is utterly confidential. Tell us about the organization of the Defenders. If someone wants something sorted out ... like travellers moved off their land ... no questions asked ... a brown envelope job ... you know the sketch.'

Gunn shrugged.

'We're looking at the murder of Arthur Aldidge, the murder of Sandra Paull, both about ten years ago, and also at the murder of Margaret Coley a few days ago. All the murders are connected with the Aldidge house in Thaxted Green. We know of the connection between the British Alliance and the Defenders,' Hennessey prompted.

'The Alliance!' Gunn sneered. 'That crew ... think they are part of it but never do anything. Never do anything at all. It's the Defenders that get results. The Alliance think they can sit it out on the touchline then take over when all the work has been done ... cloud cuckoo land. They are just dreamers.'

'We believe the Defenders of St George had something to do with the three murders ... all three of them.'

'You do, do you?' Gunn snarled.

'Yes, we do.'

'And you expect me to 'fess up to murder?' Gunn leaned back in the armchair in which he sat. 'I am getting on but I still have it all upstairs.' He tapped the side of his head. 'I'm still at home in here.'

'Well, if you know something and if we can prove you know something ... think of murder, think of accessory before or after the fact, think of obstructing the police in their inquiries,' Hennessey growled. 'If you don't mind me saying, you're getting a bit long in the tooth to be going down for a ten stretch ... maybe even more than that. That's a lot of porridge.'

'I'm not going down ... not anymore, been there, done that and got the T-shirt. If nothing else, I've got to stay out for our Thomas.'

'Thomas?'

'My eldest.' Gunn shook his head in a gesture of despair. 'He's in Franklyn ... got himself lifted for stealing suitcases off trains. I told him to watch for the CCTV but what does he do but walk off trains at York Station carrying other folks' suitcases ... not once or twice but enough to establish a pattern ... they were waiting for him, he got lifted ... now he's in the pokey. It's not that that I mind so much, it's normal to get some

299

prison time behind him, but he can't handle himself, he's weaker than I was at that age, he's already in the hospital wing.'

'Oh?'

'Yes, somebody tipped a good bucket of scalding tea over his head ... third-degree burns to his scalp and face ... that would have hurt him. That would have been sore ... very sore.'

'Ah ... confess I did wonder if you were related ... Gunn is not common as a name. Not uncommon. But not common either. Can't be many Gunns in the York telephone directory and very few of them, if any, will be known to the police. In fact it was your son who started this investigation.'

Henry Gunn paled. 'He did?'

'Yes, he did. He did the sensible thing and helped himself.'

'He gave information?'

'Yes.'

'I told him not to do that,' Gunn gasped. 'Not ever, for no one. That's why he got burned ... he's a grass.'

'He told us about Big Phil Buchan.'

'Buchan! Buchan, the swine Buchan, did that to our Tom?' Gunn flushed with anger. 'Buchan!'

'You know Phil Buchan?'

'Yes ... Buchan's in Armley ... old and crowded pokey, is Armley.'

'Full Sutton,' Webster replied calmly. 'He's in Full Sutton.'

300

'Knew it was one or the other. Full Sutton, is it? That's a better pokey.'

'So he couldn't have assaulted your lad.'

'Prison telegraph system. Any lag in any gaol can get a message to any other lag in any other gaol. Buchan would have put out a contract on our Tom. I know Buchan and I don't like him ... this is the end for him.' Gunn paused. 'I'm not giving any evidence, not signing anything. Won't go into the witness box ... nothing official.'

'But...' Hennessey sensed an imminent breakthrough.

'But Buchan is the one you want to talk to about the murders of Aldidge and Aldidge's girl.' Gunn looked at the worn carpet. 'Don't like doing this but Buchan's your man.'

'Tell me,' Hennessey asked gently.

'He shouldn't have burned our Tom, a kicking would have done ... he's scarred for life now, Tom is ... and Buchan's behind it. Buchan pays for this.'

'He is?'

'Yes. Audrey Aldidge approached me, ten years ago now, offered a good contribution in return for a couple of jobs.'

'A couple of jobs?'

'That's what she said. I offered the work to Buchan. I mean I contracted it out to Buchan. A few days later Arthur Aldidge had disappeared, and so had his girlfriend ... Sandra somebody.'

'Interesting...' Hennessey scratched his

chin. 'Those being the "couple of jobs".'

'Buchan did that to Tom ... scalded him ... he's marked for life ... Tom is ... Buchan ... Buchan is a dead man walking.'

'So what did Buchan get out of it?'

'Whatever Audrey Aldidge agreed to. The contribution to the Defenders fund only buys the introduction, less my commission, of course ... being about half ... but Buchan wouldn't have come cheap. Not for a double event.'

'Arthur Aldidge was a tall man...'

'Size doesn't matter, not if you're taken by surprise.'

'Is that what happened?'

Gunn shrugged. 'Wasn't there ... don't know the details. Just heard stuff.'

'What did you hear? What stuff did you hear?'

'Cain and Abel...' Gunn looked at Hennessey. 'Know what I mean? Went to Sunday school, did you?'

'Cain and...' Webster felt colour drain from his face. 'You mean Derek Aldidge had a part in this?'

'That is the rumour,' Gunn glanced at Webster. 'Rumour is also that it's getting to him, the guilt thing. No matter how he seems during the day, running that pub of his ... he hits the vodka hard each night ... rumour is that he's ready to crack. He won't be a tough nut for you ... but Buchan did that to Tom. Buchan dies for that.'

'The boss says I have to say to you "swimming pool".' Carmen Pharoah walked confidently up to Yellich who stood in the hallway of the Aldidge home. 'He said you would know what he meant.'

Yellich tapped his jacket. 'Already obtained ... nice and legally so.'

'Found anything, sarge?'

'Nope ... and I don't think we will, in fact I never expected to, I think the boss is just transmitting a message to milady. All we really need is water from the swimming pool.'

'Where is she? Where is milady?'

Yellich nodded to the closed door behind him. 'In the drawing room, fuming about all these police officers in her house. She does not like it at all.'

'Do her good,' Carmen Pharoah said with a grin.

'Yes.' Yellich smiled. 'I think that is what the boss thinks too.'

It was Monday, the eighteenth of November, 17.35 hours.

Nine

Tuesday, 19 November,
09.35 hours – 12.47 hours

*in which our tale concludes and a middle-aged
couple take a stroll all upon a summer's day.*

Hennessey suddenly realized and thought, Good Lord, he's serious. He really does think like that. They do really and actually think like that. Hennessey had been sitting quietly at his desk pondering the sequence of action to be taken in the Aldridge, Paull and Coley murders when his telephone had softly rung. He had let it ring twice as was his wont, and upon leisurely answering it had been informed by a nervous sounding constable at the enquiry desk that there were three gentlemen to see him. 'Not you by name, sir,' the shaky voice said, 'but they insist on speaking to the officer in charge of the Aldidge murder, sir.'

'I see,' Hennessey had grumbled. 'I'll be there directly.' He had then proceeded to the enquiry desk and stood beside the young and evidently inexperienced constable who had introduced the men as 'these gentlemen, sir'.

Hennessey saw three solemn-looking, well-dressed, middle-aged men, all of whom had taken off their hats as an obvious and age-old gesture of deference, upon entering the police station.

'I am Nigel Holmes,' one of the three men had said, clearly having been elected as the spokesman, realized Hennessey. 'This gentleman is Bruno Burnell –' he indicated the overweight man who stood stiffly and erect and the to the left of the small group –'and this is Toby Chesham.' He indicated the man standing stiffly to his right. He had then paused. 'Myself and Bruno Burnell have been visited by the police in respect of the murder of Arthur Aldidge. Toby Chesham has not, thus far, been visited. We have talked freely and at length amongst ourselves, not, of course, in any way to frustrate the police, you appreciate, quite the opposite, in fact, and we have decided to come and to give information.'

'That's quite correct,' Bruno Burnell added. 'We believe that we should play the white man ... indeed ... we must play the white man and do so at all times.'

It was then that Hennessey thought, Good Lord, he's serious, he really does think like that. They do really and actually think like that. 'Play the white man?' he questioned. 'What do you mean, gentlemen?'

'Yes.' Holmes remained straight-faced. 'We mean that the party has to come first.'

'The party?'

'The Alliance,' Burnell explained. 'The British Alliance disassociates itself from Audrey Aldidge. We make that statement. The Alliance is a party of law and order. We have come here to give information.'

'I see ... well ... we had better have a chat.' Hennessey collected himself. 'Off the record in the first instance, as is our practice, then if relevant, on the record, recorded interviews given in the presence of myself and one other officer and a solicitor to represent your interests. Is that acceptable to you gentlemen?'

'Fully.' Holmes nodded. 'It is fully acceptable.'

'It is the usual procedure, as I said, unless someone is under caution or has been arrested. Do you require legal representation?'

The third man, Toby Chesham, smiled. 'No, we do not, thank you, I am a solicitor, I work in the field of civil litigation, fighting insurance companies for compensation following death or serious injury, that sort of thing, but I think I am sufficiently well and fully versed in matters of criminal law to be able to protect our interests.'

'Very well, if you are happy to proceed on that basis, but if you do stray into danger, I will give fair warning. We'll go into interview room three.' Hennessey turned to the constable. 'Please be good enough to tell Sergeant Yellich where I am.'

'Yes, sir.' The constable snapped his reply.

Seated in the interview room, Hennessey said, 'So, what would you three gentlemen like to tell me?'

'I helped Audrey Aldidge remove the contents of the bank accounts that were jointly in her and Arthur's name. The joint accounts.' Toby Chesham spoke softly. He was immaculately dressed, smelled strongly of aftershave, and in Hennessey's view, was running a little to fat, but middle-aged lawyers tend to be, he had often observed, and as a civil litigation lawyer, he assumed Chesham to be in receipt of handsome fees. 'Nothing illegal ... perhaps a little suspect, perhaps a little underhand but not illegal. Very simple these days ... online banking ... amount of money that can be moved across the world by pressing a button or two. A trifle frightening I sometimes think.'

'Is that what you did?'

'Yes.' Toby Chesham paused. 'Yes, I did ... upon her request ... from the computer in her home ... at her request, I moved it to an account she had in her name only in the Cayman Islands.'

'An offshore account?'

'Yes.'

'How much money?'

'Seven million.' Said without blinking an eye.

'Seven million pounds was in a joint account?' Hennessey gasped.

'Accounts, there was more than one joint

account, but yes, she was able to access seven million sterling. I assumed it was a tax avoidance ploy.'

'That might be illegal,' Hennessey observed.

'Well, it might be but the Alliance is pledged to massively reduce income tax. So it wasn't contrary to Alliance policy. But murder is.'

'Go on.'

'Well, we ... I moved the money on her request. It all went into an account in her name only, as I said.'

'So she was siphoning off money from the joint accounts into her own account?'

'Yes ... but siphoning is the wrong term, it gives the wrong impression. She didn't skim a little bit here and there over a long period of time; she moved it all in one afternoon. It was earlier that very same day that she had reported Arthur as a missing person.'

Hennessey leaned back in his chair. 'And you didn't think that was suspicious?'

'Well ... like I said –' Chesham began to fidget and sound uncomfortable – 'the money was in joint accounts, it was hers as much as it was his ... and he was reported as missing. Like everybody else, I thought he'd gone off with his girlfriend ... Miss Paull. We only took money from the joint accounts. Arthur was a financier, he had his own accounts, he had money enough for himself and Miss Paull. We assumed he had left the money in the joint accounts for Audrey, as a sort of divorce settlement, so she took it. The news that he had been murdered is only a few days old, as we speak. Only now does the transfer of seven million pounds become suspicious.'

'I see,' Hennessey said, allowing a note of despair to enter his voice. He thought that, especially for a solicitor, Chesham was more than a little naïve. 'Mrs Aldidge is reported to have destroyed the computer and files in Mr Aldidge's office, do you know why she did that?'

'Probably just a clumsy attempt to cover her tracks,' Chesham suggested, 'but destroying the computer won't destroy the information. It will be accessible on the bank's computer. You'll need a court order to access it but in the case of a murder inquiry that will be easily obtained, I would think.'

'I would think so, too,' growled Hennessey. 'Right, we'll have to get this down in the form of a statement, and in the presence of another officer.'

'Did Helena tell you where to find me?' The man leaned against the tree, wrapped in a duffle coat. 'The fair barmaid who has everything going for her?'

'Yes,' Webster said. 'We called at the Vine, she told us where you were likely to be ... they want you back ... it's going to be busy.'

'But I won't be going back, will I?' Derek

Aldidge held eye contact with Webster, then with Ventnor and forced a smile.

'Not on this tide,' Webster replied.

'Kipling.' Aldidge nodded. 'I like reading him too.'

'You were expecting us,' Ventnor observed, 'you were tipped off.'

Aldidge shook his head and turned to look eastward across flat green and brown fields to the North Sea, just visible, cold and inhospitable looking, in the distance. 'I come up here to think, to escape ... it's the highest point around ... the sea, you see ... and the air ... fresh, clean ... still a little salty. I won't be getting much of that in the next few years. Yes, I was expecting you and no, nobody tipped me off, not in so many words. Got a phone call from Bruno Burnell, he told me that he and Nigel Holmes were going to see you ... the police ... he also wanted to know Toby Chesham's phone number ... they were taking him with them, for the sake of the Alliance. It was obvious what they were going to do. So I thought you would be calling on me. No point in running any more. I can't hide, so no point in running. So I came up here to take a last few lungfuls of fresh air.'

'Mr Aldidge, you are cautioned not to say anything that might incriminate you...'

'It doesn't matter.' Aldidge held up his hand and continued to gaze out across the fields towards the North Sea. 'I feel a strange sense of relief. The guilt has been eating me up ... a bottle of vodka each evening. Useful stuff vodka, so few impurities that you can demolish a full bottle each evening, have a good sleep and wake up without a hangover ... useful and dangerous. Doesn't have that built-in aversion therapy that red wine has. Demolish a bottle of red wine with all those impurities and it'll take two days to recover, during which you'll say, "never again ... never again", but not vodka.' He paused. 'So, I killed my brother.'

'Mr Aldidge!'

Aldidge again held up his hand. 'No, I want to tell you. I need to tell for my own peace of mind. We were not close, often fought, even as adults, but at the end of the day he was still my brother. Thanks be that our parents are no longer with us. Tall guy but he bent down to pick something up ... and I brought a pickaxe handle down on to his head a couple of times. If that didn't kill him out-right, then the plastic bag that Audrey pulled over his head would have done so. She knew about his affair with Sandra Paull, you see, but he didn't know about me and Audrey.'

'You and Mrs Aldidge?'

'Yes,' Aldidge said and smiled. 'I had an affair with my brother's wife and then I killed him. Neat, don't you think?'

'No, but the stories we uncover seldom are,' Webster growled.

'Audrey's idea ... get rid of Arthur then we,

me and her, can settle into a more open affair, no more secret rendezvous ... Mmm, smell that air ... had to get rid of Sandra Paull.' He looked away, towards the north. 'That was messy. We lured her to Audrey's house. I phoned her ... my voice sounds like Arthur's did, especially on the phone. She came to the house, Audrey invited her in, then she saw me and ran ... screaming ... ran into Audrey's bedroom and then crawled under Audrey's bed. Funny thing, that's always puzzled me, she had stopped screaming, held her mouth shut ... made it easier though.'

'She had taken a small gold locket from Audrey Aldidge's dressing table and put it in her mouth, probably was attempting to swallow it,' Ventnor spoke coldly.

'She knew what you were going to do,' added Webster. 'She left a little something for us. Brave girl.'

'Oh ... clever girl.' Aldidge smiled. 'Clever, clever girl.'

'So why hide her body but leave your brother's body where it was going to be found? Not immediately, but eventually.'

'Audrey's idea ... it was all Audrey's idea ... she wanted the life insurance money so she told Buchan and his team to leave my brother's body where it would never be found and we could then argue that they had run off together. In the event, Audrey and I never made public our relationship ... but

312

she always had the fact that I had murdered my brother to hold over me ... and also that I had murdered Sandra. She likes to be in control ... she's not known as the Colonel for nothing.'

'You murdered her?'

'Yes ... Audrey got hold of her ankles and pulled her from under the bed and I cracked her across the skull with the pickaxe handle ... then Audrey made sure with a plastic bag. Same way we murdered Arthur ... and just twenty-four hours later.'

'And Margaret Coley. She was drowned in the swimming pool in Audrey Aldidge's back garden?'

'Yes ... poor, harmless woman ... but she annoyed Audrey because she gave the police too much information. As to who actually drowned her –' he shook his head – 'I don't know, I can't help you there, it would have been a private arrangement between Audrey and some thugs from the Defenders. I was told ... asked ... told to get rid of the body.'

'Why didn't you?'

'Don't know. I had time ... really all the time I needed, and look at these fields, just look around you ... you can cut a body up and distribute the bits over ten or twenty square miles, or take the bits out to the coast and leave them on the wet sand at low tide, at night, nobody will see you, the high tide will swallow them ... never be found. Don't know why I didn't do that. I think it was possibly my way of giving myself up ... leaving Margaret's body not only where it would be found and quite rapidly so in my derelict cottage, but also next to a concrete mound which I knew you'd think suspicious. It was my way of saying my first loyalty is still to my brother ... not to the woman he used to call The long-haired Colonel ... but thank God our parents are not alive.' He stood upright 'Well, you'll be taking me now.'

'Yes,' Webster spoke solemnly, 'we will.'

'A favour?' Aldidge asked. 'A small but important favour?'

'Depends.'

'I have told you what happened. I'll sign a full confession ... in return can we detour via the Vine. I want to close up, pay off all the staff from the petty cash ... and give them a bonus. Can we do that? Please?'

'Yes,' Ventnor said. 'Yes, we can do that. And you know I used vodka the same way once.'

It was Tuesday, the nineteenth of November, 12.47 hours.

The middle-aged couple strolled arm in arm along the seafront. The woman wore a light-weight cotton skirt with a floral pattern, white sandals, with a modest heel, a blue T-shirt and shoulder bag, and a wide-brimmed straw hat. The man wore white trousers and a red short-sleeved shirt, and a panama hat. They both glanced up at the Royal Hotel as

314

they passed it on the other side of the Esplanade.

'Too posh for us,' the man said.

'I'll say.' The woman smiled, then glanced in the other direction, out to sea. 'I like visiting the south coast, but wouldn't like to live down here. I can never escape the notion that I am cheating somehow. I like the north where it's grim.'

The man laughed. 'I like both. As a Londoner I like the south but I've grown so used to the north now ... could not relocate.'

They strolled on in silence, shielding their eyes against the glare of the sun.

'Convenient,' she said.

'What ... the case ending when it did?'

'Yes.'

'I was worried that it would have dragged on, I would have had to cancel the holiday.'

'Yes, it could have been awkward for us ... the children being with their father this fortnight, and only this fortnight. But a good result.'

'Yes, pleasing. Three life sentences for Audrey Aldidge.'

'Will there be black prison warders where she is going?'

'Don't know ... do her good if there are. Buchan didn't get out when he thought he would. He collected ten years for conspiracy ... and Derek Aldidge, two life sentences and ten years for conspiracy to murder Margaret Coley. He is the only one to have shown

315

genuine remorse. He might be out before the system destroys him.'

'So who did murder Margaret Coley?'

The man shrugged. 'Don't know ... don't think Audrey Aldidge knew their names. Arrived one night, did what she told them to do and then they disappeared back into the night ... leaving Derek Aldidge to clean up after them ... but by then he was a bit deep with guilt and didn't clean up in the way they expected him to clean up. Lucky for us, and for the Paull family who now have some closure.'

'The British Alliance? Your views? And the other lot?'

'Harmless but unpleasant fantasists. The Defenders of St George are thugs hiding behind some claim to respectability ... dare say we'll pick them up one by one ... might even collar the two who murdered Margaret Coley at some point in the future. That's still an open case ... but it will be closed ... someone will inform on them in return for charges being dropped, so they're on borrowed time. Ah –' George Hennessey smiled as they came upon an ice-cream parlour – 'you know I could really fancy a chocolate sundae.'

'So could I,' replied Louise D'Acre. 'So could I.'